Dedication

To God the Father, To Jesus Christ, To Holy Spirit

First and foremost this book is for You. Thank you for the quest! You have shown me Your great goodness and poured your mercy upon me. You know my heart and You still love me, and You've never forsaken me. I'll **love You forever** *and I'll follow You anywhere You lead. I pray this be a book that You would hold dear to Your great heart for all* **Eternity**.

To my beautiful wife Emely and adorable children Samirah and Jeremiah

This book is also for you. Thanks for becoming the **Tribe** *that I've always wanted to be apart of. Keep being brave, virtuous, and above all things,* **True**! *My prayer is that you each will take this book and find the* **great adventure** *I've told you all about so many times……..*

To all the spiritual warriors who read this

I salute you, my Friends. My prayer for you is that as you turn this page, you find an infinite supply of tools to help you obtain **victory** *in every area of your life. In* **Jesus' name**: *Charge forth bravely, friends!* **FOR ZION!**

Printed in the United States of America
Eternal Kingdom Publishing
  Charlotte , NC 28214

https://GTKPortal.APP
http://GTKPortal.AzureWebsites.Net

Book inquiries can be sent to:
gtkportal@gmail.com

ISBN: 978-1-7338855-0-8

Shamar Meditation (Pre-Release Edition) - Reader Address

My friend, I invite you on a journey filled with great treasures and mysteries.

The veil was torn long ago. Our Creator is calling us to fill the breaches and become the Agents of His Kingdom which we've been destined to be. We are a global army of Christian Disciples, and we are on the rise. We are as varied as snowflakes gently falling from the hoary winter sky, and we each carry something inside of us which is worth more than all the gold and diamonds of this physical world. We are each spiritual warriors with varied weapons and tactics.

This book, Shamar Meditation, is for this rising army. My brethren, we are one, even as the Father and Son and Holy Spirit are One. We have been separated, called, and ultimately chosen. The Creator has great purpose for all of us.

This book is for everyone to read in your quest to satisfy the inherent hunger for the deeper spiritual life. Deep calls unto deep. Everyone has something special inside them. There is something very special inside you and all those friends and family members you hold dear. Perhaps you've released part of it already. With the principles of Shamar Mediation, you will accomplish great and mighty things in your quest for personal excellence. This book will help you to:

    a. Build up your body, soul, and spirit.
    b. Increase your confidence and knowledge of spiritual gifts.
    c. Arm you with additional reserves of virtue.
    d. Tune you to the Heart of the Father like never before.

e. Allow you to traverse into deeper dimensions of the Spirit.

f. Decrease your carnal mind while increasing the Mind of Christ within you.

g. Protect, watch over, and guard every person, idea, and thing that Jesus has given to you.

This book has nothing to do with religion. This book is all about interfacing with the Kingdom of God to release more of His Glory in your life, in your ministry, in your family, in your home, and ultimately all over the Earth.

How this read this book

This book, Shamar Meditation (Pre-Release Edition), is the 1st part of a 7 part epic accounting of God. Each book will contain 4 sections:

1.) Mindset
(Short Read)

2.) Application
(Medium Read)

3.) Epic Parable - Christian Fantasy
(Long Read)

4.) 30 Day Journal
(Daily)

This book can certainly be read from start to finish like most books, but it doesn't have to be. Pray about it and see where you feel led to start, and I believe that God will direct your path as you step into this journey!

If you are most interested in spiritual growth/spiritual warfare training, then start with Chapter 1 - "Who Do You Say That I AM?". It will open doors of fresh intimacy with God, whether you're a baby Christian or a seasoned Disciple.

If you love Super Heroes, Fantasy, and/or Science Fiction, then Chapter 3 - "Birth of a Hero", the action packed Epic Parable is where you need to start! As you explore the fantastic world of Aretz and are introduced to three special heroes (Trizzen, Jaza, and Katheros), you will have your heart filled with Godly adventure!

If you want to fast track the process of seeing some positive changes in your life, Chapter 2 - "Seek the Kingdom, Aggressively" is your best starting point. Start working towards the vision God has placed in your heart today, and watch God begin manifesting His promises in your life tomorrow!

As you make your way through any of these paths, the 30 Days Journey to Greatness Devotional is here as your daily companion. It's pretty action packed with the day to day adventure of our lives during the hectic Summer of 2017, as we were just starting to pray about this project. You will witness the actual birth of Eternal Kingdom Publishing! The devotional is largely raw and uncut…two warriors putting their hearts on the line for a vision, taking risks, and looking to please God in all things. The included notes pages are there to journal your own progress as you seek your next level in God!

As you finish a chapter, you can then explore the other chapters as God leads you. All of the chapters will build your spirit up in different ways. Be encouraged to think outside the box and use this book to choose your own adventure!

At the end, you will get a sneak peak of the rest of the books of Shamar Meditation and more information about the 21 book series they belong to, SuperNatural Humanity. These are in the process of being created, 1 prayer at a time.

Hopefully you'll love all of the book and be willing to leave a 5 star review on Amazon! Thank you for your support everyone. You're a blessing!

Table of Contents

Section 1 - Christ Brings Division

Chapter 1 - "Who Do You Say That I AM? (Mindset)

"There are many things which I want to show you.", says the Lord. "There are things I want to teach you directly. There are things I have patiently waited for millennia to reveal to you in this quiet place which I have prepared for you. For Us. Meet Us in the Beloved."

"Won't you come?", asks the Lord.

When Jesus was on that cross two thousand years ago, it was these moments of quiet intimate fellowship with you which helped sustain Him through the agony and pain of the situation. The suffering paled in comparison to Him being able to spend this time with you. You are fearfully and wonderfully made, and He cherishes time One on one with you!

It starts during your journey on Earth and will continue for Eternity, in Heaven.

"You see, My noble and beloved child, when you meet Me in the quiet place from Earth, I will meet you from Heaven. The moments we share will be the moments of legend. The moments we share here on Earth, we'll discuss in Heaven at full length, and we'll laugh and rejoice."

***

Spending time alone with God daily is crucial to your disciple walk. It is during this time alone every day that you can meet God in the secret place. The secret place is that focal point of relationship with God. It is the Throne Room.

It is the Damascus road where you can meet with Him at will. As your desire to truly know Him grows, it is these consistent daily meetings which satisfy your innermost desire to experience Him. Even as you meet Him in the secret place and that desire is fulfilled, you will receive even more desire for Him.

Look at these precious words of Jesus from the Gospel of Luke:

49 I have come to cast fire upon the earth, and how I wish that it were already kindled!
50 I have a baptism with which to be baptized, and how greatly and sorely I am urged on (impelled, constrained) until it is accomplished!
51 Do you suppose that I have come to give peace upon earth? No, I say to you, but rather division;
52 For from now on in one house there will be five divided [among themselves], three against two and two against three.
Luke 12:49-52 Amplified Bible, Classic Edition (AMPC)

The more you desire the baptism of the Holy Spirit, the harder you'll be able to seek Him in your individual secret place. This baptism isn't a once and done sort of thing. This baptism of fire is a continuous resource available to you, and it is accessible to us all even now!

Christ says of Himself that He will cause division. How can a God who relishes unity and family condone and even actively cause division?

In this case, it is a **division of degrees**. Christ doesn't want the Body to be separate. No Kingdom divided against itself can stand. However, there is a separation of degrees that must occur within your Christ-walk in order to reap the maximum benefits of life with Him.

For example, if in one circle of people, someone has decided in their heart that there is something that God won't do, or some way in which God won't operate, that may **influence** God to NOT operate in a particular fashion. If in that same circle, someone has chosen to accept that God, being sovereign and completely in control, can operate outside of our understanding, then that **looses** God to operate in a much higher capacity. Since God's ways are completely higher than our ways, then attempting to limit God only limits ourselves.

> **8** *"For My thoughts are not your thoughts,*
> *Nor are your ways My ways," says the* LORD.
> **9** *"For as the heavens are higher than the earth,*
> *So are My ways higher than your ways,*
> *And My thoughts than your thoughts.*
> **10** *"For as the rain comes down, and the snow from heaven,*
> *And do not return there,*
> *But water the earth,*
> *And make it bring forth and bud,*
> *That it may give seed to the sower*
> *And bread to the eater,*
> **11** *So shall My word be that goes forth from My mouth;*
> *It shall not return to Me void,*
> *But it shall accomplish what I please,*
> *And it shall prosper in the thing for which I sent it.*
> **Isaiah 55:8-11 New King James Version (NKJV)**

God is so far beyond human perception that He literally can't be limited in any form. He is more than we can truly fathom. However, if we come into agreement with certain limiting beliefs about God's nature, we can be limited in our baptism of His fire.

Here's an analogy to illustrate. Imagine we were all separate flames of fire, and one of us had certain beliefs which will only allow us to be heated to 100 degrees. However, once we make the decision to go higher by dropping all limiting beliefs and are no longer in agreement with anything false and limiting, we are able to go higher. We are able to experience more of the baptism. We are able to heat up and jump from 100 degrees to 1000 degrees overnight. We have free will, therefore we ultimately decide how hot we want to be and live for God.

The Lord says to you, "It is your choice. I desire greatly that you will come deeper into Me. I desire that you will have pure relationship with Me as the Chief Desire of your heart. I will not force myself upon you, for I love you too much for that. At certain crossroads of your life however I will visit with you directly and One on one. In that moment, I will give you the harvest you diligently worked for in the previous season. That harvest may be wisdom. It may be material abundance. It may be healing, whether physical or spiritual or emotional. It may be anything I have in My heart to bless you with. And I have more for you in My heart than you can ever earn. All gifts you will receive will be by My grace alone."

"However, I am a rewarder of those who diligently seek Me. Those who seek me more will be trusted with much. Those who don't really enjoy My presence will also receive, but to a limited level. I am never mocked, and what you sow you shall also reap, and more besides."

As you follow the direct will of God, there will be times

when God will need to separate you from something, some place, or someone.

If you are desiring strongly to grow in prophetic gifts, then God will separate you from anything which hinders the prophetic flow in your life. Sometimes this can even be other believers who genuinely love God, but who don't have a similar desire or understanding of how God engages with us prophetically.

If you desire to evangelize young people, God may cause separation from any ministry which is not geared towards the people group you feel called to evangelize to.

If you feel called to transform culture, God may separate you from simple minded religious circles. The Pharisees hated Jesus. The modern day Pharisee system, which is the system of simple religion for religion and continuity's sake, hates and resists anything which actually transforms culture.

These are all just used as examples, but the list goes on and on. In every season of your life as you continue to live a life centered around pleasing God, He may separate you from something, some place, or someone.

The more time you spend alone with God habitually, the greater the likelihood that you will feel led to explore new territory. Sometimes, you'll need to explore new spiritual ground with the Holy Spirit as your only companion.

The beautiful thing about this is that it allows you to get to learn new things directly from the Holy Spirit. As you honor His Presence with your time, He will get your attention and move you towards the next step in your destiny. Some seasons are going to be more centered around building foundations. Whereas others will be more centered around launching into new territory. Having a good feel for what Holy Spirit is leading you to do in each season is a skill which **all** of us have the **ability to grow in**.

Spending daily time with the Lord will help you get to know Him continually better and better. Of course, good fellowship is to be honored and respected always. We should never forsake the assembling of the brethren, as the Word commands us as such. However, we are also commanded to love the Lord our God with all of our heart, mind, and soul. As we mature in the faith, our personal relationship with the Father becomes paramount in assuring that we don't become stagnant or complacent or satisfied with the status quo.

Seven years ago, as a one year Christian, I met a street evangelist (let's call him) Wallace in Uptown Charlotte, North Carolina. Soon, we began ministering together on the streets of Charlotte. Every Friday night for some time, we fought the good fight of faith by passing out Daily Breads and Christian tracts. Every night that we went out the Lord was with us. We experienced many miracles and healings, prayed with people, and made many Kingdom connections.

At the start of this, I hadn't yet joined any church and all I knew was that I had a passion and a fire for God. Over the course of many months, we had formed a tight bond and had enjoyed numerous adventures together in the streets of Charlotte. We had shared many discussions surrounding the faith. With my understanding at that time, I figured that we would be lifetime friends and build and grow in ministry together.

As I matured in the faith, I became attached to a local church and starting working as a deacon. With months of dedicated service, I was elevated to the position of Chairman Deacon. Wallace was happy to see me growing in the faith, and we continued to enjoy great fellowship.

However, as I began embracing the prophetic call on my life, a clear shift occurred in our friendship. Wallace did not believe that God still moved prophetically and still called saints into the Office of the Prophet. I simply listened to his point of view, but knew that I'd not be able to persuade him of the truth of the matter. Then, God gave me a series of dreams which signified that He would be separating the friendship.

Next, the Lord used my dad to give me a message one morning over breakfast. The message was about how sometimes relationships in the Kingdom of God run their course and God shifts us. I hadn't told my dad anything about the situation, but God used him to deliver words of wisdom and words of knowledge. Within a week of that conversation, our fellowship was dissolved and Wallace and I went our separate paths. I would see Wallace again years down the road, and we shared a few laughs reminiscing over the adventures of old. However, we were in two completely separate realms, with two separate mindsets.

The Lord would not let our differences come to light in any negative fashion, as the Lord is always moving us toward reconciliation in the Body of Christ. Over time, this would not be the only relationship which the Lord would separate me from. As I continually yearn and press for more of His Presence, many friendships in the Kingdom have come and gone.

Unfortunately there have been several times over the years without this understanding in which I attempted to take matters into my own hands. Ultimately, this caused lots of heartache, both to myself and others. Thus, I needed to repent and refocus all of my efforts and energy on Christ, Himself.

I have had the pleasure of having friendships with many disciples over the years. During the season(s) of our friendship, the fellowship was fantastic! We each connected and were blessed by one another. However, at certain crossroads, there was a discernible shift, as the Lord moved each of us in different paths.

When certain gatherings take place, I've had the opportunity to reconnect with some of them and hear about all of the great things the Lord is doing in their lives, and share likewise. Since we're connected in the love of God, the fellowship is instant in season and out of season.

When you have an ever growing and expressly more intimate relationship with the Creator, you'll be more and more satisfied with Him. As you allow Him to separate you from anything and everything except direct connection with Himself, you'll come to the awesome revelation of how strong that personal bond with Him is. Nothing can separate you from the love of God.

35 Who shall separate us from the love of Christ? Shall tribulation, or distress, or persecution, or famine, or nakedness, or peril, or sword? 36 As it is written:
"For Your sake we are killed all day long;
We are accounted as sheep for the slaughter."
37 Yet in all these things we are more than conquerors through Him who loved us. 38 For I am persuaded that neither death nor life, nor angels nor principalities nor powers, nor things present nor things to come, 39 nor height nor depth, nor any other created thing, shall be able

to separate us from the love of God which is in Christ Jesus our Lord.
Romans 8:35-39 New King James Version (NKJV)

Since this bond with God is so strong, spending time daily alone with God will strengthen your ability to **pull the spiritual realm of Heaven** into Earth. This means that you will have **instant access** to all of the resources of Heaven when you pray, asking the Father for whatsoever in Jesus name. Yeshua (Jesus) told us:

23 *"And in that day you will ask Me nothing. Most assuredly, I say to you, whatever you ask the Father in My name He will give you.*
John 16:23 New King James Version (NKJV)

Jesus asked the disciples this, and He's asking you right now, "Who do you say that I am?"

If you say that Jesus is the King of Kings, and the Lord of Lords, you have done well. If in your heart you believe that you have full access to everything that He has access to because He is your King and your Lord, your heart is able to access the great spiritual riches of Heaven, and pull them into the physical realm of Earth.

In honoring Jesus by spending time with Him every day, you set yourself up to be a useful instrument in the hand of the Lord. We all have a desire somewhere inside of us to be used by God. You should desire that God allows you a baptism of fire which is hotter than 100 degrees. In fact, how about hotter than 1000 degrees? What about 10,000 degrees? Who do you say that He is? How worthy is He of your time, energy, commitment, and effort?

The Sons of Zebedee set a great example for us in their passionate pursuit of Jesus. They went to their Lord, and before telling Him what they wanted, slyly asked Jesus to make them a promise.

35 Then James and John, the sons of Zebedee, came to Him, saying, "Teacher, we want You to do for us whatever we ask."
36 And He said to them, "What do you want Me to do for you?"
37 They said to Him, "Grant us that we may sit, one on Your right hand and the other on Your left, in Your glory."
Mark 10:35-37 New King James Version (NKJV)

Jesus wisely asked them what it is they were desiring, before agreeing to grant it. This is fortunate for you and me. As far as Scripture reveals, the two who will sit on His right and left and are still up for grabs! We also see that a **great baptism** of the Spirit of God is required for those who will be close to Jesus in Heaven.

38 But Jesus said to them, "You do not know what you ask. Are you able to drink the cup that I drink, and be baptized with the baptism that I am baptized with?"
39 They said to Him, "We are able."
So Jesus said to them, "You will indeed drink the cup that I drink, and with the baptism I am baptized with you will be baptized;
Mark 10:38-39 New King James Version (NKJV)

James and John, the Sons of Zebedee (meaning the Sons of Thunder), declared that they are able to be baptized with the baptism that Jesus was baptized with. Once they declared this truth, Jesus confirmed that it was so. **Declare that you are able to be baptized** with the ever increasing fire of God. **Maintain a mindset** that you will continually be able to receive more and more of the baptism of fire that Jesus freely gives. Receive the revelation in your heart that every moment you spend with Him is literally **increasing the temperature** of your baptism!

Jesus goes on to give us a very important key in the very next verse. If you take this particular scripture, and **hold it in your heart** as you aggressively seek Him in the quiet place, you will see **tremendous spiritual growth.**

40 but to sit on My right hand and on My left is not Mine to give, but it is for those for whom it is prepared."
Mark 10:40 New King James Version (NKJV)

Due to what is revealed in this verse, it is quite possible that amongst the untold number of saints and angels in Heaven, you could be seated directly beside Jesus, for eternity. This is a great prize! I believe The Sons of Thunder prophetically discerned this possibility, and aggressively sought after it! They even had their mother ask on their behalf. Thank God for interceding mothers! (See Matthew 20:20-28)

Now, when the Sons of Thunder asked this of Jesus, it created a **level of separation** between themselves and the other apostles in training.

41 And when the ten heard it, they began to be greatly displeased with James and John.
Mark 10:41 New King James Version (NKJV)

As you begin and continue to seek God for deeper and deeper intimacy with Him, you should be prepared to take risks for more of His glory. Everyone around may not always agree with every move you make, unless God has revealed it to them. As it has been insinuated all throughout this chapter, that is okay! **It is perfectly acceptable to be different, peculiar, and driven in your desire to increase the heat in your passionate pursuit of the heart of the Father.**

For two other scriptural examples of this, let's look at specific moments in the life of both Abraham and Jesus.

After God gave Abraham the promised son Isaac, He then requested a very hard thing from Abraham.

Now it came to pass after these things that God tested Abraham, and said to him, "Abraham!"
And he said, "Here I am."
² Then He said, "Take now your son, your only son Isaac, whom you love, and go to the land of Moriah, and offer him there as a burnt offering on one of the mountains of which I shall tell you."
Genesis 22:1-2 New King James Version (NKJV)

Now this is obviously a major heat check moment for Abraham, as God tested his heart in this way. Abraham didn't attempt to put God in a little box by shrugging the command off as only his imagination. Although conceivably God never spoke such a thing to any of His followers before this moment, Abraham was able to move in obedience at the pioneering request from God.

9 Then they came to the place of which God had told him. And Abraham built an altar there and placed the wood in order; and he bound Isaac his son and laid him on the altar, upon the wood. 10 And Abraham stretched out his hand and took the knife to slay his son.
11 But the Angel of the LORD called to him from heaven and said, "Abraham, Abraham!"
So he said, "Here I am."
12 And He said, "Do not lay your hand on the lad, or do anything to him; for now I know that you fear God, since you have not withheld your son, your only son, from Me."
Genesis 22:9-12 New King James Version (NKJV)

So once Abraham proved to all of creation that his love for God was far greater than his love for his beloved son, God blessed him tremendously. Abraham sacrificed Isaac in his heart, and this proved enough for God. If you were to analyze what could have been in Abraham's heart at that moment, you may come to the conclusion that as dearly and passionately as Abraham loved Isaac, it **paled in comparison to his love for his Maker**. We should **model this behavior continuously** in our own friendship with God.

The near sacrifice of Isaac foreshadows the eventual sacrifice of Jesus thousands of years later. Jesus continued that level of commitment to the Father, as evidenced here in this passage.

41 His parents went to Jerusalem every year at the Feast of the Passover. 42 And when He was twelve years old, they went up to Jerusalem according to the custom of the feast. 43 When they had finished the days, as they returned, the Boy Jesus lingered behind in Jerusalem. And Joseph and His mother did not know it; 44 but supposing Him to have been in the company, they went a day's journey, and sought Him among their relatives and acquaintances. 45 So when they did not find Him, they returned to Jerusalem, seeking Him. 46 Now so it was that after three days they found Him in the temple, sitting in the midst of the teachers, both listening to them and asking them questions. 47 And all who heard Him were astonished at His understanding and answers. 48 So when they saw Him, they were amazed; and His mother said to Him, "Son, why have You done this to us? Look, Your father and I have sought You anxiously."

49 And He said to them, "Why did you seek Me? Did you not know that I must be about My Father's business?" 50 But they did not

understand the statement which He spoke to them.
Luke 2:41-50 New King James Version (NKJV)

Any parent who has a child missing for three days would likely be worried sick! Once finally found, Jesus just casually explains that He's obviously doing the Father's will. This would imply that Jesus' heart was more attuned to please His Father in Heaven more than satisfy the needs of His earthly parents. As we receive more so and more so the mind of Christ, we should always be willing to even do the spontaneous things which God places in our hearts even if it causes heartburn in our loved ones. This may be expressed differently in each one of us.

The Father, in all of His creative glory, has taken careful action to make each of us uniquely different. You can look at the beauty of nature all over the earth and within the universe, for that matter, to see the great variety of His creation.

Every human being is completely different. In looks, in thought, in heart, and in a vast variety of other ways. As you make your walk with God more and more personal, you will discover aspects of His Being that no-one ele has personally discovered yet. He is too vast for any one person or one group to know everything about. However, He reveals Himself to us, and His great treasures which are available to us via His Spirit.

9 But as it is written:
"Eye has not seen, nor ear heard,
Nor have entered into the heart of man
The things which God has prepared for those who love Him."

10 But God has revealed them to us through His Spirit. For the Spirit searches all things, yes, the deep things of God.
1 Corinthians 2:9-10 New King James Version (NKJV)

In your personal relationship with God, there is access to treasures which are deeply hidden in Him. For those treasures, only you are uniquely qualified to obtain and possess them. Ultimately, these treasures are for you to wield wisely, as you build His Kingdom all around you.

No one else is able to fulfill your role within God's heart. He loves you uniquely. As any parent with multiple children knows, each child you have is vastly different, and although none are perfect, each one is a completely different expression of love. You are a wonderfully made vessel of humankind. You are a great treasure, which the Lord has invested His Spirit into. In order to ensure that He receives the maximum return on investment for you, you can **express your fullest self** in your special bond with Him.

God desires all of us to be the very best version of ourselves for His own glory, and our brothers and sisters in Christ are each on their own journey. Our journeys often intersect at various points as we are all seeking Him. We are able to receive much wisdom from fellowship with other disciples of the Messiah. In the second phase of the SuperNatural Humanity series, Ro'eh Shepherding, we will explore fellowship and pioneering new ways for groups of disciples to build up one another.

As each member of a company of believers deepens their individual walk with the Creator, corporate meeting times will lead the group deeper into the heart of God. To expand upon this concept, see below:

26 "If anyone comes to Me and does not hate his father and mother, wife and children, brothers and sisters, yes, and his own life also, he cannot be My disciple.
Luke 14:26 New King James Version (NKJV)

The 'hate' here obviously isn't real hatred being alluded to. It's **degrees of love** that is being addressed. The deepest love you can ever feel is towards God. He is Love. So you should love your spouse, children, parents, and friends with a passionate longing sort of love. You should live your life willing and ready to honor them all deeply in your heart.

However, when that deep passionate yearning love is compared to the love you have for Christ, it should pale in comparison. If the love you have for your greatest loved one on Earth were to be compared to the love you have for your Creator, it should reek of hatred!

What a fabulous paradox!

Let's look at the Peter the apostle. When Jesus approached on the waves, walking and scaring the disciples who thought He was a ghost, Peter alone asked the Master to allow him to walk on the water (See Matthew 14:22-33). Something which conceivably had never been done before by any human being, Peter was willing to separate himself from his brethren, and attempt the impossible. Peter loved his fellow disciples.

However, when the idea to ask Jesus to allow him to join Him in walking on the water occurred in his mind, Peter didn't hesitate. His love for his brothers in the faith didn't lead him to turn to them and calm their fears. He didn't pat them on the shoulders and tell them everything was going to be okay. His love for Jesus lead him to take very different action! He fearlessly began to walk towards the scene which frightened them to their core.

His love for the other disciples paled in comparison to his love for his Messiah. He made the personal decision to **leave all reason behind,** and **seek to meet Jesus in an impossible place**!

Everyday, God is calling us to the impossible. In the age which we live in, information has become abundant. We have more information than the early Church did. However, we also have more distractions than any other time in history. How many times while reading this chapter did a cell phone buzz or vibrate or ding? Therefore, Jesus must sometimes cause separation from the world at large and consecration to Himself.

When we keep the eye on the prize of blissful eternity close at His side, this separation is easy and not burdensome at all.

Look at the John the Apostle. He is the notorious disciple whom Jesus loved. He had the tenderness of heart to simply lay upon the chest of the Master and listen to His heart beat. When Peter didn't want to ask the Master who the traitor among them was, he motioned to John to do it.

23 Now there was leaning on Jesus' bosom one of His disciples, whom Jesus loved. 24 Simon Peter therefore motioned to him to ask who it was of whom He spoke.

25 Then, leaning back on Jesus' breast, he said to Him, 'Lord, who is it?"

John 13:23-25 New King James Version (NKJV)

I want to contrast the love that these two great disciples and Apostles had for Jesus. One walked on water with great courage. One listened to His heartbeat with great tenderness. They expressed their radical love in different ways. They each had a deep connection with Him, which was truly personal. That love manifested itself in different ways at different times.

You, too, have a personal love and relationship with God. **You are special to God!** This is part of the reason spending daily time alone with Him is so important for you. If you've failed to do this in the past, it's not a big deal at all honestly. Cover it in grace, receive of His fresh mercies, then seek Him. **Hunt for Him as a hungry lion hunts for its prey. Hunt for Him as a shark hunts for its constant meal.**

Knock on the doors of His heart until He lets you in. **Be aggressive in your pursuit of Him!** Tell Him that you desire great things in Heaven. Then, live your life and believe it's yours.

Follow His leading in allowing separation to occur.

Another great thing about personal relationship with Him is that you will come to understand that He knows you. In fact, **He actually knows you better than you know yourself**. To journey deeper into Christ is also to **journey deeper into yourself**.

He alone has the secrets of why He made you to live at this time in this age. He alone knows why you had the parents you were born to. He alone knows why you grew up where you grew up. He alone knows why you may have been attracted to a certain profession. He knows why you ultimately chose certain specifics when it comes to your eduction. He knows why you chose the spouse you have, or even who you'll ultimately choose. He knows every joy you've ever experienced. He knows every pain you've ever felt, whether it be physical or emotional. He alone holds the keys of revelation of why you are the way you are. He is your Maker, after all, aye? **He personally crafted you to be a specific individual instrument of His glory.** Spending quiet time with Him everyday will lead you into an even deeper understanding of yourself and the world around you. Spending time with Him everyday will lead you to **walk on water in every aspect of your life**, as He will indeed carry you through situations. You will be able to **hear His heartbeat in the stillness of your secret place.**

God says to you "Come to Me, My child and lay all of your burdens on Me. I have reasons and purposes which the greatest minds of your time have never figured out and won't be able to figure out. I have reserved them for no ears but yours. I want to give you the best I have to give. I made you special and different from all of the rest of My creation. I have you in My heart every moment of every day. I yearn to fellowship alone with you. I yearn to give you secrets. Both secrets of yourself and secrets of Myself. I long and desire passionately to give you secrets of the past age. I yearn to give you secrets of the age to come. Won't you come and meet Me here, in the secret place?"

Chapter 2 -Seek the Kingdom, Aggressively (Application)

"I have given you the keys of the Kingdom, My disciple and My agent. I have placed numerous gifts inside you. Some you know already. Others are hidden just beyond the surface. As you aggressively seek My Kingdom's will to be done upon the Earth, these gifts will flourish within you. I will aggressively transform you into a mighty avatar of My Glory. When the trumpets blow, how close do you desire to be by My side?"

Summary

- Co-control your life w/ God
- Set personal goals daily
- Body Goals - Discipline
- Soul Goals - Discipline
- Spirit Goals - Discipline
- Personal Devotion Time
- Scripture Meditation and Memorization
- Find new ways to be intimate with the Lover of your soul

In the Hebrew language, the world Shamar means to guard, to watch, to keep. Essentially, it means to protect.

Shamar Meditation is a lifestyle that I've developed at the side of Jesus Christ. Shamar Meditation, simply put, means to live a life in which you are covered and even radiating with the power of God. This book and my website:

https://GTKPortal.App

Or
http://GTKPortal.Azurewebsites.net

were both created with the mindset that you are capable of doing amazing things in the name of the Lord Jesus Christ. As God's Holy Scripture becomes engrafted into your heart and soul, the greatness that God placed within you from before the beginning of time…..that same Scripture will guide you concerning all things. This is one of the functions of the Holy Spirit surging inside you. He truly is a Strong Tower!

To begin, please examine the way Jesus operates in the below excerpt from Scripture:

22 Immediately Jesus made His disciples get into the boat and go before Him to the other side, while He sent the multitudes away. 23 And when He had sent the multitudes away, He went up on the mountain by Himself to pray. Now when evening came, He was alone there. 24 But the boat was now in the middle of the sea, tossed by the waves, for the wind was contrary.

25 Now in the fourth watch of the night Jesus went to them, walking on the sea. 26 And when the disciples saw Him walking on the sea, they were troubled, saying, "It is a ghost!" And they cried out for fear.

27 But immediately Jesus spoke to them, saying, "Be of good cheer! It is I; do not be afraid."
Matthew 12:22-27 New King James Version (NKJV)

Before Jesus walked on water, He was alone. Jesus was deliberately alone, right before He demonstrated mastery over all things, including matter. At the beginning of starting to embrace the Shamar Meditation lifestyle, I recommend you take some time to be alone daily with God having this same expectation for yourself in mind.

Being alone, separate as possible from everything else, away from everyone else for a time allows us to focus on something to an entirely new and different level. And periodically in life, it is very helpful to take time away from as much as possible, and focus purely on the Word of God. This may be for a season or for a time, but building this sort of personal devotion time will generate tremendous benefits in both your present and future.

Now, you should always have a strong focus in your life on the Word of God. It's Eternal. It's life giving. It's JESUS on paper.

If you have been a disciple of the Messiah for a while, I salute you fellow warrior. I honor the work you have done for Him in the Kingdom, and I pray that this information blesses you. I encourage you to start thinking about all of your favorite Scriptures and the ones most meaningful to you. These are the perfect priceless gems to craft your Covenant Armor with. Covenant Armor is a term I like to use to describe the Scriptures which you take the time to commit to your memory and use as tenets in your heart to guide your decision making. These are your go to Scriptures for encouragement, warfare, worship, and every other aspect of life.

If you are new to the Kingdom of God, or if you have been apart of it for awhile and now are looking to get deeper into spiritual truth, I salute you as well. You are on the road to a great adventure. To assist you in your Covenant Armor quest, as you spend time alone with God everyday begin highlighting Scriptures which really speak to your heart.

Congratulations, you are about to experience explosive spiritual growth and the Lord your God goes before you.

If you have not had the luxury of having a deep and passionate relationship with Jesus Christ as of yet, please just keep reading. I also salute you, and I pray that He reveal Himself to you soon.

10 With my whole heart I have sought You;
Oh, let me not wander from Your commandments!
11 Your word I have hidden in my heart,
That I might not sin against You.
Psalm 119:10-11 New King James Version (NKJV)

Make a strong push for a season to commit more and more of the Word of God into your memory. If you already have a strong word base working in your memory, great! You have a solid head start.

If you've never spent time memorizing Scripture before, you're at the right place! It's nowhere near as scary as it may sound.

Shamar Meditation is going to require that you have the Word of God firmly planted in your heart and your memory. Let's practice. I recommend starting with easy Scriptures. Take for example:

Matthew 5:14.

"You are the light of the world. A city set on a hill cannot be hidden."

Visualize a city of bright lights, shining at the top of a

31

very tall hill. Imagine that you at the bottom of that hill, looking up in amazement at the brightness. Then start memorizing it little by little.

"You are the light"

Think that in your head, and say it aloud.

"You are the light of the world"

Think it, speak it. Let your mind wander to something else briefly. Then bring your mind back to the task. This technique will be very helpful and very useful as you move forward in SM (Shamar Meditation).

Now, think and speak this:

"You are the light of the world. A city"

Imagine that you're a full city, all within yourself. Imagine that the different parts of your being, your body, your soul, and your spirit are all glowing brightly like the city you imagined earlier. Close your eyes, and imagine the bright city of lights, and yourself being in it.

Let you mind wander for a few seconds...it's ok. Now, back to the task at hand. Think and say aloud:

"You are the light of the world. A city set on a hill".

Got it? If so great!!

If you don't yet, don't worry. Start from the beginning, and remember to breathe. If doubts or other concerns come to mind, simply let them flow out of your mind and heart.

Then patiently restart stepping through the Scripture until you improve. Follow the path of memorizing it. Little by little. Easy does it. You can do it, I believe in you! Keep working through it until you're ready to move on.

Now that you've mastered 90% of it, finish the rest:

"You are the light of the world. A city set on a hill cannot be hidden"

Now, spend a few minutes remembering the verse information. Matthew 5:14.

What chapter is it in? What is the verse number?

***

Great! Now you have the mindset required for Shamar Mediation. The next focus will be applying that mindset to your everyday life.

Since Christ is calling us all to a progressively higher calling in Him, we need to constantly make ourselves ready for that next level. God calls us all from Faith to Faith and from Glory to Glory. Every day that we are allowed to wake up, we have a resource given to us that we should never take for granted. Time.

Christ was very concerned with how His disciples spent their time. He prefers for us to spend time wisely and grow His kingdom. Spending time daily to build up your spirit, body, and soul will pay enormous dividends in your life. Incorporating Scripture into everything we do is an amazing way to keep all three parts of yourself strong.

I have personally searched high and low in many places to help me find resources which help me truly unpack the treasury of Scripture. On my journey, I have found many trusted resources and I will share those with you, reader to reader. I love the explanation of body/soul/spirit which I discovered in this book:

Spirit Life Training: If You Knew What God Has Put Within You, You Would Train It To Become Your Greatest Asset (Jorgensen, 2011)

by Timothy Jorgensen. He breaks down how we are three part beings, and our spirit should be the king, our soul should be the servant, and our body should be the slave.

I believe the book gives insight to what it takes for one to tap into the same anointing which John G. Lake himself operated under. I implemented much of what he encourages in SLT (Spirit Life Training) in my own quest for spiritual growth and it was very helpful, so I recommend it to everyone I know who is excited about spiritual growth.

This leads me to a funny story. I'd like to introduce you to Martie, a friend of my wife and mine, who once attended our Guardian Brigade church service. She is a young lady very passionate to know the deep things of God. Like many young adults she sometimes found it difficult to really connect with God in stuffy religious situations. Since I knew exactly what she was going though, I was able to recommend this book to her from my library. I let her borrow it. I figured I'd get it back in a few months, since it is definitely a book I keep on the top of my bookshelf (where I keep all my favorites).

We saw Martie a few months later, as she would come to

worship with us sometimes on Saturdays when she was free. I asked her about the book and the look on her face told me everything I needed to know. She had worked through the book, making notes and using it in her quest for growth. I knew then that I wouldn't be getting the copy of the book back, and I was happy that she was able to harness the power held within it.

As a leader, I was glad to see her growing. As a friend, I was even happier to see that the knowledge from the book was helping her to live a more empowered life. From that moment in time, I vowed that when I released my first book, it would have the same capability to change lives and help a person achieve their God given destiny.

It left me with a small problem of needing to buy the book again, but I promptly did so. I knew that when I got to this portion of writing this book, I was going to want to reference it.

However, now that this moment is occurring (my past just became my present), I am fully aware that the first podcast I'd like to produce would be a podcast where I am able to serve as host, as Martie speaks with Timothy Jorgensen, its author. Although I don't know Tim personally, I would love to offer him the chance to to make prophetic future history come around full circle.

So reader, I'll reach out to him and see what I can do, but stay tuned to me on social media for further information.

Timothy, thanks for all that you do for the Kingdom of God!

And to Martie G. our friend….Emely and I send you

much love! And note to Martie… gotcha! lol

As I already stated this is a fantastic book that I highly recommend you get your own copy of. And this is why.

52 Then He said to them, "Therefore every scribe instructed concerning the kingdom of heaven is like a householder who brings out of his treasure things new and old."
Matthew 13:52 New King James Version (NKJV)

What Timothy did in his book was take some things out of Heaven as well as some personal treasures which he had learned from his life and testimony, and presents it to the reader for consideration. After reading his book and applying the principles contained within I started to operate at a higher capacity, spiritually. I pray that this book and my website will begin to immediately have the same effect upon you. To sum up what Timothy says I present to you several key concepts to keep in mind.

- We consist of spirit, body and soul.
- Our spirit should be the king (or queen)
- Our soul should be the servant to our spirit
- Our body should be the slave to the spirit.
- Our soul consists of our mind, will, and emotions
- Our spirit, as born again believers, is one with God

Since you are royalty, a king or queen, you have an infinite ability to transform into a better version of yourself. Personally, I see this as an eternal blessing upon royalty. We are infinitely capable of rising to ever greater and greater occassions. Your life is your specific dominion. Rule well, mighty one!

My GTKPortal App is another resource which can help you on your own quest towards greatness. I've built this website primarily to lead my own family towards receiving the fullest blessing of God upon our household. In our quest to "Grind for God's Glory", we incorporate the working of body, soul, and spirit into all things we do. Getting my kids Samirah (9) and Jeremiah (8) acclimated to the deep things of the spiritual world at a young age has had tremendous benefits.

For example, recently my son Jeremiah inspired me greatly. In his school there was a certain (alleged) problem child bullying a student in his 2nd Grade class. Jeremiah, in defense of his classmate, was able to diffuse the situation. The problem child verbalized to my son that he would kill him.

In this world, the endless struggle of the powers of light versus the powers of darkness is found even in our elementary schools. I strongly believe in arming both children and adults alike in spiritual armor to lean into during times of trouble.

Instead of retaliating at the threat, my boy came home and told my wife what happened. She alerted my sons school teacher, who notified the appropriate authorities. The next day the boy wrote a letter to my son saying sorry.

My son, on his own authority wrote him back a letter saying "I forgive you. God forgives you and God bless you." 10 words in all, but hearing the story of the event was such a huge blessing. In my heart of hearts, I felt like our family had crossed a major milestone towards something I had set out to do over seven years ago when I became a Disciple of Jesus Christ. I had sought to find a community where spiritual growth in God was the center of activity.

I started the quest in the church. I found tons of wonderful teaching and preaching there, and God Himself made many appearances. I served in any and every capacity I could. However, after the service and outside of the weekly meetings, I realized that what I was seeking would only be possible is if time is being spent by all members to take the necessary time out for spiritual growth in between meetings.

I began to see some inconsistency in things here and there as well, so ultimately my wife and I felt led to begin our own church plant, which is where Guardian Brigade started. We met and worked with many wonderful disciples. After a year and a half of this effort, we decided to switch gears and focus on not just building up those around us, but the whole world.

If you've read any of the 30 Days to Greatness devotional which is at the end of this book, you should know that after the end of that 30 day Covenant I was led by the Lord into a season of what I would consider a prophetic cave. For me, it was a season of honing every skill that I had.

In that cave, I was shown many treasures and keys to wisdom, wealth, and God's unlimited mercy. He truly is a masterful God, who adroitly brings things together full circle.

When I heard the tale of my son who had responded with love in a very demanding and challenging situation, I knew in my heart that it was possible to change the world, one minute with God at a time.

I encourage you to begin working on improving your body, soul, and spirit every day. Even if you're only able to spend one minute on each of these three parts of your being, it is a powerful thing to do consistently!

Body

One key is making sure that as you focus on your body, you're doing so with the understanding that your body is just a tool of your spirit (which is one with God). As you do this everyday, I assure you that your spirit will be more in control. Maintaining the discipline to keep your body at its optimal conditioning is a great strategy to help ensure you're crucifying the flesh, daily.

If you're already physically fit and capable, great! I encourage you to add to your routine anything which helps you to honor God. If you're a marathoner who runs ten miles a day, be a marathoner who runs ten miles a day and finishes it with a prayer. If you're new to staying fit, you can't go wrong with stretching for a minute, while thanking God that you can do so. God receives the prayers from both equally, as long as hearts are seeking Him. He is an amazing God who has no respect of persons!

We each may have different physical fitness goals, so my advice to every one is that resistance training and cardio of some sort will go a long way into helping you stay healthy longterm.

In addition to exercise of some sort, do your part to eat healthy. In the next installment of Shamar Mediation in Chapter 5: Internal World Building, I'm going to talk more about food and it's properties within and upon the human body. An excellent resource that I've found on this subject is this book by Dr. Caroline Leaf:

- Think and Eat Yourself Smart: A Neuroscientific Approach to a Sharper Mind and Healthier Life (Leaf, 2016)

If you'd like to get a head start, I strongly recommend getting your own copy of this book. The authoress does a fantastic job of presenting her in-depth research on the subject matter.

Last, focus on ensuring you become adept at managing your sleep schedule. When you are able to live life fully refreshed, you can be alive in the moment. Every moment.

Sleep, dreams, and night visions will be covered in further detail later in further installments of Shamar Mediation. In the meantime, if you can wake up early and start putting your best self before God, you can then help speed along the process of your soul maturing in the Faith of Jesus Christ.

Giving Him the first fruits of your day as often as possible, is one of the wisest decisions a person can habitually make. As you develop Godly habits and keep them, it gets easier to incorporate other beneficial habits into your life. Someone once said that what we think, we ultimately say. What we say, we ultimately do. What we do often eventually becomes our habits. Our habits become our character. Over time, our character becomes our destiny! So, remember that as you continually work towards exercising Godliness with your entire being early in your day!

17 I love those who love me, and those who seek me early and diligently shall find me.
Proverbs 8:17 Amplified Bible, Classic Edition (AMPC)

The human body is an amazing machine which God has created. He has given our spirit a vehicle to navigate life on this Earth by. The body that we are in right now is a reflection of our values. If we're in the best shape of our life, that shows that we value good health and the abundance of life which Jesus promised us. It means that we've been good stewards of this temple which was given to us for the journey through Earth. But another key is to remember that this life is just a fleeting thing. We'll one day **receive glorified bodies**, so discipline your body, but be more concerned with the **development of your soul and spirit**.

If we know that we've haven't made the effort to reflect appreciation for this body to our Creator, it's okay. There is no day like today to start! The human body is really a miracle all by itself. It heals itself. As we demand more of it and **put into place the processes** to **continually strengthen** it, build it up with more **endurance**, and make it more **flexible**, it responds to us **favorably**.

Now, everyone who spends time working out in some capacity has a choice to make. We can do it for our own vain glory, or we can do it for the glory of the Creator who made us. It is infinitely wiser to **keep our temples in good shape for His glory**, and not our own.

If we allow selfish pride to be the driving factor for staying fit, God will need to work that out of us. God opposes the proud, but gives grace to the humble.

As we realize in humility that God has made us wondrous and that each of us is a marvelous creation, we will desire to reflect God in our temple. Our God is strong. Jesus, when He walked this earth was a carpenter. Can you imagine how strong He must have been to perform that sort of manual labor as a profession in the first 30 years of His life?

Peter and several other disciples were fisherman. Can you imagine the strength that they likely had, pulling in nets of fish and rowing boats on the sea? Can you imagine how much exercise the disciples and our Lord got as they walked from city to city and town to town?

In this day and age, it is even more important to develop an individual physical fitness plan for ourselves. Many activities such as work and recreation in the past included strenuous physical activity of some sort. Not anymore. There are many things we can accomplish with just our fingertips in this great Information Age. With the advent of more virtual reality systems and new technologies, our mind will be able to go more places and do more without much involvement from our body.

I believe Christ wants your body to be strong. He literally crafted you so that your body will respond to the stimuli you subject it to.

Try to develop the application of **eating to live, not living to eat**. I'm sure most of us have heard the old adage "You are what you eat". It is true!

Seeking to control these three factors (exercise, food, and sleep) and bring them into subjection to God will do wonders for our sense of self discipline. With a strong body, we'll be able to lend a helping hand. With a strong body, we'll have an alert sense of focus and ability to concentrate on spiritual things. With a strong body, we'll be more adept at combating sickness, disease, fatigue, and will be resistant to injury. God created each of us with an ability to grow. If you separate time to strengthen your body every day, even if it's only 5 minutes a day, you'll see results over time. Consistency daily is the key.

Soul

The soul can be defined as our mind, will, and emotions.

God has given you an unlimited access to His very own power. This means that your soul is unlimited in what it can become. Your mind is unlimited. Your will and drive can be used to accomplish great things. You can have a high level of mastery as it pertains to your emotions. Your soul is to be the servant of your spirit. You can use your soul to build up your spirit, and propel you and everyone around you to new previously unfamothed and unchartered territories in God.

Our soul, once properly harnessed, can become a dynamic power source for us to tap into in order to release waves of God's glory. Here is a terrific Scripture which really pinpoints the relationship between spirit and soul.

12 For the Word that God speaks is alive and full of power [making it active, operative, energizing, and effective]; it is sharper than any two-edged sword, penetrating to the dividing line of the breath of life (soul) and [the immortal] spirit, and of joints and marrow [of the deepest parts of our nature], exposing and sifting and analyzing and judging the very thoughts and purposes of the heart.
Hebrews 4:12 Amplified Bible, Classic Edition (AMPC)

God's Word functions as a mirror, showing you the state

of your own heart. When you consistently put the Word of God before your eyes and allow your heart to reflect on it, you allow Holy Spirit to highlight to you what the current state of your mind, will, and emotions are compared to God's Holiness. This serves as a powerful barometer as you seek intimate fellowship with your Maker.

2 Do not be conformed to this world (this age), [fashioned after and adapted to its external, superficial customs], but be transformed (changed) by the [entire] renewal of your mind [by its new ideals and its new attitude], so that you may prove [for yourselves] what is the good and acceptable and perfect will of God, even the thing which is good and acceptable and perfect [in His sight for you].
Romans 12:2 Amplified Bible, Classic Edition (AMPC)

Mind. What you focus your mind on, you will eventually become attuned to. Whatever you continually put before your eyes, you will hook into it. If you use your mind to focus on Godly thinking and reasoning, you will consistently become more like God. You will eventually become more and more like Jesus Christ. You will think the way He thinks. You will love the way He loves

However, if you focus your thinking more so and more so on the world around you, you will be moved by the world around you.

An application principle to keep in mind is that this world that we see is passing and fleeting. It is the unseen world that we should keep our thinking attuned with. Another great resource from Dr. Caroline Leaf is this book:

- Switch On Your Brain: The Key to Peak Happiness, Thinking, and Health (Leaf, 2015)

I chanced upon this gem in my local Christian book store one day, and I thank God for the knowledge it contains. One of my many take-aways from this book was the study of Epigenetics! What we think about in our mind (soul) literally changes our physical body (brain) and our spiritual development. I highly recommend getting your own copy of this book for your own exploration!

What we focus on with our mind is going to eventually and consistently grow around us. The mind is a gateway to the heart. The mind (soul) is a gateway to our spirit. It sits between our body and our spirit. Guard the Kingdom of Heaven. As a born again believer in Jesus Christ, the Kingdom of Heaven is accessible to you at the very core of your being. You are His. He purchased you with His blood, and He will never leave or forsake you. He will never abandon you. Keep your mind focused on this fact in the midst of any trouble or dilemma. Christ told us we would have tribulation. He then turned around and told us to take cheer, because He has already overcome the world.

As a spiritual warrior, there will be days when it feels as if the forces of hell are mounting for an attack. Having a close relationship with God allows you to receive comfort from the spiritual realm with much more ease. You'll essentially be controlling your emotions and mind from your spirit, which is one with God already. Fear will flee from before your face. Doubt and discouragement will dissipate when you remember that Jesus is the same yesterday, today, and tomorrow.

23 Keep and guard your heart with all vigilance and above all that you guard, for out of it flow the springs of life.
Proverbs 4:23 Amplified Bible, Classic Edition (AMPC)

The peace of God is a strong defense, and you will be poised to release what God has put inside of you. The world needs you to do so. Creation is literally groaning at every moment awaiting the Sons and Daughters of God to arise. Let's **arise to the occasion**, friends.

Will. What do you want to accomplish? Actively draw closer to God with your will. Drive forward the plans that God has purposed in your heart. The dream will be birthed in our spirit. **See it constantly with our mind's eye**, then **drive it to completion. Take actions every day.**

If you are consistent and show up time and time again, eventually something is going to happen. Develop a will like Rocky Balboa. Develop a will like Apostle Paul. Develop a will like Alexander the Great. Latch on to all that you find personally heroic. As you achieve milestones towards whatever vision God has placed inside you, your confidence and faith in God will grow to previously unexplored heights.

Seek to please God in your life with your will and drive. Take time to reflect on what you've accomplished previously. Don't dwell on failures, but harness the wisdom from them. Be willing to try something new for a season. If it produces and maintains results, continue it. If it doesn't take the lessons you've learned then try something new.

Every day that you receive from God is a blessing. Harness it and make a goal for yourself to DO

SOMETHING every day towards the end game.

If you want to start a business, set aside 5 or 10 minutes every day to read up on your industry. Maybe read up on success stories of similar businesses owners.

Then, move from reading up on business owners to 10 minutes a day writing a plan. Elaborate on the plan. Spend 10 minutes a day just thinking and writing down inspiring thoughts that come to you. God will meet you in that place or He will direct you towards another path. Trust Him.

Once that's done, spend 10 minutes a day researching ways to get started. Howe can you drum up the finances? Can you take a part time job doing something for a season that will give you some extra capital? This is just an example, but please apply the general tactic to your own dream, whatever that may be. **Your mind has great potential.** As you exercise your will, it will be strengthened. Using a **God centered strong will to advance the dream or vision** that He placed in your heart before Eternity began is going to pan out. **Believe in God, and believe in yourself.**

After weeks or months of this strategy, I guarantee you that something good is going to be the result.

Emotions. This is where the fighting is fiercest for the souls of this earth. If the enemy can't stop a born again disciple of Jesus Christ from advancing in God, he'll attempt to cause pain in the emotional realm for that individual. Once you learn his tricks and snares, you will be able to sidestep his nonsense and counter attack. **Praising God is a powerful weapon** to use when your emotions seem to be out of whack.

Emotions are very powerful. Positive emotions can really serve to build us up. Negative emotions can really serve to bring us down. The good news is that we can train our emotions. Try this. Set aside 5 minutes to think of something positive. Just spend the entire 5 minutes focused on that positive thing.

EXERCISE
(try below to help train your emotions)

Spend 5 minutes focused on something positive. Fire focus all your energy on that 1 thing.

How do you feel?

Can you still feel the positive emotions?

Do you feel victorious?

Now if you want reinforcements that what I tell you is truth, focus on something negative for 30 seconds.

How do you feel?

How did thinking about it help you?

If you get nothing good out of thinking about it, what is the purpose?

Spend 30 more seconds focused on the positive thing. If the negative things pops up in your mind...let the thought drift away, refocus on the positive thing.

This is a simple exercise which you can do often. You can tailor it to fit your schedule and your way of thinking.

If you find that thinking about the positive thing doesn't keep you at peace, examine the motives of your emotions. Is this positive thing something God would rejoice in? Is this positive thing something which God placed in your life, and if so, what reason could He have done it for?

For the negative thing, anytime you feel heavy or burdened, spend some time meditating and seek to get to the root of why a certain situation has you down. Is the situation or circumstance something that God has the capability to bring you out of? Can God heal your heart of this matter?

When you refocus your attention towards the positive thing, can you feel a difference in your internal feelings?

This is easy for some. For others it may take work to accomplish. However, I certainly believe that all of us will have a grand adventure in the pursuit of improvement as we seek to understand the root causes of our emotions. This exercise only scratches the surface of understanding our emotions, as this is a vast topic. Future Application chapters of the Shamar Meditation line of books will press much deeper into this realm of humanity which has great influence on all of us.

The Imagination is a key concept for Shamar Meditation. Using a Holy and sanctified imagination often will lead to breakthrough moments and epiphanies in life. God has an effective and oft-times transparent way of preparing us for these moments of sudden world changing revelation. I want you to consider that if this below verse from Jesus is true, then it applies both to the positive and negative connotations:

27 "You have heard that it was said to those of old, 'You shall not commit adultery.' 28 But I say to you that whoever looks at a woman to lust for her has already committed adultery with her in his heart.
Matthew 5:27-28(NKJV)

As far as Jesus is concerned, if we look upon someone and imagine lustful thoughts, we've already committed adultery. In the same vein, it should mean that if we look upon someone with mercy and imagine blessing them we've already blessed them in our hearts.

Example

I want you to imagine a person who has done wrong to you. Someone who has mistreated you or talked about you or not appreciated you. For 15 seconds, I just want you to focus on all the mean or even cruel things this person has done or said.

Now, for 30 seconds, I want you to imagine doing something nice for that person. Imagine giving them money when you hardly have it to give. Imagine praying that God bless them with their hearts' desire, and imagine God moving swiftly at your prayer request. Imagine any wrong between you and that person being righted. Don't do it out of a sense of compulsion, but out of love. You genuinely want to see God bless that person's socks off, and you want to be a part of that blessing. Even an integral part of the blessing.

How do you feel afterward?

Do you think that God enjoyed the opportunity to condition your heart?

Do you feel that God attributed the thoughts of your

mind to you as righteousness?

As you perform exercises like this in your Shamar Meditation build up time, you will find that God will conduct many pep talks with you during these quiet times of reflection. Holy Spirit, as our Coach in a sense, methodically builds us up with what we will need with you realize the potential that God has set before you. Sometimes, forgiveness is tough to do. This imagination exercise will help you in any situation where forgiveness is needed, so that bitterness will not take root in your heart.

Conscience. God's still small Voice will flood from your spirit into your soul via your conscience. As you learn to recognize His leanings and promptings, you will be able to actively participate in God's plan for your life. This is a skill, which can be built up over time. When you feel something is the right thing to do, or the right thing to say or not say, this is likely your conscience expressing itself. At times, your conscience will likely be at odds with your emotions. Since your conscience is a gateway between your spirit and soul, the ability to purposely choose what you are sensing in your Conscience over what you are presently feeling in your emotions is a valuable skill as a disciple of Christ.

EXERCISE
(Try below to receive a "quick" fix revelatory word from God. Remember that close relationship has great benefits.)

Here is a Shamar meditative practice you can begin implementing immediately. Set specific intervals, such as the top of every hour, to take a moment out of your busy day to just be quiet.

"God, is there anything you want to tell me?"

Believe what you hear. If it's instructions, obey them. If it's encouragement, believe that it is from God and not merely from yourself. If you feel that you can't hear or sense anything from God in these moments, it's okay. Just take the time to thank Him for loving you. Overtime as you practice this exercise, you'll definitely grow in your ability to receive direction from the Holy Spirit.

In addition to a strong conscience which you can trust in, having a strong soul helps you to be able to be able to reason effectively, even in tough situations.

God has opened great doors of Wisdom to us with the gift of His Son Jesus Christ.

24 For I tell you that many prophets and kings longed to see what you see and they did not see it, and to hear what you hear and they did not hear it.
Luke 10:24 Amplified Bible, Classic Edition (AMPC)

We should apply our ability to reason into the quest to love God. A Google search supplied this definition of 'reasoning':

{ think, understand, and form judgments by a process of logic }

We should use all of our heart, soul, and every scattered ray of our mind in our worship of the Father!

2 Making your ear attentive to skillful and godly Wisdom and inclining and directing your heart and mind to understanding [applying all your powers to the quest for it];

Proverbs 2:2 Amplified Bible, Classic Edition (AMPC)

Begin applying spiritual principles to every aspect of your life. Apply everything you know about God to every detail within your life. As you do this, you'll really be able to see God's hand supernaturally moving in these areas. The Shamar Meditation lifestyle is a supernatural lifestyle, and it is only by incorporating God and His revealed principles that the supernatural will grow consistently around you.

I like to call this spiritual critical thinking, and I will make several references to this throughout this series.

When you reason, or think critically spiritually, you have an arsenal of weapons to use within your mind! You can use direct scriptures which apply to your current situation or moment in time. You can also use your memory of everything God has already done in your life. But, it doesn't just stop with what you've already seen God do directly.

You can be encouraged by testimony from others. Whenever a testimony is given, it releases the same anointing by faith for all those who hear it and honor it in their hearts. You should seek to develop a strong ability to honor the testimonies of other disciples. If you honor the testimony of fellow believers, God will repay you for that honor tenfold.

You can also use **revelations which you've received such as dreams and visions**. This is a reason that you are strongly encouraged to **record everything in a journal** of some kind. The longer you walk with the Lord, the more and more revelations will come your way. If you forget them, they can not be used as effectively to **improve your ability to think critically**.

You can also use dreams and visions which you've heard other disciples share. The list is limitless to what you can use to encourage yourself spiritually. You can begin to use virtually anything encouraging by the authority of this verse.

Meditate on These Things
8 Finally, brethren, whatever things are true, whatever things are noble, whatever things are just, whatever things are pure, whatever things are lovely, whatever things are of good report, if there is any virtue and if there is anything praiseworthy—meditate on these things.
Philippians 4:8 New King James Version (NKJV)

EXERCISE
(use the below questions to examine your sense of purpose)

Take a moment to ask yourself these three questions. Then, take a moment to use spiritual critical thinking to draw encouragement from the answers to these questions.

1.) What is the most serious issue I need resolved in my life right now?   (Prophetic Key to begin with: Has God performed bigger breakthroughs in your life, or in the Bible, or in the life of another believer)

2.) What am I most excited about in my life right now?

(Prophetic Key to begin with: How has God inspired this and what has He shown you?)

3.) What can I do to positively influence the Kingdom of God, over the next 24 hours?
(Prophetic Key to begin with: What do you feel in your heart God is telling you? Believe!)

In your secret place with God, spend time meditating and reflecting on these sorts of questions. Eventually this habit will climax in a wonderful harvest from God Himself.

Spirit

Your spirit is the greatest treasure you possess!

Of all of the three parts of your being, this is the most important by far. Your body and soul need to be as strong as possible to support the increase to your ability to accomplish greater and greater spiritual goals.

Your spiritual goals will net you the direct accumulation of treasure in Heaven. Nothing we do for the Lord is ever in vain! The soul is the breath of life. However, your spirit is **IMMORTAL**!

51 Behold, I tell you a mystery: We shall not all sleep, but we shall all be changed— 52 in a moment, in the twinkling of an eye, at the last trumpet. For the trumpet will sound, and the dead will be raised incorruptible, and we shall be changed. 53 For this corruptible must put *on incorruption, and this mortal must put on immortality. **54** So when this corruptible has put on incorruption, and this mortal has put on immortality, then shall be brought to pass the saying that is written: "Death is swallowed up in victory."*

***55** "O Death, where is your sting?*
O Hades, where is your victory?"

***56** The sting of death is sin, and the strength of sin is the law. **57** But thanks be to God, who gives us the victory through our Lord Jesus Christ.*

***58** Therefore, my beloved brethren, be steadfast, immovable, always abounding in the work of the Lord, knowing that your labor is not in vain in the Lord.*

1 Corinthians 15:51-58 New King James Version (NKJV)

In Heaven, there is a level of glory laid up for those who live their lives as spiritual champions. You don't need to die to get into Heaven. You just need to close your eyes and breathe. Since you're in the **Messiah, the realm of Heaven is that near to you.**

Jesus Christ is the ultimate Champion. As His disciple, you are all set to walk in victory in every area and arena of your life.

Similar to Christ, that journey to victory is going to include challenges. But **you are an overcomer!** Your spirit is one spirit with Jesus Christ Himself. Your life should parallel Jesus' life in many ways. Continue to draw closer and closer to Him in prayer, fasting, studying the Word, being obedient, fellowshipping with saints and living holy.

Your character and your destiny should resemble Christ's character and Christ's destiny. You can ensure that this happens by setting spiritual goals for yourself. Increasing the intimacy with God in your private time with Him becomes a key metric for spiritual growth.

Once you have that time set apart for drawing closer to Christ, there are a myriad of ways in which you can use this time to make it valuable in your growth. I'll give you some suggestions, however, like everything else that is suggested in this book, the principles will work best when you apply them to you and your own walk with God. You are literally one spirit with Christ, so Holy Spirit is the best tutor and guide you can ever directly follow!

17 But the person who is united to the Lord becomes one spirit with Him.
1 Corinthians 6:17 Amplified Bible, Classic Edition (AMPC)

The Bible. Develop a daily Bible reading plan that works for you. The Word of God is life, and it literally fuels every aspect of your life. You would do well to schedule this time early in the day, perhaps before you do anything else. The Word is fresh life into your spirit. Getting the word into your spirit will help you really connect to the Person of Jesus Christ, since He is the Word.

14 And the Word (Christ) became flesh (human, incarnate) and tabernacled (fixed His tent of flesh, lived awhile) among us; and we [actually] saw His glory (His honor, His majesty), such glory as an only begotten son receives from his father, full of grace (favor, loving-kindness) and truth.
John 1:14 Amplified Bible, Classic Edition (AMPC)

As morning routines go, I personally like to read the

book of Proverbs first. The book of Proverbs gives you information that if applied, will help you to reign in life. I like to read the chapter in Proverbs that corresponds to the day of the month. Since there are anywhere from 28 to 31 days in a month, and there are 31 chapters in Proverbs, I always have something fresh from God awaiting in my inbox, if you catch my drift.

Depending on your reading speed, this may take you anywhere from five to ten minutes, or more or less. It's certainly not a race. Otherwise, perhaps you will flourish with a reading plan which allows you to read the entire Bible in 1 year. That is fantastic as well. Whatever habits or tactics you can build into your daily routine to draw you closer to Father will ensure that your spirit stays refreshed and connected to Jesus.

Otherwise, maybe you want to simply pray and go into the Word wherever God is leading you to. This is also a great strategy. I salute you in your quest to find more of Him.

As needed, spend time really feasting on passages which directly address any situation which you are current living through. Searching on the Internet or using an additional resource to find specific passages and stories which give insight to your current season in life is a necessary tool which sometimes even grizzled old spiritual warfare warriors would do well to still keep part of their spiritual rotation.

In addition to the time I spend in Proverbs every day, I spend an additional 15 minutes of time reading the bible every morning during my devotional time. I alternate every other day between New Testament and the Old Testament. If I happen to want to finish a specific book, I may read that one specific book, for 15 minutes every other day, until I finish that book.

As I stated earlier, this works for me, but it took me much experimentation in spiritual growth to find this strategy. And still, depending on what I feel in my own spirit, I may change up that strategy at different points.

The overall goal is that we have something in place which works for us. The Word is paramount to us maintaining a strong connection with our Creator.

After you read the Bible, remember to take some time to let it resonate in your spirit. The first step is to read it and get it in your mind. After you've done this, I suggest having some quiet time to think about what you've read. You may also want to write down notes on key points from what you've read to reflect on. Doing this will allow the Word the time it needs to sink down from your head to your heart.

Imagination. The vehicle of your imagination is once again key when reading Scripture. If you're reading about Jesus and His interactions with the disciples, after you've read, spend some time thinking about it. Imagine in your mind the scene or scenes you just read. Imagine Jesus preaching the Sermon on the Mount, the Beatitudes, with fire and conviction. Imagine the displeasing look on the face of the Pharisees as Jesus rebukes them time and time again.

If you're reading the Book of Revelation, take some time to imagine the angels blasting trumpets and the scene around God's Throne-Room. Imagine the lone Apostle John on the island of Patmos being pulled into spiritual places and encountering Jesus with fire in His eyes. Oh, imagine the love that Jesus must have had in His eyes as He beheld the disciple that He loved!

If you're reading the book of Proverbs imagine putting into action the principles and parables you are reading about. If you're reading the Epistles, imagine the Early church standing against great persecution as they attempted to perform all of the commands from the Apostle Paul.

Imagine these scenes and principles with **all your heart**. Take the time to reflect on them and **make them real and personal.** See it with your mind's eye and hold to it. Doing this over time is going to strengthen your mind, and your soul and your spirit.

Prayer. We should pray ceaselessly, throughout our day, for things great and small. Since prayer is a constant communication with God, we should be making our requests known to Him, blessing and thanking Him, and simply fellowshipping with Him. Our prayer life is very important to God, and prayer builds up our spirit tremendously.

This is going to draw us near to the heart of the Father. It is through this daily offering of prayer that God is going to use to give us direction, instruction, and comfort, amongst many other things. **Prayer is a two way communication**. As you pray and bless His name, He will speak to you.

There is no right or wrong way to pray. Here are two methods you can use to super charge your prayer life.

- ACTS Method
    I first read of the ACTS method of prayer in this book:

- The Battle Plan for Prayer: From Basic Training to Targeted Strategies (Kendrick & Kendrick, 2015)

I highly recommend that book to any dedicated prayer warrior looking to advance their spiritual life. The four steps are to: **A**cknowledge God, **C**onfess any and every sin, **T**hank God for His mercy, and only then get to **S**upplication. Supplication is asking the Lord for what you need, after you've acknowledged His goodness, confessed anything and everything, and also thanked Him for being so amazing. The Lord's Prayer is a great example of this method. (**Matthew 6:9-13**) This is **how Jesus told His disciples to pray**, and I find this prayer approach to be extremely effective.

- John 17 Prayer method

In this priestly prayer by the Great High Priest, Jesus Christ, Jesus first prays for Himself, then He prays for His disciples, then He prays for all believers everywhere. I've heard it mentioned that we should never pray for ourselves, but I personally couldn't disagree more. If Jesus prayed for Himself, it is imperative that we pray for ourselves.

By **praying for yourself first**, you will in a spiritual sense be able to cover yourself in the priestly garments needed to intercede successfully for others.

Then, shift to praying for your family and or your church or ministry and or your friends and or co-workers (**your inner circle**). The point is to pray for those that are the closest to you. You will know specific needs. Be sure to ask directly for those things which they need, from the Father. It is His joy to answer your patient and self sacrificial prayer.

Lastly, pray for the **entire Body of Christ**. Will your spirit wherever the Father will direct you. If you feel led to pray for the persecuted Church, pray for the persecuted Church. If you feel led to pray for exposure of things which are being done wrong in the church as a whole, pray for that. If you feel led to pray for the leadership of the church as a whole, pray for that. Pray for those who need spiritual guidance. Pray for those who have been backslidden and need to be restored. Pray all these things and know that God is listening, and know that He will act on your prayers when the time is right. So re-enforce what you've prayed daily with more prayer. Look at this powerful Scripture:

6 I have set watchmen upon your walls, O Jerusalem, who will never hold their peace day or night; you who [are His servants and by your prayers] put the Lord in remembrance [of His promises], keep not silence,
7 And give Him no rest until He establishes Jerusalem and makes her a praise in the earth.
Isaiah 62:6-7 Amplified Bible, Classic Edition (AMPC)

You are set to be *that* watchman. Give the Lord no rest. Keep the prayer vigil non stop, every day, as you bombard heaven with your prayers.

Praying the Word directly back to God is an excellent strategy. In the next book, Grinder's Paradise (Shamar Meditation Part 2) we will be deep diving into building up your spirit by using memory and meditation. For now, as you read through the rest of this book, keep in the back of your subconscious mind that you are set to be *that* watchman (or *that* watchwoman).

Scripture memorization and meditation. God told Joshua to meditate in the Word, day and night. A great secret to taking the promised land in your own life is meditating on scripture, day and night.

Here are some helpful points to get you started, which will build off of the exercise we began this chapter with.

- Spend some time memorizing scripture. Start small by selecting key verses, then memorizing a few words at a time.

- Try to remember the book, chapter and verse number.

- Whatever you can remember, begin to recite it to yourself in your mind throughout the day as you go about your daily life.

- Meditation in Hebrew also describes a cow chewing cud (grass that it has regurgitated). Cows chew this over and over.
  ○ Although this may not be the most appetizing analogy, it is very helpful for building up your spirit. **Just keep 'chewing' on that scripture over and over.**

- The more often you bring Scripture to the fore-front of your mind, the greater your expectation and likelihood will be that God is going to bring you specific, individual revelation which relates directly (and powerfully) to your life.

EXERCISE

{Here is an example of how to begin memorizing and Shamar Meditating John 1:1}

Begin by reading and thinking about the whole scripture.

In the beginning was the Word, and the Word was with God, and the

*Word was God. **John 1:1***

Then, begin by memorizing the first few words.

In the beginning was the Word

Say this over and over until you can recite it in your mind (heart). After you feel you have it memorized, set a timer for 15 minutes, and shift your focus into doing something else. Try not to think about it at all.

Once the timer goes off, can you still recite it without trouble? If not, try again! If so, move on the the next part of the verse.

In the beginning was the Word, and the Word was with God

Say this over and over until you can recite it in your mind (heart). After you feel you have it memorized, set a timer for 15 minutes, and shift your focus into doing something else. Try not to think about it at all.

Once the timer goes off, can you still recite it without trouble? If not, try again! If so, move on the the next part of the verse.

In the beginning was the Word, and the Word was with God, and the Word was God.

Say this over and over until you can recite it in your mind (heart). After you feel you have it memorized, set a timer for 15 minutes, and shift your focus into doing something else. Try not to think about it at all.

Once the timer goes off, can you still recite it without trouble? If not, try again! If so, move on the the last part, which is the verse information.

In the beginning was the Word, and the Word was with God, and the Word was God. **John 1:1**

Say this over and over until you can recite it in your mind (heart). After you feel you have it memorized, set a time for 15 minutes, and shift your focus into doing something else. Try not to think about it at all.

Once the timer goes off, can you still recite it without trouble? If not, try again. If so, you're all done committing this Scripture to your heart!

Feel free to change this approach as you see fit. If 5 minutes works better for you in between trying to recite the verse, then go with that! If an hour works better for you, then go with that! Whatever it takes to commit the scripture to memory in the best way for you is what you're seeking to accomplish.

Once the Scripture is firm in your memory, it is in your short term memory. Try it again in a few hours, then tomorrow. Continue this practice until your long term memory is saturated with this scripture.

As you continue to build up your spirit, you are going to find a wealth of power in every area of your life. The GTKPortal App has been built with this in mind. It is a free resource to help you in your quest, and I invite you to come and fellowship with others who are willing to grind for God's Glory. As of this writing, 21,622 minutes have been tracked in the quest to give God glory! With your help, we could reverse the dark trends of the times, and increase God's Kingdom within the Earth realm.

Otherwise, thank you for reading and supporting this Shamar Meditation project. Stay tuned for the rest of this book and series, and please look me up and feel free to add me to your social networks. A bright age looms before us, my friends. Keep your spiritual weapons sharp, and stay hedged in with prayer. Let us all take up the mantle to Guard This Kingdom!

I'd like to close this chapter out by encouraging you to actively practice your spiritual gifts, followed by presenting some information on proper goal setting. We should practice spiritual gifts often so that they can grow. In the Application chapters of this book, I will focus on one or two of the 9 spiritual gifts mentioned in 1 Corinthians 12. A key for all of us to remember is that the Holy Spirit Himself performs these gifts in each of us.

God is the the same yesterday, today, and tomorrow. All of the miracles, signs, and wonders that we read about in the Bible are available to us today. God loves it when we seek to live a supernatural life, because a supernatural life is going to reveal Him to the world around us.

One way to seek the supernatural is to seek opportunities to operate in the gifts of the Spirit. There are 9 specifically listed in 1 Corinthians 12.

4 There are diversities of gifts, but the same Spirit. 5 There are differences of ministries, but the same Lord. 6 And there are diversities of activities, but it is the same God who works all in all. 7 But the *manifestation of the Spirit is given to each one for the profit of all: **8** for to one is given the word of wisdom through the Spirit, to another the word of knowledge through the same Spirit, **9** to another faith by the same Spirit, to another gifts of healings by the same Spirit, **10** to another the working of miracles, to another prophecy, to another discerning of spirits, to another different kinds of tongues, to another the interpretation of tongues. **11** But one and the same Spirit works all these things, distributing to each one individually as He wills.*

1 Corinthians 12:4-11 New King James Version (NKJV)

In Shamar Meditation, each gift will be covered as follows:

Words of Wisdom (Chapter 8) - Book 3
Words of Knowledge (Chapter (11) - Book 4
Gift of Faith (Chapter 17) - Book 6
Gift of Healing(Covering in this chapter)
Discernment of Spirits (Covering in this chapter)
Prophecy (Chapter 5) - Book 2
Miracles (Chapter 14) - Book 5
Tongues (Chapter 20) - Book 7
Interpretation of Tongues(chapter 20) - Book 7

We will focus on the gift of healing and discernment of spirits in this chapter, as these two important gifts can be used to heavily influence the world around you.

Gift of Healing. All of the gifts including healing are given as the Holy Spirit wills. This tells us that any of the gifts can operate in any believer in Jesus Christ, since God is not a respecter of persons. However, just like any other skill in life, the more we practice it the better we'll become at it.

We need to continually stir up the gifts inside us. We may

find that certain gifts we feel more attuned to. If so, that doesn't mean you can't operate in the other gifts, but you may have a certain dispensation towards one gift because God has willed it so.

Since it is Holy Spirit who actually performs the gift from inside us, we never should have any pressure to 'perform'. Keeping it simple is the best route. Either Holy Spirit is going to demonstrate the gift at any particular point in time, or He is not, for reasoning that is beyond us. However, we should be giving the opportunity to Holy Spirit within us to release the Kingdom, often.

Here are some pointers to operating and growing in healing.

1.) Know that Jesus Christ has paid the price for healing, at the Cross. That was the Atonement for all sin, ever committed. Once we've repented (more on this in a future chapter) from sin, we have full access to the inheritance of Christ, which includes this healing.

17 and if children, then heirs—heirs of God and joint heirs with Christ, if indeed we suffer with Him, that we may also be glorified together.
Romans 8:17 New King James Version (NKJV)

2.) We must have and continually strengthen the belief that God actually wants to heal, within us. If we have doubt that God can do the miraculous and perform such healing, it is unlikely that we will see many healings in our life. Faith pleases God, so it is a condition that must be met for healing to operate at it's highest capacity. If you have any doubt that God can and will use a vessel like yourself to heal, a simple prayer is "God, help my unbelief". Keep it simple and remember that completely relying upon God is essential.

6 But without faith it is impossible to please him: for he that cometh to God must believe that he is, and that he is a rewarder of them that diligently seek him.
Hebrews 11:6 King James Version (KJV)

3.) Depending on the circumstance in which you're praying for healing, it may be beneficial to speak with the person first and make sure that there is no unforgivingness at work in their heart. Unforgivingness is a major blocker to the full measure of the gift of healing operating. Any unresolved sin can block healing, but unforgivingness/bitterness/or any sort of active rebellion to God seems to really be a major weapon the enemy uses to stop healing from going forth. However, once these things are addressed and given to God, healing can come immediately.

4.) In some scenarios, having a further conversation regarding forgiveness may not be necessary. God may just want you to pray for them or command their body to be healed so that He can demonstrate His power. Being sensitive to the unction of the Holy Spirit is key in such situations. This will be covered in detail in Chapter 14.

5.) In order for the body to be healed, often the soul will need to be healed first. If someone has deep emotional wounds, you may need to pray for healing in their emotions, speak life into those places, then pray for the physical body. Discernment of spirit, Words of Knowledge and Words of Wisdom are all very important for this. The gifts are all closely intertwined, and all serve as tools which build his Kingdom.

6.) When praying for someone for physical healing, ask them to first tell you where the pain level is from a 1 to a 10. This serves several purposes. One, it gives you and the person being healed a baseline to know where you're starting at. After praying, if the pain level goes down, you can take heart that God is at work. This also helps increase faith, as even a tiny healing miracle can become the foundation of someone's entire faith that God can and wants to heal right now. If you pray for someone and the pain goes down by any measure, go ahead and pause and give God some praise and worship him. Spend a few minutes acknowledging what He just did! This is powerful in building up the forces of light in the spiritual world around you, and will be covered in detail in Chapter 17.

6.) If the pain goes down a little bit, but not all the way, pray again and repeat. If possible and as you feel led by the Holy Spirit, you can have a discussion about possible spiritual or soulish causes for the physical pain.

7.) Do this as often as possible to build up that gift. Anytime you're around someone who is dealing with pain, be quick to offer prayer, unless Holy Spirit within you is leading you not to.

In my own experience, this method of approaching the gift of healing is very effective. However, this only scratches the surface, and there are many wonderful books which focus entirely on this subject packed with great testimonies. Here is a book by Mary K. Baxter and George Bloomer which I highly recommend if you are interesting in diving much deeper in research of this gift:

- A Divine Revelation of Healing: You Too, Can Receive

Your Healing! (Baxter & Bloomer, 2009)

This book is packed with experiences, guidance, and testimonies which will help you understand and operate in this gift yourself!

Discernment of Spirits. This spiritual gift is also very important. Having a proper understanding of the dynamics of the spiritual world will allow you to understand things spiritually, as opposed to carnally. The carnally minded believer in Jesus Christ is at a huge disadvantage!

Once Jesus Christ is received in your heart, you are a new creation, and an entirely new world is opened up to you. This will be covered in detail in Chapters 13 and 14. In order to access many of the treasures that are now your inheritance, you will need to be able to discern things spiritually.

Since the realm of the soul and the realm of the spirit are both largely unseen with the natural eyes, it is important to first understand the difference between what is of the soul and what is of the spirit, in origin. The soul refers to your mind, will, and emotions. Your spirit is that part of you that is directly connected to God. As you know, the Word of God is an extremely important tool for allowing you to be able to discern spiritual things.

12 For the word of God is living and powerful, and sharper than any two-edged sword, piercing even to the division of soul and spirit, and of joints and marrow, and is a discerner of the thoughts and intents of the heart.
Hebrews 4:12 New King James Version (NKJV)

You can separate all spiritual activity into stemming from

one of two camps. Either something spiritual is coming from God in Heaven who commands the armies of angels or from the devil and his demonic horde.

God makes his angels into spirits, to perform spiritual tasks of varied nature.

7 And of the angels He says:

"Who makes His angels spirits
And His ministers a flame of fire."
Hebrews 1:7 New King James Version (NKJV)

The enemy of mankind has 1/3 of the original angels twisted into serving his dark will. Although they have already lost in that effort, the price for their treachery looms before them even to this day. Desperate to inflict as much harm and trouble as they can before the sound of the Trumpet (any.....second......now......), these miserable rebel angels, known as demons (and/or fallen angels) conspire to slow God's advance on the souls of mankind.

However, the call to action is presented to the reader. Jesus Christ is in full control of all things, and as we advance His Kingdom, great things are going to happen in the Earth.

The spiritual world operates 24 hours and day, 7 days a week. It is never asleep. Being able to properly discern (know, understand, and realize) what sorts of spirits are operating within a person, including yourself, is vital to optimal spiritual growth.

God gives his angels charge over you, to guard you in all

your ways. This means that God's angels are with you always. However, we see from the example in Scripture that the enemy has tools and means to bind your angel from helping you properly.

13 But the prince of the kingdom of Persia withstood me twenty-one days; and behold, Michael, one of the chief princes, came to help me, for I had been left alone there with the kings of Persia. 14 Now I have come to make you understand what will happen to your people in the latter days, for the vision refers to many days yet to come."
Daniel 10:13-14 New King James Version (NKJV)

As you begin to spend time alone with God, you will know when you hear His voice.

27 My sheep hear my voice, and I know them, and they follow me:

28 And I give unto them eternal life; and they shall never perish, neither shall any man pluck them out of my hand.
John 10:27-28 King James Version (KJV)

The more you can recognize God's leading, and submit in obedience to it (like a sheep), the more you'll be able to move with the confidence that God is with you. This should be kept *close to our hearts,* as disciples of Christ in order to become more and more intimately acquainted with your Lord and master, Jesus Christ. This will go a long way in keeping your spirit strong in the power of God.

Now, understanding the inner workings of other people around you is another key to developing the gift of discernment of spirits. A scripture that is useful is this one:

You Will Know Them by Their Fruits
15 *"Beware of false prophets, who come to you in sheep's clothing, but inwardly they are ravenous wolves.* **16** *You will know them by their fruits. Do men gather grapes from thornbushes or figs from thistles?* **17** *Even so, every good tree bears good fruit, but a bad tree bears bad fruit.* **18** *A good tree cannot bear bad fruit, nor can a bad tree bear good fruit.* **19** *Every tree that does not bear good fruit is cut down and thrown into the fire.* **20** *Therefore by their fruits you will know them.*
Matthew 7:15-20 New King James Version (NKJV)

Observing someones actions, whether they are good or evil, is paramount to understand what spirit is empowering them. If someone is primarily concerned with operating out of love and truly displaying Jesus Christ to the world, you can rest assured that Christ is leading them. If someone is using Christ's name to control, manipulate, or coerce others, you can rest assure that Christ is not leading that person. All of us need work, so there's no need to be too critical. As a watchman/watchwoman, **we need to keep our eyes open to the realization that the physical actions are just the natural manifestation of what is truly inside of a person**.

If someone is displaying a willingness to help others unselfishly, you can rest assure that Christ is leading that aspect of a person. Every good and perfect gift is from God. If someone is selfish with their time, money, and/or energy, you can rest assure that they haven't completely surrendered all of them selves to Christ, yet.

Since no one is perfect, and we have all fallen short of the Glory of God, all of us are a work in progress. Just because someone makes mistakes doesn't mean that Christ is not with them, nor does it mean that that person doesn't genuinely love Christ. It just means they are in the process of getting closer and closer to Christ, and certain parts of our souls likely need to serve our spirit a bit more. **Grind hard until the harvest.**

Being able to recognize spiritual maturity in others, while all the while seeking your own salvation with fear and trembling is another key to operating in the discernment of spirits, on a day by day basis.

Now, in deliverance ministry (casting out of demons), discernment of spirits is an essential gift. You may be able to hear what spirits a person needs to be delivered from. Or, you may be able to clearly see with your eyes or have the understanding impressed upon your mind what the Holy Spirit wants to show you. He loves interacting with you in this way.

Deliverance is the children's bread, and as children of God, **we all need this at some level, from time to time** and possibly more than that. Chapter 11 of this book will discuss deliverance in detail.

These tips I've included only scratch the surface of the gift of discernment of spirits. These are application guidelines which I believe will serve to help you grow as you practice them. I've personally read many books on this subject as I find it absolutely fascinating, especially when people who are naturally inclined seers write them.

I have a habit of giving books away to spiritual seekers who happen to visit my home, so the only two I can pull off my shelf right now are below. However, I know of many more, and if you're interested in this subject, please don't hesitate to email me a gtkportal@gmail.com or contact me via social media. I'd be glad to point you in the right direction of other great resources for any of the gifts of the Spirit.

- Open My Eyes, Lord: A Practical Guide to Angelic Visitations and Heavenly Experiences (Oates & Lamb, 2004)

- Secrets of the Seer: 10 Keys to Activating Seer Encounters (Galloway, 2017)

Both of these books are filled with dozens of accountings of the manifestation of this gift. Both are fantastic teaching resources to help you in your quest to develop and sharpen this gift. One thing I find in virtually every book I've read on the subject is the need to keep a pure heart. Those who have a pure heart will see the Lord! Enjoy!

8 Blessed are the pure in heart,
For they shall see God.
Matthew 5:8 (NKJV)

Proper Goal Setting

Now, bringing everything together from this chapter, I encourage you to start working towards a better body to sustain you while you enjoy this pilgrimage through Earth. I encourage you to begin strengthening your soul by honing your mind, will, and emotions. I encourage you to start really pressing after the deep spiritual things of God. This will be the same process for all of us, however every believer will be best suited to different methods. **Ask God what methods will help you the most, and believe what you hear!**

The person who has no goals is going to be used by the

person who does have goals. Setting goals for yourself is paramount to transformation. You can't sit back and wait for great things to happen to you. We are at a point in history where change is happening more rapidly as technology disrupts the business, social, and economic spheres quicker than ever before.

If the world is changing rapidly, we as sons and daughters of light need to be transforming more and more into the likeness of Jesus Christ in order to stand as guardians of all that is holy, pure, and right in the eyes of God. Eternal Kingdom Publishing is aimed at creating resources to help you and the entire Body of Christ continually transform into greater and greater versions of yourself.

As the world spins, God's will for mankind is communicated to us more and more each second. The enemy is looking to steal every Godly seed that he is allowed to, and disrupt God's perfect plan as much as possible. It is high time we shut down his disruptive network, and render him ineffective at his duties. He has to report to God as his Boss, who also happens to be your best friend.

You, because you have chosen to make the wise choice of serving Christ, are recruited as a warrior in this major fight. Eternity looms before you.

As you set Godly goals for yourself, you will grow as a disciple of Jesus Christ of Nazareth. As you grow, you will not only transform yourself, but the world around you. Here are some keys to proper goal settings. Goals should be measurable and attainable, and usually repeatable.

I'd like to introduce you to Zane the Disciple of Christ. Zane has many goals and is passionate about becoming the best version of himself that he can possibly be. Zane has many goals, and he will have the luxury of being featured in all of the Application chapters of Shamar Meditation.

Zane has one major goal for each part of his being. Body, Soul, and Spirit.

Body: Zane is 30 pounds overweight, and it is affecting his health. He wants to lose all of this extra weight and have a healthier appearance.

Soul: Zane has a job, but he would like to setup a blog to promote the Kingdom of Jesus Christ, and generate some passive income for himself. Zane needs more cashflow coming in! Get that money Zane!

Spirit: Zane goes to church, but he's just coming into the realization that he is the church. He wants to be much more intimate with God, and be able to help others outside the four walls of the church.

Goals should be measurable.

A overall goal should be broken down into individual goals which you can measure and either complete or fail on a daily basis. Zane, after consulting with his Transformation Coach, decided that for the first few weeks, he should focus on certain daily goals to help promote all three of his goals.

Body: Zane setup a 15 minute exercise regiment, which includes cardio and resistance training. He began by using GTKPORTAL.app to set a daily recurring goal to exercise for 15 minutes every day.

Soul: Zane set a daily goal of spending 10 minutes a day to read other Christian blogs on the Internet. He also had the takeaway action of sending atleast 1 encouraging email every day to the blog owner, and bless the blogger with positive feedback about their blog. This he added as a goal which took 5 minutes to complete.

Spirit: Zane began a two step approach to building up his spirit. He had a 10-minute Bible Study goal, where he reads for 10 minutes anywhere in the Bible. Wherever he felt led on a particular day, Zane opened up the Bible there and started reading. Then, for 5 minutes, Zane would simply pray to God about whatever was on his heart right after reading the Bible. Zane made the conscious effort to repeat as much Scripture to God in prayer as he could remember, asking God for more revelation.

After two weeks of this approach Zane had achieved the following results.

Body: Zane is already down three pounds, and feels like he has more confidence and a bit more energy. He is happy with the results so far, and is looking forward to pressing more.

Soul: Several bloggers connected with Zane and reached out to him and let them know how much his kind words really impacted them. A few even offered to help him with information and resources for whenever he was ready to start his own blog. This really encouraged Zane a lot.

Spirit. Zane begins to notice that he feels much more spiritually empowered throughout his day. Things which used to stress him or make his imagination get a little too active in the wrong direction now no longer phase him. He feels like God has something new in store for him in the upcoming season, and he has a holy excitement that he is going to tap into something new.

Remember, GTKPORTAL is a resource which is available to help you chart your growth in body, soul, and spirit. Although you can use old fashioned pen and paper to set and track goals, I invite you to come and Grind for God's Glory at my side, along with the rest of the world! Oh, what adventure it will be, my friend! Imagine the outcome! You should be able to use GTKPortal on any device which has Internet access from anywhere in the world. So far, we've recorded grinding over 21,500 minutes for God's Glory. I am currently building and adding more features to this application day by day, so please feel free to check it out!

My website was also built around the idea of accountability. Having an accountability partner or several partners checking in with you is very vital. Sometimes we may get discouraged if we don't see results right away, or we can get busy with the many other things which are happening in our life. Having some accountability partners will help you to stay focused on the goal or goals at hand, and provide positive feedback as you step through the goals on your journey.

As you stay consistent, many positive results will begin to flourish within your life. As you learn to embrace the Grind, respect the grind, and learn the biblical principles of the grind, you will arm yourself with a fabulous array of tools which you'll be able to use to conquer all of life's obstacles. You are more than a conqueror through Christ who strengthens you. In the next installment of this series, **Grinder's Paradise: Shamar Mediation Part 2,** we will explore one of my favorite subjects in explicit detail, **The**

Grind. This book will arm you with ammunition against procrastination and every device of the enemy aimed at keeping you from becoming all that you can be, in Christ.

Chapter 3 - Birth of a Hero (Epic Parable)

The young woman stood upon the cliff of the highest mountain in the range. Below her the snow covered caps of the lesser mountains poked through the misty cloud covering. Above her the darkened portal to the Nether realms pulsed just once, then the dragon raced through. Its red scales were translucent and iridescent as it reflected the dusky light of the waning sun.

She looked closer however, and she somehow knew that she was the only one upon all of Salvatia who could see its true form. It was an undead thing, a dracolich, and death radiated from its very being. It knew she could see its true color. She could read its mind and see the creatures soul (or lack thereof) bare.

It saw her and screeched. She felt more than heard its thoughts "DIE GUARDIAN!". It altered its course and bolted towards her, death bubbling forth from its stomach. It meant to devour her and her world entirely. It would not stop until all that she had ever known was no more.

She knew she could not possibly stop such a being. But her green eyes were set firm, and her hands tightened on something powerful which she held in her hands. She felt its power comfort and soothe her in the face of the oncoming certain disaster.

Then, she saw him. The one who was prepared for such a fight. The one whom had lived his life in preparation for this very fight. He was running as fast as he could up the trail to where she alone had stood. Two others were running behind him, one slower than the other.

He caught up to her and smiled. His smile calmed her as it always had in the dream. There was confidence there, but it wasn't just that. There was an eagerness beneath the surface which he was trying his very best to subdue. If he gave in to that eagerness, it would turn into rage. If he gave in to the rage, it would turn into madness. If he gave in to the madness, it would turn into failure. If he failed in this crucial moment, their entire world would perish. Perhaps even other worlds would perish as well. They both knew the severe price of failure.

"Good job Jaz!" he exclaimed. He nodded to the other two who were with them. "We found the other stone, but only you can lead them there. Buy me as much time as you can." He exchanged stones with her, dropping the stone he gave her in his belt pouch. The stone she gave him had an otherworldly Power exuding from it. The stone he gave her radiated with the energy of some great and benevolent Being.

They clasped each other at the elbow, and stared briefly into each other's eyes. They heard the dragon screech again and knew that the seconds were few until its arrival. She felt a turmoil and doubt within her which gave her strong unrest. She subdued it somehow, then assured him by confidently stating "I believe in you, brother Triz. We shall dine well on the open trail under starlight this night, indeed. Do not give in to the rage, but do not hold back either." She took strength from their bond of friendship, and she imparted all the strength she could back into him in that fleeting moment.

His eyes transformed from an earthy brown to a fiery lavender in an instant. His clothing changed from greens and browns to lavender and white. He dropped her arm, grabbed his weapon, and leaped into the air to meet the dragon head on. Both ranger and dragon disappeared in a flash of blinding light.

The other two reached her then. They held the silence for just a moment. Then, impossibly, after they discussed something, the three of them ran together, and jumped off the cliff. She felt the sensation of free falling down the mountain with her gaze locked on something specific beneath her.

She awoke in her bed at that moment, with adrenaline coursing through her veins. She took a few moments to steady her breathing. She sat up, and placed her delicate feet into her running moccasin boots. She was already ready for her morning run, already dressed perfectly for the cool dawn air.

She was into her daily run within minutes. This night it was the dragon dream again. The streets were quiet as usual, with a handful of merchants waving and calling greeting to her as she ran. She smiled politely and waved, but hardly noticed them otherwise.

Why was she having this dream or another similar dream almost every night? What were the stones? Why was she fighting a dragon? Who were the other two comrades in the dream? Why was she jumping off of a cliff? More importantly, why did she know Trizzen? In waking life she had heard of him, everyone had. But she would have been only fourteen summers when he had left the city of Heart, they could not possibly have ever met.

Her run helped calm her from the adrenaline high of the dream. But her mind raced with the bizarre recurrence of it all. One of her professors from University had lectured on these things once, but none of that guidance had prepared her for this. She smiled. This was a mystery which she was determined to solve. If there were one thing that Jaza Soulbinder enjoyed, it was a good mystery.

***

Trizzen stood atop the high walled ramparts of Guardian Fortress. Many memories flooded through him. The war had been brutal, savage, and era altering. He had seen many good warriors fall. He had seen heroics. He had seen his God do some incredible things. And, in the end, the free people of Salvatia had triumphed against the forces of DarckNex. DarckNex was a merciless land, separated from Salvatia by both mountain ranges and sea, a land which was ruled by ruthless anarchy. Unless a warlord claimed himself the title of king for a time, in which it was temporarily ruled by tyranny.

Yet, in the end, the free people of Salvatia had triumphed. "Triz!" exclaimed someone below him.

Trizzen turned around and smiled.

Giston Lefrox was a Barbarian, who hailed from the snow covered caps of Icing Hills, far to the northeast of where they now stood. Icing Hills surrounded the great keep of Stronghold. The two were old friends, being veterans of many of the same campaigns. They had saved each other's lives more times than they could possibly count. Giston stood nearly seven feet tall, with broad shoulders, short blondish hair, and eyes bluer than the sea which separated Salvatia from DarckNex.

Trizzen started down the rampart to bid farewell to one of his dearest friends on all of Aretz. Giston stood near the bottom of the rampart stairs patiently waiting for his good friend Triz to make it to the bottom. Gist smiled from ear to ear, a wide toothy grin which Triz found difficult to not return.

The two were nearly as different as two human men could be. Trizzen Stealthkin, a mixed breed human of both Native and Nubian descent, was hardly five and a half feet. His hair, which was usually pulled into a tight warriors pony tail during times of battle readiness, was hanging freely in bouncy curls to his shoulder. His eyes were brown as the earth itself, and often changed hue depending upon his mood. Trizzen, with his tannish olive skin and peculiar ways was a mystery to most people he met.

He reached the bottom of the stairs, and the two men firmly took hold of the insides of each others elbows with their outstretched hands, as was a proper customary warrior's greeting.

They paused for a moment and gave each other a knowing glance. Then they embraced each other in a brotherly hug.

The two had been in numerous battles together, more than they could possibly ever hope to count. They had saved each other's lives more times than should be possible in one lifetime. They had been on adventures deep in exotic places, and had stood shoulder to shoulder against impossible foes. Even in situations where certain death seemed imminent for the both of them, somehow, someway they had always escaped and were victorious. They were two members of the band of seven adventurers known as Legend and Lore.

In the 10 years the band had fought together, they had all become something of legends in Salvatia. The famous Bard,

Marbin Jay, had even penned a ballad about their heroics at the famous and war deciding battle of Shimmieria, some 3 years ago. The song was a favorite of soldiers and little children, not to mention the fair maidens of the land.

Soldiers relished the song as it stirred fiery courage in their hearts. Many soldiers hummed the inspiring tune as they prepared for the fateful last days of the 100 Pence war. The heroics of Legend and Lore had inspired them all. As special operations scouts, they were the first forces into enemy territories, and the soldiers knew who their leaders were.

In Salvatia, there had not been a proper king for thousands of years. The forces which defended Salvatia were all volunteer basis. Either defend Salvatia, or accept brutal tyranny. Heroes from all walks of life had risen up and fought for all that was Good.

The side of Good had won the war. Yet, there were rumors of dark stirrings in certain parts of Salvatia. Everywhere, the Scorpion Cult known as the DragonBorne operated from the spiritual realms, carrying out missions to appease their dark master.

Children, specifically orphans, loved the song because of the legendary duo who defeated 8 DragonBorne with the help of an orphanage, which otherwise would have surely perished. The orphans had been activated supernaturally during the encounter. Trizzen Stealthkin had taught the orphans how to pray for the power of the One God, just hours before the inevitable battle while on the run from the approaching dark horde.

The children learned fast, and their innocent child like faith had produced a Supernatural portal to Heaven. From the portal, Archangels poured into the very heart of the continent of DarckNex. With the timely assistance of the One True God, the two soldiers and ragtag group of orphans were able to slay the entire patrol of DragonBorne. The DragonBorne were ferocious evil beasts, who had once been angels, but had lost all hope of salvation. They manifested themselves in many gruesome ways. The children had lived in fear for their entire lifetimes, the ages ranging from 3 to 13. Now, they traveled the continent of DarckNex and fought against the remaining DragonBorne through prayer, fasting, and blades when needed. They inspired many in DarckNex to fight back against the unseen spiritual forces which sought to penetrate the veil and become something more than spirit.

And finally, the fair maidens loved the song, since Trizzen was rumored to be unattached and eligible as a bachelor, and Giston kept the Barbaric practice of having multiple wives and was not shy in letting it be known that he was hunting for one more. Trizzen on the other hand was looking to stay elusive, since several of his past relationships had become a bit too complicated.

***

The Throne room erupted in laughter.

"Oh PawPa, surely you jest with us!" roared his son, the Prince Emmanuel Stealthkin.

"His daughter, the Princess Natalia looked to her mother for confirmation. Tell us if this tale is true or if PawPa is just pulling our leg again!"

"No way PawPa!" blurted out the young Prince, not wanting to believe that his taciturn father was ever that unattached and free spirited! He knew his dad was a hero. But Emmanuel wanted to know if this was a real hero exploit, or a bit of embellishment. He loved a good story, but he loved truth even more.

Trizzen Stealthkin, King of Salvatia, smiled upon the two almost adolescent children.

"Never interrupt a Story-Teller! I was just getting to the good part!" jokingly he commanded his chap-chaps. That was his special name for them.

The children laughed all the more, and looked over to the Queen of Salvatia.

"Mommy, is he pulling our leg again?" asked the oldest to their mother, even as Trizzen playfully feigned ignorance and did whatever he could do to enhance the telling of this story. The story would unlock many great mysteries in their young hearts. He relished the opportunity! He knew that soon their own journeys as disciples would begin.

The wife of Trizzen Stealthkin playfully glared at him. She was as beautiful this day as the moment he first laid eyes upon her. In fact, even more so. She looked into his earthy brown eyes, which were glimmering the way they do when he was telling the story of the olden days. She looked to her children. They were fully engaged, and she was relieved. The king had recently returned from a long journey recently, and would only be in the city of Heart for a few days. She missed him and she had deep spiritual revelation to share with him. She was his seer as well as his wife. Her husband trusted in her with all his heart.

They had a love like none other. She had many deep and

serious things to speak with him about concerning the other city-realms of Aretz and other dimensions besides. But, tonight she would simply enjoy her family. She would speak to the king soon.

"Children, would you dare question the exploits of Legend and Lore?" she asked, smiling. "Legend and Lore is your legacy. Love fiercely!" she exclaimed.

The children repeated the family slogan, and listened attentively to the Ranger-King's every word.

As he began to speak, his Seer Queen saw angels flood the king's throne-room. They were mostly there to record the revelations which would be unlocked in the minds of the young listeners. She smiled. At least she would be able to bring him a good report when she was finally able to tell him of some of the things on her mind. Some of her closest friends were rulers of other city states of Aretz, and other dimensions besides. Spiritually, too many vicious attacks had been launched against them for her to possibly keep track of it all.

Salvatia, was comprised of many great city-states, with all of them in constant transformation. Heart was the legendary domain of her Triz. As her own private knight in shining armor, he had unlocked deep love within her heart. She focused on the peaceful thoughts, and tried to focus on his tale. His gentle voice had the effect of calming her nerves. She had seen dark things in the spiritual world recently, and she needed to let her husband know so that he could dispatch warrior forces to the other city states.

A gentle voice spoke to her in her heart. "Are there not others who can call for help from on high?"

Da. The One True God had spoken to her, and she felt His Presence and relaxed. She shifted her concerns onto His mighty shoulders, and immediately felt calm and serene. Within minutes, she knew she would likely find much needed rest, and cozied herself up on her throne.

Across the room, Trizzen continued with the desperate tale. He had alluded to finally revealing to them mysteries which they were too young for previously. Soon, their own journey would begin. The Father had shown him as much. With his diplomatic schedule becoming increasingly more involved with the affairs of other dimensions, he doubted he'd have another chance to tell them this tale directly for some time.

"Tell us everything you figured out over the years, PawPa!"

"Ah, you have asked for a wise thing! If you pay close attention to every word, you shall have it!" answered Trizzen.

"Now, at this time I was only 10 years into the service of the Eternal One...."

***

After a few minutes of rough banter and recapping of cherished memories, Triz and Gist said their farewells. The other five members of Legend and Lore had departed to their homes the previous year. Triz and Gist had both stayed back to ensure that no other Archon Warlord would rise in attempt to take advantage of the confusion caused in the wake of the previous Warlord's total loss. DarckNex was an ambitious land which gave birth to many twisted, dark, and ruthless villains.

They were also the grizzliest two members of Legend and Lore, and loved battling on both Aretz and within the NetherRealms. After the official victory of Salvatia at the catastrophic battle of Shimmieria, The two men alone had done an impressive job thinning the numbers of imps, familiar spirits, and DragonBorne which were very abundant on DarckNex. Although many DarckNex natives had taken the Archon Pact and became agents of evil, none could muster enough strength to seriously threaten the heroes. The evil entities which secretly ruled DarckNex and the majority of its peoples were not fully destroyed, but were severely weakened on the entire continent.

Gist was heading to the north of Salvatia, to the grand mountains of Icing Hills, his native homeland. His plan was to take the jewels and gold coin he had earned in the war, and build up walls and protection in the many towns there. It had been some time since he had last heard from his family, but he kept high hopes that everything was fine.

"Are you sure I can't talk you into accompanying me on this next adventure? I could use your sharp eyes and even sharper blades." asked Giston. For good measure he added "I'd even let you tell me more about this One God of yours."

"Bah, your great poleaxe is legendary enough to keep away imps and other foul creatures, so you've no need of my bow or swords." Trizzen responded. "And besides, my Father has inspired me in my heart and I know that a great quest awaits me in the City of Heart. But you will have my prayers. I have heard of a new Quantum Technology released which will allow us to talk often, although we'll be hundreds of miles apart. And if ever you need my blades at your disposal, simply inquire of me there. I think we've a few more adventures in us yet, yes?

"Yes" bellowed the mighty barbarian. Gist never had much use for gods and whatnot. He preferred the clang of his weapons against any foe. But fighting alongside Trizzen Stealthkin had made Giston reconsider some of his ideals to say the least. Gist admired how passionate Trizzen was about protecting his home and loved ones. He liked the wily and zany fighting style which was always a dance of spirit, body, and soul. And when the ranger transformed from greens and browns into whites and purples, evil creatures died in multitudes. It was exciting to watch. Paired with his own ancestral elemental knacks and innate powers, the two made quite the deadly duo.

Gist had quickly befriended Trizzen Stealthkin 10 years ago, and now the long war was finally over. The ferocious war centered around the daily spawning of the Portal of Nexus. With the fate of the free world hanging in the balance, the forces of good had triumphed. But now, all of the evil which had once accessed the world of man through the main Nexus point had to find lesser portals to carry out its dark work.

Gist was returning home, to see his beloved family. Often his three sons and daughter were on his mind. Now, he would be able to wrap them in a huge love filled bear hug when he got back. Both of his wives would be ecstatic that he had returned as well. He had intention of adding another wife to his flock, since neither of his current wives would likely be able to bear him any new children.

"Farewell, noble ranger. I will seek this One God you have demonstrated to me these 10 years. If my three boys would grow up to be half as brave as you, whether they've inherited my ancestral gifts or choose a deity, even your

Eternal, I'll consider my task as a father a huge success" he lavished on his friend.

Pretending to be serious in his authoritative voice, Trizzen didn't miss a beat as he quipped "The Eternal is a jealous God. He'll have either all of you, or none of you. You've seen His might and power on the battlefield. I've yet to see simple positivism and right thinking do that, my friend. Why live as your own god any longer?" reasoned Trizzen.

"Aye…makes sense ye' ol' own brain" slashed Gist. He enjoyed the banter with his friend. He would miss it.

Trizzen knowingly smirked at the comment. Gist has joking within a joke back at Trizzen, but only the two would understand. Such was their bond. He decided he would bless the noble warrior with a prophetic declaration.

"Gist, all of your boys will grow up to be 10 times the man I am, 10 times the man you are, and more besides. And your girl will become 20 times the victor that even her father is."

Gist felt a spiritual rain fall upon him. As quickly as it fell, it disappeared. Gist smiled to himself. Yes, he vowed he would indeed look deeper into this One God. This One known by many warriors simply as the Eternal. But for now, travel and adventure awaited to the North.

"And I've heard dark reports that the north is crawling with imps, orclings, and all sorts of other vermin."

"Well, my friend and brother, you can rest assure that I'll be visiting once I've been able to peer into the mysteries I've been shown. I speak that the Eternal will protect you, and that He will send others to your side. I'll be keeping you covered in prayer. And if you ever have need of my blades, send me for. May your pole-axe avenge the blood of your people, always!" exclaimed Trizzen.

"Aye, my brother! And may you convert this entire land to your One God!" jokingly responded Giston.

Trizzen smiled, as in jest, but something resounded within him at the last statement from his beloved friend.

Trizzen raised his longsword and shouted his war cry. "For Zyon, for Zyon!"

Giston, not to be outdone, lifted his poleaxe and shouted his own warcry, "Let us eat giants for our bread!" Simply for emphasis, Gist slammed the butt of his poleaxe into the ground. Orange elemental fire spurted all about as he released the powers which his ancestors had maintained in his bloodline for many generations.

The two seasoned warriors parted company, excited about the new adventures they would each face, and secretly hoping to enjoy the other's company sooner rather than later.

It would be three years before they met face to face again.

***

Later that night, Trizzen found himself with his new company. He was asked to accompany two eastward traveling families, toward the Native forests of central Salvatia, to a region known as the Heart Forest. This was an enormous multi terrianed forest located near the very center of the continent of Salvatia. It would be odd for Trizzen, he reasoned. He had left ten years ago not much more than an orphaned child who had hardly survived his savage life in the deadly Undercity of Heart. He had left a boy. He returned as a man.

The two families, who were a mix of the different human races of Salvatia, were extremely happy that Trizzen Stealthkin, the Ranger of Legend and Lore was accompanying them on this 3 week trek. They had heard rumors of DragonBorne who were still in the land, not to mention zealots and goblin bandits who were taking advantage of the end of the war to cause havoc. Although the Nexus points over DarckNex were properly closed, the ten years of war had taken a toll. Most of the spiritual warriors who had battled in the fierce combat and survived to return to Salvatia were looking to live a quiet peaceful life.

There were many decisions to be made concerning the next chapter in his life. Triz was a little overwhelmed with going back to being a civilian. This is what he was pondering before Gist had called to him on the ramparts.

The group he traveled with was led by a man named Derius. He was a leather maker and a battle hardened vendor who had taken his entire family into the very heart of DarckNex. Many said he was crazy! Derius was 27 summers young, and a humble patriarch of a Nubian clan.

God had called him to the battle. Had given him the ridiculous command to take his family there. He had some skill with a blade, but his skill set of leather making and leadership made him a valued friend to Trizzen. Many times his family was attacked in the wilds, but always the blades and bow of Trizzen Stealthkin helped repel the attacks. Now, due to his obedience to God, Derius was granted high favor. Trizzen Stealthkin realized this long ago, and was thus drawn to protect Derius and his clan with his own life. The two had formed a hearty bond.

'Yo man, I see the gleam in your eye. You know it is time for you to settle down and find a good wife." He jested with his friend. Derius loved to attempt to get under the ranger's skin when the opportunity presented itself.

Trizzen laughed easy. Nothing could be further from his mind! He had mysteries to unlock in the spiritual realm. A wife could surely wait.

As the One True God prompted and began downloading fresh revelation into Derius, the man closed his eyes and perked up. Trizzen had seen the look on his friend's face many times. Derius was younger than him, but Trizzen understood in his core that Derius was chosen just as he was. That tranquil look only happened when God had shared some bit of revelation with Derius, and Trizzen was suddenly intent on gleaning from it.

"You know, ranger, there are some wives who prove very useful to seeking out God's heart. Such a woman will bring God's blessing upon your life more than ever. Even your Transformation State will increase in manifested power."

Now it was Trizzen's turn to perk up. It was an interesting concept, and one he had not considered before. A wife such as that would be a useful ally to have at his side, he thought to himself. Trizzen had a string of complicated relationships over his lifetime, and he had vowed within himself to avoid attractive women like the plague. He could figure out battle strategies galore and was brave enough to rush into mortal combat against any known or unknown foe, or even multitudes of foes. He, however, had not figured women out one iota, and was no where near brave enough to even think about entering into a relationship. This heavenly inspired word from Derius however had given him some much needed hope.

Derius gave a knowing grin. His friend would not be talkative this day. He would be too busy ironing out the details of this inspired message with his Heavenly Father. Derius understood that Trizzen didn't need to barrage Heaven with prayers inquiring further, like he was surely about to do. The One God knew fully well how to accomplish His will, and Derius remembered very well the circumstances by which his own wife was given to Him by the One God. Indeed, he who finds a wife finds a very good thing. And Derius also knew that Trizzen Stealthkin the honored hero, who also happened to be ruggedly handsome, mischievously brave, and now more than a little famous in Salvatia would be sought after by more than one lass, here or there.

Knowing some of the ranger's past woes with women, as Trizzen had confided in him over the years things he had told none other save Gist, understood the ramifications of the word he had just delivered. Knowing his friend needed some time alone to process the words which had just passed both Trizzen's ears and strongly walled defenses on the subject matter, he simply asked the ranger to scout ahead of the party for danger. Derius also took time to thank the Eternal for allowing him to play such a part in His grand design.

Trizzen, who knew that he did his very best scouting when he was chewing on a new revelation of some kind, quickly disappeared into the forest ahead of the group. Unknown to Trizzen or Derius at that time, in the Spirit world, an angel who had three finely crafted jewels wrapped as presents for the ranger raced ahead into the Quantum realm. The Quantum realm is a buffer between the world of Spirit and the physically bound world of man. The angel moved quickly and carefully, for as soon as he finished his task, the angel could get back to the Father's Throne Room. He loved serving God in this capacity. The angel's name was Hunter, and the Father often used him to train His human spiritual hunters. Hunter enjoyed doing missions for Yeshua , and had delivered many such revelatory packages to Trizzen over the years. The ranger kept his spiritual armor in tact and polished by daily prayer, so Hunter didn't have much concern of a dark one binding him while on this mission.

The binding wasn't painful if it should have occurred, however it would have kept Hunter from being directly back in the Presence of The One True God. Once the spiritual badges were found, Hunter was free to appear in the Throne Room of God, also known as the Great Nexus. It was connection with the very Source of Life Himself. As Trizzen moved effortlessly and quietly through the dense brush flanking the path, Hunter drew near unto him. As usual, Trizzen was barraging Heaven with questions, being silent for a few moments, then continuing with supplication and gratitude. This made Hunter's delivery simple. He released the three gems near Trizzen, and immediately Trizzen received the revelations into his spirit man. He felt the joy of communion with the Father, although his natural mind did not understand at all what had been deposited. Hunter smiled at what little he could see occurring in the spiritual and quantum realms at the receiving of the revelation. He loved serving God in this capacity. With that thought, Hunter vanished from the spiritual realm surrounding Trizzen, and was translocated back to the Throne Room where he experienced the euphoria and bliss of worshiping God directly. Although he could freely travel wherever he wished to, his joy was worshiping The One True God directly, and would remain there until there was need of his skillset again within the perfect will of God.

As for Derius and his family, he had befriended a leather making family from DarckNex. Jerle FitzGordo had come to receive the favor of the One True God upon his family as well. Although his lineage was once mired deep in the wicked practices of his ancestors, he had come to know the One God directly. Now, he was apprenticing with Derius Silvereye. Jerle was just beginning to comprehend some of the ways of the One God. He watched the Ranger of Legend and Lore move quietly ahead and then out of sight of the group. He would learn from both Derius and Trizzen. As for his own family, the Lord had blessed him with twins, a great blessing of God. Jozua and Izias. They were the apple of his eye. He spoke to the boys.

"Ah my sons" he smiled at them. They mumbled some baby talk. Oh how their little hearts wanted to be able to speak so that they could tell their Pa how he took them back into Eternity when he looked at them lovingly. Although their precious hearts could not say it, their gleaming exuberance at their dad was all they needed to do to melt his heart anew for them. "I will protect you with my life" he spoke over them.

The war had produced a strong demand for their skills, for leather armors, tents, clothing, boots, and much more. They had done well for the past seven years, and now were looking to move to the northern tip of the Oriengal Outlands, near the great floating island trade city Hamsaon. This would allow the families to continue their prosperity. They would accompany Trizzen to the City of Heart first, however. Derius had something in the works for his friend.

Trizzen had met Jerle in the Sanctum a few years back, which is where the servants of the Eternal One gathered on Sabbath, which was the Eternal's name for the Seventh Day of the week.

In some ways, it was families like this which spurred Trizzen to fight as hard as he had. In battling against the hordes of the DragonBorne, he had come to know what true evil was. Evil which would eradicate anything and everything in its power, for the sake of just that.... more power. Even some time before the war had began, he became very aware of forces beyond the world as he knew it. He had come to know that great darkness had existed. He had reasoned within himself that surely there must be some great forces of light. Although he had known of the Creator, he had not known or understood that he could have a personal relationship with Him.

However, coming face to face with other-worldly forces of darkness caused him to question his assessment. Then, he had begun to seek the Truth for himself. From there, he had entered into covenant relationship with the One God, and he had become something not simply human.

He became a disciple of the One True God.

He was trained as a scout, a ranger to be exact. He trained hard, he practiced, and he stayed in the best physical and mental shape he possibly could. He was agile, courageous, and had a sharp wit as well. However, even this was of little use against certain forces. Not long into his service of Artez as a *warscout*, he had come to realize that the One God had been training him his whole life, even as an orphaned child. At that point, every night for some time the Commander of the Lord's forces would train Trizzen personally. Trizzen knew immediately they were more than just dreams. He learned to both battle and navigate in the spiritual realms.

Everything changed for Trizzen after that season of his life.

In battle, since his spiritual senses had been sharpened through much intense interdimensional training, he could move impossibly fast to evade an arrow aimed perfectly for him, or he would decapitate a DragonBorne with one slice of his sword when that was the only way to survive an extremely pressing battle, or wake up in the darkest of night from a dead sleep to throw one of his ranger axes simply on instinct, perfectly and uncannily finding the middle of the forehead of a creeping dark assassin.

The rag tag orphan who had left the seedy undercity of Heart a decade ago no longer existed, as the transformation in God had worked wonders on his physical being as well as in the inner life of his soul.

And now he was returning home.

***

Far away on the continent of DarckNex, a dark mage stood within a shrouded chamber. He was speaking an arcane language, a foul language long since forgotten by most cultures. He swayed side to side in a dark trance. The dark radiance of death emanated from him. His eyes were blazed with the fire of the underworld. Suddenly, he fell to his knees and cried out in great pain.

"No! Noooooo!" He cried out in futility.

A dark shape entered into the room, materializing out of thin air. The dark shape took the form of a humanoid, but with multiple arms. "You ssshall ssserve me!" it mouthed though a spectral forked tongue.

The mage's eyes returned to normal. "No, foul creature. It is you who shall serve me!" he defiantly yelled while searching his mind for a spell of bindage.

The mage was lifted into the air and casually tossed against the wall as the spectral figure stretched forth just one of its many arms. "You have ssseen the underworld, and you now know your fate. Would you go now or later? Foolisssh mortal!"

The mage struggled for a few moments, then surrendered. It was futile. He had seen the torment which awaited him in the underworld, a world of no hope. He quit resisting internally, and silently thought the words, "I surrender."

A terrible voice boomed in his head. "Very well. Open your palm."

A black dagger with a red jeweled hilt, appeared out of thin air, and began to carve a bloody pentagram on his palm.

"You sssoold your ssoul. So preccssiouss! You wanted power. You ssshall have more than you ever imagined possssible. Take the dagger!"

Finished carving into the mage's palm, the dagger dropped unanimated to the ground.

He picked it up. He felt raw power surge through him. It was so much power that he stumbled back and fell.

He stood up, with a sick grin on his face.

"It ssshall lead you. Take many lives as you journey. The more lives you sssteal, the more your own life ssshall be preserved and sssstrengthened. Spend some time getting your revenge here, then I will arrange for your passage to Ssalvatia. There is one there whom you must dessstroy, but you must be muccchhh ssstronger than you are now."

The mage, Magon, adjusted his sight, then started looking clearly. He was able to see into the netherworld, and could even sense the flow of aether as it ebbed and flowed. He peered throughout what he could see of the spiritual world and the quantum worlds as well.

Typically it would take a deep trance, animal sacrifice, and enhancing drugs to see even a fraction of what he was seeing and sensing beyond. Then he noticed that through his connection with the nether realm that he could sense information pertaining to items and objects around him. He glanced over at a quill which he recently purchased. The street merchant who sold him the quill was an unbearable man who figured how much Magon had needed it. He was able to drive the price up five times its typical value. Just by focusing on the quill, he was able to get a sense of that merchant's soul at that moment. He then envisioned the man, grasping for breath, his throat painfully not responding to his desperate command to draw breath.

The implications of the power which he felt began to dawn upon him.

He bowed the knee to the demon, Biaal. "I will sserve you faithfully, Dark One".

He had never had speech impediments before, but if that was part of the package, fine. He had thirsted for this sort of power. He began to forget the awful torment he had just seen and witnessed. His mindset shifted to the carnal pleasures he could obtain with this much power.

Across town, the peaceful dinner time silence was suddenly disturbed in a neighborhood as a wife wailed out in horror and shock, and her three children ran out yelling for someone to help.

The street merchant died right at the dinner table, exactly as Magon had willed.

***

The company had traveled for close to a fortnight, and the journey was smooth. Trizzen had ample time to read, journal, and fellowship. He was always happiest out on the open road. Wind on his face. Friends at his side. Dangers to prepare for. The spiritual world was before him. Derius had taught him some spiritual gems recently. One was the mystery of the Calah.

This was an ancient word of power for the disciples. It referred to the soon to be bride of a king. In a much deeper sense, it referred to the bride to be of the King of Kings. There were many blessings upon those selected as friend to the Bridegroom. Trizzen understood the implications of what Derius had taught him, and for the first time in his life began praying that the Father bring himself a wife in His own timing.

Another revelation he had come upon in his studies was that of the mysterious Deisis. It was a mystical connection with God, which allowed God to meet concrete specific needs. Although Trizzen had a deep relationship with the Father, and had walked at the side of the Son for some years now, that study birthed a new desire for deeper intimacy.

Being truthful to himself, he realized that he was more than a little anxious about returning to Heart. Before he left ten years ago, he had a handful of friends and more than a few enemies. As an orphan in the undercity of Heart, survival was a by any means necessary sort of job.

Realizing that he was allowing his thoughts to spin towards the past, he changed the direction of his thinking. Ah, he began to visualize Zyon and let his mind drift into the mysteries and wonders of his faith.

Some scholars and sages debated that the writings of this place called "Ysreal" proved that it was simply a land of milk and honey far on the other side of Aretz, and one could take a ship there. Others claimed that Ysreal was a planet which circled a neighboring star. Others still claimed that Ysreal was a separate dimension from their own.

Whether or not any of these theories were true was not much of a concern to Trizzen. In his dreams, and in visions, and through many other means the Father had shown him many many things over the years. He was a revelation seeker, and his life was full of them. Whilst it would be amazing to understand it all, he knew that the ways of the Father were higher than his own ways, and that His thoughts were higher than his own thoughts.

And although he had been semi-conscious of the existence of the One True God before joining the Militia, he had come to really have a deep relationship with Him during the war. This was something very important to Trizzen. He wanted to have a close relationship with his God. He loved the testimony of the disciples in the Book and their walk with Yeshua. Especially that of the disciple Yochanan, who seemed to have a special understanding of the role of the Son. Trizzen had only recently had the advantage of plenty of time to think. It usually wasn't a great idea to be lost in thought in either the jungles of DarckNex or when traversing the Nether realms.

None could know the Maker, unless the Son brought him into Himself. Yeshua was and is the Gate, by which all things are possible. Yeshua even came and died, long ago! Whether it was this planet, or another place similar to Aretz, Trizzen did not know. But he did believe that Yeshua was exactly who He said that He was, and that the Book is one hundred percent true and accurate. After all, he knew Him face to face.

Trizzen had collected several scrolls over the years when he could. The continent of DarckNex was not the ideal place to find scriptures of the Holy Book, but still he had managed to scavenge a few. However, he was told that there was one special book, which was written by Yochanan, which was extremely rare and powerful. He had committed in his heart to search this book out.

He chuckled to himself, and he remembered a passage which the crew had discussed together. It was the Glory of the Maker to conceal a thing, and it was the glory of kings to search them out. Imagine! As far as the Book was concerned, Trizzen was a king! Salvatia had never had a king, and most only knew of the tales of royalty from children's stories.

The families he was traveling with had begun to share testimonies about their journey. They told him about many miracles that they've witnessed as a result of prayer. Hearing these things made his heart leap with joy and excitement. Understanding the spiritual realm and its complexities in an all out war zone was exciting, but Trizzen knew that there was much he had not explored yet. For an explorer and a ranger, this stirred up an urge to explore this unseen world all the more.

He was reflecting on these many testimonies as he scouted ahead of his party one afternoon. Many memories, some sweet, and some bitter sweet flooded his soul.

As he was pondering this, suddenly an image of a camp of goblin impish bandits flashed across his mind. Immediately, his eyes flared purple. A heavenly purple mist began radiating from his eyes, and his clothing instantly changed from greens and browns to whites and purples. His heavenly armor and weapons appeared in a flash, quicker than a lightning bolt strikes the ground from a cloud.

He quickly doubled back to his companions.

Upon seeing him hurrying back to them fully manifested as the Ranger of Legend and Lore, the company stopped. The leather makers picked up their crossbows and frantically began loading quarrels. They looked to him for direction.

He heard a still small Voice say to him "Two miles away. Their scout has seen you from afar. They prepare."

He smiled. He recognized the Voice of the Holy

Phantom. He looked to the families, and measured their grit. Pulling upon his training as a leader within the scout operatives, he said, "Steady yourselves. Keep moving. A group of imps is watching the road two miles ahead. Prepare your weapons as we move."

He smiled. "It has been some time since my blades have tasted goblin flesh. It has been too long since my arrows have pierced a goblin heart. Remember the things I've been teaching you. And I will remember the things you've been teaching me. For Zyon! For Zyon! " he ended emphatically.

He was glad to see the grins on their faces. These were a hearty folk. He saw knives unsheathed, then hidden under cloaks. He saw crossbows calmly fitted and locked in carry ready position, casually placed beside carriage riders. He saw mouths quietly uttering prayers.

His recent combat training of this group of his friends had been remembered in this critical moment. Keeping his end of the bargain, he began muttering warfare Scriptures. "Yeshua, give us the necks of our enemies. Let them look for one to save, even to You, but then do not answer them. Let us beat them as fine as the dust of the earth, and trod them like dirt in the streets, and spread them out.". As he spoke the Scripture, he could feel the lightning of God surge through his body.

***

Trizzen scurried off towards some foliage near a very shaded part of the road. He had told his companions to wait for his signal. They would know. He ran off, quietly but quickly. The imps would not suspect him coming ahead of the party.

Imps were mean, brutish, nasty, and above all cruel servants of the dark forces. They had always been around in Salvatia, but since the war they had become bold, and looked to stake as much claim as they could to that which was not rightfully theirs. They showed no mercy to humans. It did trouble Trizzen a good deal that they were so boldly encamped this close to a major city.

None the less, he shifted his focus back to the task at hand. Silently, deftly, and with a murderous intent as he ran. He had spotted a path which angled up into a higher elevation, then around to where he prophetically suspected the imps would be camped. He had instructed his companions to slow the procession, but only slightly. That should give him enough time to scout the enemies forces, without tipping the imps off that this particular party was more than prepared.

If the imps had been a proper band of warriors, they would have closed off such an angle of attack. He smirked to himself. He let his mind drift to the many hunts himself and Gist had been on since the other Legend and Lore members had departed. The two warriors had played the ages old hero game of who could slaughter the most baddies for every fight. Giston, with his deadly pole-axe and generational abilities, was a tough opponent. He could take out a dozen foes with one swipe of that mighty weapon. Whenever Gist won the day with more slain heads, Trizzen would hear about it incessantly until the next fight. He smirked at the multitude of memories of their banter. Their friendship had deepened over the past year, and the fact dawned on Trizzen that he would dearly miss Gist. He threw up a quick heartfelt prayer for the mighty yet humble Barbarian, then focused solely on the task at hand.

He easily penetrated their left flank position, and saw them preparing a crude war machine, an over-sized spoon looking device, along with a boulder which was doused with oil, ready to be lit on fire.

They were literally minutes away from launching a flying fireball at his companions. He would need to move soon.

Trizzen closed his eyes, and focused on his Father. In the spiritual Realm, Trizzen had been transported to his secret place with God. There he received blessings from God directly to his soul. Triz looked at it like the cradle of Life itself. Intimate union with the Father, before time began. All of the Disciples of the One God possessed this ability in some capacity. He became transparent, no more than a mist in the physical realm of Aretz. Time itself had no bearing on the union between the Eternal and Trizzen. Although only seconds would pass by in Aretz, Trizzen took the time to connect to the heart of his Father.

Quietly he mouthed an urgent prayer. "Father, I find myself in great need of You and Your mighty Arm again. I will defend this land of Salvatia, even to the point of my life. Thank you for your grace! Thank you for your mercy! Allow me to be useful to you on Aretz! Father, please bless my physical body once again!" he exclaimed passionately to the Father.

The Father responded, "You have my full Davidic Warrior Rage blessing upon you, My noble son. Also, the Strength of Samson I speak into you as well. My full Wisdom is with you as you go."

Trizzen teleported himself directly into the center of the

camp, but appeared as not much more than wind to the spiritually blinded imps. He was far from alone. In the flash of light which he appeared again, there were millions of Warrior Angels at his side. His armor was illuminated brightly as the mysterious White Ranger. He had a white otherworldly translucent ball surrounding him as well. His face had a thin strip of white raiment covering the area around his eyes, which now radiated a majestic purple. From head to toe, the white jerkin, breeches, boots and cape which covered him appeared to have life even within itself. Besides the pure white, the only marking was a symbol of a full eclipse, surrounded by a band of swords across his chest. This was the mark of Legend and Lore.

Yeshua looked across the way at Trizzen. Jesus was as He usually appeared, when He wasn't as a Lion. Yeshua was chowing down on a freshly prepared leg of lamb. He always liked to do that before battle. He glanced over at Trizzen, who was clearly awestruck by the sight of the Commander of the Lord's Army. It had been 10 years since his initial training as a ranger in His army. Jesus looked upward, and the sky was suddenly filled with the sound of a Heavenly Choir playing an Earth number.

Trizzen stepped out into the imp's camp and started dancing his war dance. Pandemonium and confusion erupted in the goblin camp. The imps (goblins), frozen in panic, tried to find the courage to attack. But spiritually all around the imps the Angels of the Lord were moving impossibly fast. The imps at one time were somewhat akin to the mighty angels which now sealed their fates, but they had chosen to rebel against the source of all Light, Jesus Christ (Yeshua). Once all of the imps were spiritually bound, and none had the seal of the Lord upon their forehead, Trizzen's chief guardian angel , whom went only by the codename WarShade, materialized in front of Trizzen. "Well met, ranger friend. The forces of Shamayim are with you. Be sure to leave none of these wretches alive."

Trizzen took note of the command with a nod. The dancer went away and the warrior came out.

It was rumored that the Heavenly blessed blades of Legend and Lore sent evil directly to hell for Eternity. No more floating around looking to inhabit another host. If DragonBorne encountered those blades, their Eternity was forfeit. It was directly to the dark pits to await the final sentencing to the Lake of Fire and torment.

The spectral DragonBorne, operating from their base of power on the plane of Gehenna inspired and directed these imps to do evil. As soon as the White Ranger appeared, along with the backup from the plane of Shamayim, the specters instantly cut all spiritual ties, leaving the impish goblins without support. Trizzen could feel the distant sensation, as the spiritual covering for these low levels minions was completely eradicated.

Trizzen's eyes froze them in place. The radiating majestic purple pupils had an otherworldly glow about them. Friends to the ranger often revealed that when he looked at them behind those purple orbs they could feel the love of the Creator flow through their veins. When enemies dared to looked into those eyes, there was no such warmth. Typically, there was only death there. He smiled upon them.

"Flee, you fools!"

Snarling with hatred, the imps looked to one another for support. They realized the connection with the higher spiritual powers, the DragonBorne was no longer with them. But they could not discern that the Angel of the Lord had shown up, nor understand that their fates were sealed. And although these simple goblins had indeed heard of the heroes of Legend and Lore, they were too prideful to think that a lone man could defeat them.

Yelling out to their dark master in war cry, at once they grabbed their weapons and rushed him.

He had counted around 30 imps total, including the 1 who was dancing a shamanic ritual dance with hopes to restore the spiritual connection to their higher powers. Trizzen nocked an arrow unto his bow. He let it fly and it found its aim to be true. The arrow ripped through the shaman goblin's neck and then into the heart of one of its comrades.

Both goblins fell without any screams. "Ah, looks like your deity couldn't save you. How pathetic.", jested the ranger as he began moving and loading another arrow into his blessed bow. With the first bloodshed, Trizzen received a flash of prophetic insight into the lives of the two dead goblins and the rest of the group. They had slain more than a few men, women, and even children. The goblins were savage murderers who had harmed innocent people. Today, Trizzen was sent as the arm of judgment for the Eternal. Trizzen smirked and recalled Warshade's guidance to let none of these wretches live. The purple radiance of his eyes flared dangerously as his heart was now totally bent on absolute destruction of these wicked creatures.

Trizzen's second arrow went high into the air, far away from any goblin target. It whisked over the goblin camp, and its purpose was to signal to his companions that he had obtained the desired position.

Before the imps could even register the blinding speed which Trizzen was operating in, two arrows, one right after the other, were sent toward the biggest goblin, who had the appearance of being their leader and chief. Goblin (or imp) war chieftains always hung in the middle of their camp, where his or her position would be safest. One arrow found the middle of his forehead, the other his heart.

As those arrows penetrated their target, the signal arrow exploded in mid air, sending up a shower of bright yellow and blue sparks. As the signal to begin executing the plan was executed, the companions started shouting and whooping and hollering and making the noise of a group twenty times their size.

The imps, seeing both their shaman and chief fall lifelessly to the ground, compounded with hearing the outrageous sounds of what they thought was a small force easily defeated, quickly lost what little heart they had, and were completely bewildered.

Trizzen then suddenly drew all attention to himself with his battlecry, "For Zyon, For Zyon!" Running and dancing and kiting the majority of the goblin forces who were brandishing swords and clubs by keeping them at a distance with bowshots, he downed two more imps before any serious defense could be mounted. With no other target for the alarmed imps to attack, they rushed him with pure hatred and malice in their eyes.

Deftly and confidently, Trizzen nocked one more arrow into his bow, and wildly running in a zig zag fashion while maneuvering out of the way of enemy spears, Trizzen dropped to his knees at a specific point, and fired that arrow.

To the surprise and chagrin of the imps, his arrow went directly through the campfire upon which a small pig was roasting and continued in the perfect trajectory towards the giant bowl of oil that was used for their war machine. Immediately there was a deafening explosion, and the goblin body parts of those closest to the explosion cascaded though the air.

Trizzen hurriedly dashed towards the campfire to save the roasted pig from any goblin matter ruining it. Goblins were surprisingly good cooks. Well, not so surprisingly since they maintained the standards of the fast food industry on Earth. Delicious but far from nutritious. He took a bite then and savored the moment. He looked up at the remaining goblin forces. Dropping the roasted swine into a separate pouch within his belt pouch, he turned his focus back to the imps, who were finally attempting to form a fighting wedge so they can rush him all at once.

In one fluid and quick motion, Trizzen dropped his bow to the ground and brandished one ranger axe and his long sword. He flung his ranger axe at the leading goblin rusher, and it penetrated deep into his throat. Dark green goblin blood sprayed high in the air, giving one moment of hesitation to the attackers directly behind it.

The moment of hesitation would be their last.

Pulling his shortsword out with his left hand, Trizzen closed the gap between them quicker than a leaping panther, deftly setting both swords into motion. The first goblin he attacked tasted his longsword's steel as Trizzen plunged it into the foul creature's mouth and out the back of its neck. As

Trizzen pulled his sword out, the steel flared brightly with a pulse of purple light and the corpse of the goblin began disintegrating into nothingness, blowing away with the wind. The next goblin lunged desperately at Trizzen with its sword, only to be stopped cold by Trizzen's parrying shortsword. Yelling and gaining strength from his battle cry again, "For Zyon, For Zyon", he leaped forward and high into the air at the same time, landing in the middle of the bulk of the remaining imps. Although he was easily outnumbered twenty to one still, he stoically slashed his shortsword and thrust his longsword as he spun and ducked and defended. Many goblins were returned to the dust from whence they came.

They came at him from every direction, but his shortsword parried every attack with ease, and his longsword pulsed with an ever increasing purplish glow. Minutes later, the imps had lost any hope of confidence. Almost as if it were on queue, they began to flee any and every which way, anything to get anyway from the chaotic scene and deadly swords before them. There was no regard for their brethren, there was no community amongst their hearts. There was only survival, each to his or her own.

Seeing the end of the encounter drawing near as the imps begin fleeing, he sheathed his swords. Trizzen threw another ranger axe at one fleeing goblin, the one which happened to be furthest away. The axe found its mark in the middle of the goblin's back, bringing it down in its tracks. He then ran to retrieve his bow. Although several imps were still rolling around frantically trying to put out the flames which were burning their dark green skin from the oil explosion (which was not proving too successful of an effort), Trizzen's concentration was unerring. One by one, his arrows sizzled through the camp, picking off one by one in scary speed. Oh, how he missed this carnage and bloodshed! His heart yearned for the adrenaline which was now coursing through his veins.

"Ah, my comrades from Legend and Lore. How fare ye all? Do any of ye dream of the days of old, when The Seven quested side by side through both fire and cold?" the ranger lamented. He missed his friends in that moment. But then he remembered a promise which the Father had given him. There would be new adventures a plenty, and his Savior would not forget him.

Trizzen didn't think, too lost in admiration for the Glory of the Father. He simply reacted. His eyes scanning the camp, realizing that there were no fleeing imps left, save the one which he had let run directly in the direction of his friends.

And, as quick as his onset had began, it was done. He quickly retrieved his ranger axes and even managed to salvage a few arrows. He took a moment to take a few deep breaths and focus inwardly. As he did so, his Heavenly whites and purples were replaced with the normal greens and browns.

Green cloak gracefully bouncing in the wind as he ran, he raced towards his companions being confident that his gamble would pay off. As he had picked off the fleeing goblins with his ever so deadly bow, he had baited this particular imp to run directly westward. The imp had tried to head towards a path to the south to begin with, but seeing two of its party get skewered right in front of it forced it to rethink that escape route pretty quickly. With the fire still raging to the north, and the ranger to east, there was only westward left to it.

Cresting over the hill where he left his traveling companions, his heart was filled with joy. Thank Yeshua!

His training sessions over the past few weeks with the settlers was not in vain. The corpse of the goblin he had let escape the clearing lay there, with numerous arrows and quarrels protruding from its lifeless torso. He wasn't able to relish the sight very long before he heard the twang of a bow release.

Looking up, he saw that one of the leather makers had just fired an arrow directly at him! Deftly dropping and rolling to his right, he was able to easily evade it.

"Oh no! What have I done" cried out the would be assailant, even as the quarrel left the crossbow.

The projectile harmlessly flew beside Trizzen. The shot was straight and true, and would have been perfectly placed at his chest had he not moved.

Trizzen smiled, realizing what had happened. His training was perhaps a little too good. Seeing the green of Trizzen's cloak, as opposed to the white in which he was wearing when he had left them, Jerle had fired away. The settlers were now running towards Trizzen, wanting to make sure he was okay.

"I'm fine, my friends", he assured them. "I'll know where to look should I have need of archers in the future.", he consoled them further, exchanging a warm glance with Jerle.

Jerle visibly relaxed and began to explain what Trizzen had already surmised. Trizzen cut him off with a friendly wave of his hand, and embraced the man.

"You did exactly what I taught you to do, and I couldn't be more proud". He looked around, directly in the eyes of the others as he continued speaking. "I'm proud of all of you.

Yeshua has called all of us to be warriors in some capacity. Today, you defended yourselves. Tomorrow, you may need to defend others who need you." He encouraged them, drawing deeply upon the leadership training his own mentors had given him over the years.

"Keep this victory in your hearts. Meditate upon it in the lone of night. Imagine and relive the excitement you felt when that goblin ran over the hilltop, screeching at you! Bring up the vision of those perfectly placed arrows and quarrels exploding in its chest, ending its lifeforce and the threat to your safety. You will need this courage and boldness again. The war is over, but dark denizens walk the lands here and there, and many nexus portals still need to be closed. Yeshua has called you all to be warriors! You have responded well to the call, and He is pleased with you!" he emphatically and excitedly finished.

Cheers went up from the settlers. He saw a shift in them, before his very eyes. "For Zyon, for Zyon!" they yelled in their celebration.

Trizzen knew not what things awaited the lands, but he knew these would be ready for that challenge. He suspected that sooner or later their mettle would be tested.

***

Not many days after this, Trizzen and his companions arrived at Heart Road, the main entryway to the majestic and iconic city of Heart.

Heart was a massive city, nestled in a grand valley surrounded by a circle of mountains. Waters from Northern Sea, along with melted waters from the snow-caps of the magnanimous Icing Hills far to the north, as well as from many other locations streamed into the many gushing rivers and lakes located throughout the Heart Circle Mountains. The waters naturally formed a massive bowl at the bottom of the Heart Valley, out of which Heart City itself was built.

Out of the water, massive and deep rooted trees had long ago sprang up. In the very branches of these immense trees was the city of Heart itself built. Limbs were crafted together to create roadways large enough that teams of oxen could be driven over. Massive multi-layered farms of berries, fruits, grains and other substances were harvested, primarily along the outer edges. Some of the insides of the massive ancient trees had even been transformed into multi-floored apartments and places of commerce. At any time, the surrounding mountainous region and the city of Heart itself hosted several million people, both residents and visitors.

Heart was an important and honored city on the far stretching continent of Salvatia, and it was legendary in its majestic appeal. As legend had it, long ago there was a significant drought throughout all of Aretz. The valley of Heart was positioned in such a way that although there was significant drought, there was still some steady streams of water at various places within the valley. As the ancient settlers gathered and began building infrastructure, over time, Heart became a nexus and a melting pot for peoples of all tribes and cultures. The Natives were credited as being the original inhabitants in the great valley, before the cataclysmic drought, and they possessed a deep knowledge of the land, creatures, and ecosystem of the valley. They were instrumental in the building and maintaining of Heart.

Some of the early arrivals during the drought were the Nubian peoples, who hailed from the deserts of Southern

Salvatia. Naturally, the camel hording desert nomads were the
first majorly affected by the drought, and they had brought
with them a deep knowledge of craftsmanship and love for
the Maker.

Soon thereafter, the Oriengals, the chief studiers of
astronomy and stars of the heavens, had read the signs of the
skies, and added to the budding population of Heart. Being
extremely in touch with nature and having a strong desire to
still be able to read the stars and sky, it was the noble idea
within the Oriengals camp to begin building Heart higher, in
order to see over the surrounding mountain ranges. This
called for skilled labor from every people's population in
Salvatia. Many Oriengals practiced the ways of their ancestors
similar to the Barbarians, although their practices were more
attuned to oneness with nature as opposed to raw strength
and forceful use of knacks and ancestral powers.

Although it was virtually unheard of for the different
cultures to mix previously, the cataclysmic drought had
brought all of the peoples of Salvatia into one central
location within the Valley of Heart. Prejudices and
preferences from long kept generational lines became a thing
of the past, since the peoples intermingled heavily as sons of
one people fell in love with daughters of a different culture.
There were some standouts and opposition to this, but it was
the minority.

The Latani peoples, long respected for their deeply
erudite and scholarly nature, brought with them philosophies
and ideas which the other peoples had not been previously
exposed to. The fair skinned Barbarians from Northern
Salvatia brought with them advanced knowledge of war
strategies, as they were a hearty folk who had long protected
the rest of Salvatia from imps and other threats by

maintaining the northern fortress aptly named Stronghold. Salvatia was linked by a one mile across, one hundred mile strip of land to a smaller northern peninsula region, known as the Fizz.

Although not much was known and recorded about the Fizz, save the sparse drawings of it from seafarers, who dared not port there but rather safely sketched the coastlines. The Fizz was also known to be full of goblin, orc, ogre, and even giant civilizations. It was left solely to the brave Barbarians of the North to defend against this threat. For this reason, the Barbarians received many trade goods at steep discount or free willingly from the rest of the peoples of Salvatia annually.

Along the fortress walls of Heart, the citizens stood this day in celebration. Scouts had confirmed that Trizzen Stealthkin, one of the chief most heroes of the war would be arriving today. As his company was spotted around noon approaching from the base of Heart Road, as expected , the cheers began to go up.

Those who were followers of the One God all knew of his signature battle cry. Cheers of "For Zyon! For Zyon!" erupted from his brethren of faith. Even some of those who chose not to serve the One God, or simply didn't know enough to make an informed decision, echoed the war cry. Some of the population who served other gods still cried out "Hail Trizzen! Hail Stealthkin!", wanting to honor the hero but not anger their chosen deities.

Among those unbelievers there was one certain young lass, Jaza Soulbinder. She had dreamed of this moment for months, and now that it was finally here, she didn't know how to respond. She had anticipated this very moment ever since the word went out that Heart's last hero was returning. She had a great respect for this hero, as she understood that he was a primary leader for keeping order in the realm. She had encountered the DragonBorne face to face on a spiritual expedition, and had hardly escaped with her life. Although she followed no god herself, she was extremely thankful that others such as Trizzen were as guardians to the rest of all humanity.

But, Jaza could never solve the riddle and mystery of the continuous dreams. She had visited the fortune tellers and soothsayers, she had consulted the magicians and the wizards, and spoken at length with the ones known as the Sages. All of this had cost her a miniature fortune in gold coins. However, there was only one thing Jaza truly enjoyed in this life, and it was solving a brand new mystery. She had graduated from Heart University two summers ago, and was making a reasonable living solving riddles of an arcane nature. She didn't practice magic herself, as she wasn't willing to pay the cost to her soul and body for it. But, she understand the quantum sciences at an expert level, and found easy employment within the Quantum Guild. She had spent virtually all of her coin, to no avail. The magicians, wizards, soothsayers, and fortune tellers had each given her a different answer. The Sages she had consulted had atleast given her the same answer, which was the dreams were prophetic indicators from the God known as the Eternal. She had resolved that she would seek information about this Eternal, although she typically despised the practices of some of His followers.

Now, however, she knew that her destiny was at a crossroads. She understood the Law of Quantum Entanglement enough to understand that. She was connected to this hero Trizzen, in some way. And now he was here. She resolved in herself that she would have answers this day.

125

"Well well, hello there Jaza. Look at you, looking like sunshine itself" said a familiar voice as Jaza was interrupted in her musing.

Not even turning her body to respond, and wishing she had taken up magic so that she could teleport herself far far away, she answered "Good mornin' Jol".

"Surely you mean afternoon, milady" Jol reminded Jaza that it was just past noon.

And herein was her dilemma. Jaza was deeply introverted by nature. She abhorred useless small talk.

She turned towards Jol and nodded with a slight smirk. She didn't want to be overly rude, as she had learned it was never wise to burn bridges. And Jol wasn't the worst company, just shallow and not intriguing to her. Never had the man been.

Jol was a handsome enough fellow. He was tall, broad shouldered, and outgoing. He had been the captain of the Smashball Team at their University. Jol just couldn't understand it. Although Jol was practically the dream of every girl at University, with those large hawkish eyes and sharply defined muscles, Jaza didn't fancy him in the least. She in fact went to great lengths to avoid him whenever and wherever possible.

But, Jol didn't seem to catch the hint, which only made Jaza want to avoid him more. Jol however, was very observant. His powers of observation were eclipsed only by his powers of persistence.

Jol walked up uncomfortably close to Jaza and leaned against the walls of the gate with his back to the approaching parade. He desperately wanted her attention. He had been eying Jaza as a potential wife since before University. She was everything he could possibly ask for in a woman. She was beautiful, athletic, extremely intelligent, and seemed compassionate, at least where he wasn't concerned.

He looked at her longingly again from bottom to top. He admired her athletic frame and her sense of style. Whatever perfume Jaza wore must have been made from a flower from Heaven. Inhaling even the slightest whiff of her sweet fragrance always took Jol back to the first time he had seen her. Although she didn't know it, they had once participated in a race together, when they were youths. It was a jamboree of all of Heart's Borough Schools, and she was the only girl who passed him in that race. He would never forget the fluid sight of those legs whipping past him, nor the chase in his heart to pass her on the road. He ran with all his might that day, but she still finished the ten mile race before him, although by less than a minute. She was the first girl to finish, and had beat the vast majority of boys that day.

Since that very moment, he was madly in love with her. Other than her athletic grace, her exotic look didn't help matters. She was an exquisite mix of both Barbarian and Latani heritage. She had a cinnamon complexion, long curly dark-blondish hair, dark green eyes, a gorgeous face, and she captivated his entire being.

He had been keeping track of Jaza since they both graduated University. She had never shown much interest in having a mate-friend, so he figured if he could stay on the scene, eventually she'd fall for him. After all, all the other girls always did, whether he wanted them to or not. But Jaza was

127

so different from all of the other girls at University, which simply attracted him all the more. All of her time was spent studying, training for different athletics, practicing Quantum principles, or figuring out some new mystery. Even after University, she had continued more or less the same schedule.

But recently, she had been walking in strange circles inquiring about this Trizzen fellow. Naturally, Jol understood that a woman like Jaza must be saving her virtue for her ultimate husband. Typically, only the followers of the One God made that sacrifice. Jol had never heard of Jaza serving the One God. But now, all of a sudden, she was inquiring about this Trizzen character and here she was at the parade, and he had walked up on her deep in thought. Imagining the possible thoughts she could have been thinking spurred him further into the rage of jealousy. Putting all of that into perspective, Jol did not like the direction his mind was pointing him into. No, Jol didn't like this situation one little bit (or as Jaza would be quick to say "I don't like this, one little bit, aye, not even one iota"), and he had every intention of slyly getting to the bottom of it.

"So, the great hero returns. Do you think all of the hyped up stories have any truth to them?" he asked her point blank. Internally, he winced a bit as he saw her flinch.

She regarded him coolly.

"I'm not going to dignify that with a response." She peered at him with penetrating eyes. She could clearly read his envy. How pathetic. Very little got past Jaza. She could literally feel a jealous and possessive energy stemming from the man.

"While we enjoyed freedom from tyranny and worse, Trizzen and the rest of the Militia risked their life, left behind whatever they held dear, and crossed the sea to defend that freedom. What have you done besides lead a Smashball team to a second place tournament finish?"

Immediately Jaza's heart sank. Her sharp wit had got the best of her. She wanted to retort, but she hadn't meant to cut that low.

A momentary flash of rage crossed Jol's face. But then the next moment, still captivated by her beauty, he smiled. "Well met, Jaza Soulbinder, well met."

He turned to see the approaching party getting closer to the city gates.

Wanting to soften the mood a good bit, he tenderly asked "Do you mind if I enjoy your lovely company for a few minutes?"

"It is a free city, thanks to certain efforts. I don't see why not, Jol Rockhammer." she light heartedly retorted once again and stood beside him.

Immediately deep in thought once again, she didn't notice the quick side glances he cast her way over the next few minutes.

Jol had once heard one of the Expounders of the One God giving a message about marriage. He didn't typically listen to the town criers who would periodically set up stations at busy intersections within Heart, to herald their message. But after his parents had got a divorce during a tough time period in his life right before the start of the war, he was so broken and the Expounders always seemed to somehow make him feel a tad bit more whole, atleast for a little while. He thought back to the particular message now:

"Men, when you find that woman who will stand her ground and set you straight with Wisdom, who will turn your heart towards Understanding, and in who you know that your heart can trust all your days, you better be willing to shake all the continents of Aretz and the dimensions of the Shamayim's to take her hand in marriage. There is nothing more precious on all of Aretz, and nothing you can possess which will compare to her."

Jol wasn't much into the One God stuff, as it was all so confusing. But messages like this had stuck with him. And unlike all of the other women he had known, none ever talked to him like Jaza did. He looked out at this Trizzen character once again. Aye. Hero or not, if there was to be a battle for Jaza's heart, Jol began scheming on ways to make sure this Trizzen would not win that battle.

***

Trizzen's heart was overjoyed. He was not expecting anyone to be awaiting his return to the Heart Region. Instead of his expectations, seemingly the entire population of Heart was cheering him on the the walls of the city! Wow!

He looked around at his companions as they journeyed together, and his heart felt the sincere love they all had for him. He knew that they must have alerted some scouts somehow that he would soon arrive. Thinking deeper about it, he shot a knowing glance over to Derius. The leather maker was indeed resourceful.

"Thank you, I'm humbled and honored" was all he could say as emotional tears streamed down his cheek. It was all he could muster, as he was overwhelmed with joy.

Trizzen had left all those years ago, with no blood family and only one friend and was actually quite a broken individual. Life had been rough for Trizzen before joining the Militia service of Salvatia. He had learned so much, he had seen so much, he had experienced so much in the years he had been gone. He had left a lonely boy with only one real friend. Now, he was returning as a hero of the land, a man grown, chiseled, and accomplished.

The road hadn't been easy, but now Salvatia was free from threat of tyranny. He looked to the top of the wall and simply let the admiration wash over him. In his heart, for the first time in his life, the thought entered that he was truly great amongst men, and a true champion amongst his kind. He smiled as his heart beamed with pride.

Unbeknown to Trizzen, in that instant, a dark cloud had gravitated towards him in the spiritual realm. In the midst of the dark cloud, servants of the darkness were watching him intently. Finally, after surveilling him from afar for several years, in that moment they were able to penetrate his heart with a smidgen of the spirit of pride. Great celebration went through their ranks.

A chief demon who served the Court of Pride, left the cloud, and took spiritual form behind Trizzen. The evil being focused with all of its might, and started transforming from a mist of dark cloud matter, into the likeness of a human. Its goal was to emulate Trizzen's every move. It would require time, effort, patience and cooperation with the vast army of darkness at its beck and call.

This so called hero of the War needed to be stopped.

The Dark Master had seen in the Library of Shamayim that this one had a great destiny. However, in order to achieve such a destiny, a string of many correct decisions would need to be made with this one's free will. This evil spirit had taken up the call to stop him, which would be no easy feat.

This human was strong of mind. But the chief demon Azmodeous had been studying humans for centuries in this dimension and others, and he had thousands of tricks up his sleeves. This one was sharp, yes. But this Trizzen knew little of the higher operations of spiritual warfare. A great warrior with swords and bows and axes, yes. But these things could not pose any threat to Azmodeous.

But Azmodeous knew too, that this one's faith in the Eternal One was real. If Trizzen somehow became aware of this assignment, he could quickly force Azmodeous back to a place he didn't want to go. Back into dry places. Dry spiritual places. Places which could take days, weeks, or even months to reach the DarkCloud again. No, that simply wouldn't do. Azmodeous quickly began barking out orders to minions.

"Imp Battalion 3, prepare the way before me. Move! All of the disciples who have been praying for this one during the war, go to them. Don't engage directly, lest one of them discern. Don't even attempt to remove them from their prayer places. Instead, suggest to them other good things to pray for. We'll take hits here and there, but the most important thing in this dimension right now is to keep this Trizzen from his destiny. The other humans are attached to him spiritually."

"You, Sezikar. I command you to leave this dimension at once. Travel to the dimension of Earth. There is a strongman spirit there of False Humility. Receive of impartation from her, and travel back here at once. Pride will be ineffective on this one I sense. However, False Humility will achieve the same effect. He shall fall to it."

"Yes Leader. But Earth.....isn't there were Yeshua walked originally?"

Gasps and concerned looks emanated from all over the dark cloud. Azmodeous belted out "SILENCE! Do not speak that name, ever!"

Seeing Sezikar accept the command and realize his error, Azmodeous relaxed.

"Yes, Beware. The disciples there are the absolute strongest there are. They are the only realm fully anchored in Truth, and the only dimension with the full understanding of News of the One." answered Azmodeous, although his patience was already growing thin. He typically didn't entertain questions from minions.

But the stakes were high here. There could be no chance of failure allowed. This was the most important mission since the Slaughter of the Son. And that mission had backfired and damned them all forever. If this mission went sourly, that day of Judgment was closer than ever. Azmodeous quickly reflected on this, and decided to discuss the mission and its importance at length.

He grabbed the young DragonBorne spirit then, and transported it to a high place, deep in the dense jungle of DarckNex. This was Azmodeous's very own seat of power within this realm of Aretz. The spirit Sezikar was surprised, and began calling up innate defenses and planning to escape back to the DarkCloud, thinking that it had angered its senior and was now in for the scorning.

"Relax. No harm will come to you from my hand." Azmodeous said evenly, yet Sezikar could pick up on the hint of hastiness. This must be important. Sezikar listened intently.

"At this point, your mission is grave and carries great importance. I have faith in the absolute darkness of your heart, and the cunning which you employ. You are DragonBorne. Young, yes, but you have courage, wit, and heartlessness when it comes to these humans. These qualities and more will be needed in the coming months."

"But should you fail, you will find that my kindness is only outmatched by my ability to cause pain. Do you understand?"

"Yes, dark one" Sezikar bowed and visibly relaxed.

"Good. Now prepare your heart to understand all that I shall teach you of Earth. False Humility at the side of Pride is amongst the strongest strategies we can employ, and this Trizzen Stealthkin will fall to it." Azmodeous declared. He continued on in his tutelage of dark operations.

***

At the gates of Shamayim, The Son of God stood in all of His radiant Glory.

He smiled. It had began. His Bride was now closer than ever.

He looked to the Great Cloud of Witnesses, intent on His every Word.

"My Father has heard your request and prayers. You will be allowed to serve Us in the newly created dimensions."

A great roar went up which shook the Heavens! The saints loved serving the Father in new capacities! How exciting!

Jesus Christ, the King of all Kings, the Lord of all Glory, looked upon them and smiled.

"Task Angels!" He called. Instantly an innumerable multitude appeared in shining raiment.

Prepare the way for the saints. Father has allowed the inspiration for your leadership assignments to bubble up. You will each pair up with one of My saints, and be dispatched into the new Realms. Remember, Father is always a prayer away. Victory is assured, walk by faith, and not by sight. I bless each of you."

Jesus looked intently. In a moment of time, He individually blessed the trillions of pairings. Every saint and every Task Angel heard His voice in their hearts with an individual blessing to strengthen them. Some yelled out in worship. Some sang. Some blessed Him back. Others began meditating on the truth which was revealed to them immediately. Still, others began discussing their prophetic word with the Father in their heart. Others began instantly reciting their favorite Scripture. More than a few went directly to the Throne Room to surrender all their hearts afresh, directly before the Father. Others celebrated in other ways. In Heaven, free will for each of His worshipers is one of the Creator's greatest delights.

Jesus smiled. The saints had waited long for this. The

angels had waited even longer.

In that instant, Jesus turned back towards the gates. He transformed into the Lion of Judah, and roared a great and mighty roar, which every dimension of existence felt the effects of.

With a deafening ferocious roar, He leaped towards the gate in front of Him, which immediately opened. His form spread into the constellation of Leo the Lion and disappeared from all of their sights.

Excitedly, each one followed suit. The angels sought their assigned saint, and the saint their assigned angel. As the inspiration bubbled forth in every task angel, the instructions were shared with the saint. The cloud of witnesses went to and fro. Some departed to Earth to begin assignments. Others were dispatched to realms such as Aretz. Others dispatched to special places in Heaven. Other pairs connected with other pairs, creating multi assignment focused teams.

It had begun.

***

As Trizzen and the companions approached the final stretch of the main entrance into Heart, trumpets began to blast. Then, an orchestra of the cities' most talented musicians began to perform the ballad which detailed Trizzen's and Giston's heroics. Trizzen, with tears pouring down his face could hardly continue to walk, overcome as he was with emotion.

His companions gently hooked their elbows under his arms to keep him moving forward. As the party finally reached the gate, everything stopped all at once.

The Ambassador of the Heart Region, a Latani man by the name of Buwark Amana, stood standing on the ledge above the gate.

"Trizzen Stealthkin! Welcome home, and thank you for your service!" boomed the powerful man in a loud voice.

Cheers went up loudly from the peoples. As the crescendo finally died down, Buwark continued.

"On behalf of the Region of Heart, this day, the day of your return after the War, shall be celebrated in Heart for generations to come. This day, from this year forward, will be known as Trizzen's Return!"

As the cheers roared, Trizzen dropped to a knee. Tears of pure elation flowed freely from the man's face. He looked up, and coming out of the newly opened gate were dozens of fellow soldiers. Trizzen recognized many of them from the war. He had battled at many of their sides.

They began welcoming and hugging him, and cheers of "For Zyon, For Zyon" echoed throughout the crowd. The soldiers escorted Trizzen to the Militia campaign center, which was where Trizzen had departed from Heart those many years ago. Now it would be where Trizzen received the debrief from his time of service.

There was official paperwork to sign, final coin to to be paid to him, some awards were given, and later that night, it was official.

Trizzen was a veteran, a national hero, and ultimately a

man with with several important decisions to make.

As Trizzen was finishing up the necessary paperwork, he saw an old leader and mentor of his. Shyla Ann Brightstar. She and her husband, Tye Louis Brightstar were Trizzen's first leaders. Trizzen smiled when he saw her, and he noted that she was with child. Trizzen had last seen Shyla about four years ago, as she was leader of some of the healing forces near the shore. He had accompanied her and several others on a dangerous mission near the DarckNex capital city, Menzonarn. The mission was a success as three important connections were made which would ultimately help Trizzen and the other scouts begin the process of closing one of the main Nexus portals over DarckNex.

Even as she exclaimed "Welcome back!", he was telling her congratulations on the pregnancy. She beamed proudly, and Tye Louis walked in at that moment. Tye and Trizzen gave each other knowing glances. Tye and Shyla were Trizzen's leaders on his first campaign. They witnessed his transition from street orphan to notable ranger first hand. They had been tough on him, as they saw both his commitment to excellence and tendency to get distracted easily when direct combat was not taking place. They were instrumental in pushing him to develop strong discipline, for which he was appreciative now. This had led to some serious discussions in which harsh words were said. Now, after so many years none of that mattered anymore. They had all survived!

"Ah, so the ranger returns! I'm proud of you!" excitedly stated Tye.

"You taught me all that was necessary." He looked at Shyla and Tye as he spoke to them. "Thank you for your service as well. I remember well the heroics of Tye

BrightStar."

Tye smiled. Tye clasped Trizzen at the elbow in a customary warrior's greeting. Trizzen was specifically referring to a situation which had made Tye BrightStar a hero to be remembered. That battle occurred at the northern edge of the continent of DarckNex, where the enemy forces had latched onto a Nexus ring, and used the ring to open doorways into the nether realms.

Through these doorways, nightmarish creatures which had been created in the Netherstuff from the minds of the increasingly wicked DragonBorne entered into the realm of Aretz. The Militia forces had been camped out in the North for several months, fighting the forces and attempting to close the Nexus portals which were in use. Tye had been placed in charge, as he had a strong gift to bind forces at the gates. Tye become a hero on that campaign. Although he didn't have the resources to close the Nexus portals, he was crucial to the operations of keeping the Netherstuff Beasts contained in the realm of the Nether as opposed to the realm of Aretz.

Once Trizzen and the rest of Legend and Lore had arrived, they were able to enter stealthily into the Nether portals, and close them from the other side. Trizzen had worked closely with Tye to complete that mission, before Legend and Lore were summoned to expediently rush to the southern tip of DarckNex. The DragonBorne caught wind of the dismantling of the Nexus portals in the north, so they began barraging the portals in the south, knowing that even Trizzen and his crew would be hard pressed to get there in time. Tye held the northern tip of DarckNex, and it was a useful strategic holding for the rest of the War, although Tye was not involved in much direct battle from that point.

Trizzen looked to Shyla and Tye both, and beamed a lavish and charming smile upon them. These had fought at his side. These had survived, and were directly responsible for the lives of many people, many of whom he held dear. He looked toward the protruding bump of Shyla's womb and said "Woah! Woah to the forces of darkness which one day must stand before the seed of Tye Louis and Shyla Ann BrightStar! Surely it would be better for those forces if they had never existed!" he exclaimed with a wink.

Shyla blushed, and hurriedly asked Trizzen if he would do them the honor of having dinner with them, as they had someone that wanted to meet Trizzen.

Trizzen easily said yes, and was quite relieved to have the invitation. He was beginning to feel lost with all of the attention, and knew that spending time with some humble yet heroic people like these would be good.

An hour later, Trizzen was seated at a scrumptious dinner table. Roasted fowl with honey glazed topping, baked sweet-bread, an assortment of fresh vegetables, and a few flagons of mixed wine.

The person that Tye and Shyla would introduce to Trizzen was indeed someone very interesting. Although Trizzen was the unwitting celebrity in the group, he was captivated by the other dinner guest. A guest who would ultimately be one of the most important connections ever made in Trizzen's life.

***

Magon stood on the balcony of the inn room he had purchased for the next few months. He looked down at the busy populace of townsfolk. Most simple laborers, but many others not quite what they seemed. He had been busy the past three weeks.

In the spiritual world, many of these folks bore his mark, which is to say, bore the stamp of his dark master. He had subverted their minds making use of the vast army of demonic thralls under his command. By the month's end, all of them would be his willing but unwitting servants. Murders. Robberies. Curses. Adulteries. They would commit these crimes and many many more.

He saw a young married couple walking. He focused on the man, and was pleased to see that adulterous thoughts were already in his heart. Magon conjured up an image of Shelda Soarings, a town wench. Magon called forth a familiar spirit, a low level demonic spirit which happened to specialize in lust and sent it towards the thoughts of this young husband's mind. It wouldn't be long before the inevitable happened.

Magon then focused on the man's young wife. "Musch heartbreak you shall receive, sssweeet thing" he declared. He peered beyond the sweet motives of her live consciousness, which was only attuned to making her husband happy. He saw the emotional wounds she had suffered from her father and step-brothers over the years. Yes, this would be easy. He spoke a curse over all of that unresolved baggage. In the end, that curse would cause her to do the unthinkable to this beloved husband of hers. How pathetic and small their lives were. Their minds were putty in his hands.

It was so easy. Soon, the entire village would be cursed and under his control. This was only a starting point however. His real mission was far from this place. That would be far from easy, but he would use the latent soul power of these sheep to spur his own lust for power. Then, the dark prophecy he had seen would come to pass. He would subvert the entire continent of Salvatia. He would rule not just that place, but all of Aretz. Then, and only then, could he avoid the awful torment which awaited him for selling his soul. In the legendary tales of old, wizards had obtained long lives which went on for centuries.

No, failure was not an option.

He walked back into his inn room. Drawn on the floor was a sinister pentagram containing a goat's face with a mocking smile. He laid his body on it, and then projected his spiritual body into the Nether realm. Spiritually, he saw the limits of his power, which had grown leaps and bounds. He smiled to himself, and began visiting every curse which he had spoken over this village and its inhabitants. He was diligent and thorough. He could see spiritual wounds festering in their lives. He touched those places and poured bitterness deep inside the unsuspecting citizens. He then returned to his spiritual throne. It was a dark iron throne, built in the throws of dimensional boundaries on the edge of the Nexus veil.

In his meditation, he saw the fruits of his dark actions. Around his throne, a fortress of dark bricks was beginning to form. He craved more of that unending power.

More ruthlessly then did he begin calling forth spirits of wanton evil and pronouncing curses. He had a lot of work to do and a lot of mayhem to loose.

Behind him and unknowingly watching from a deeper spiritual plane of darkness, a sinister evil chuckled. Failure or not, I am going to enjoy the torment of your soul, the evil spirit mouthed, with pure malice and hatred in its eyes.

Such was Darkness.

****

Trizzen listened wide eyed to the stories of the Sage.
Caldolmork Beauford was a Sage from the Order of the
Eternal. He had served the Eternal for close to 100 years. He
was far traveled in all of Aretz. He had seen dimensions and
localities far from Aretz. He had been allowed to visit the
Highest Shamayim on more than one occasion. And he knew
the Maker in a deeply personal way, which allowed him to
express His heart in ways which mystified Trizzen.

After several hours of stories and fellowship, Tye and
Shyla went off to bed with farewells made and blessings
spoken. Trizzen and the Sage began walking through the
Nobles Garden section of Heart, which was near the dwelling
place of Tye and Shyla. Trizzen had a hundred questions
bubbling forth from himself that he wanted to ask the Sage
about the Eternal One. The Sage had a personal story as
answer to every question, which captivated Trizzen all the
more. Trizzen had never met anyone with such a profound
and deep relationship with the Eternal One. His heart leaped
within him as Sage Caldolmork expounded on many deep
truths previously unknown to Trizzen.

Trizzen had come to know his Creator on a deep level
but he was beginning to realize that he had only scratched the
surface. Finally, deeply contemplating everything the Sage had
told him, Trizzen drifted into a self searching silence. A
silence which the Sage clearly understood all to well. Even
after walking in silence for over 20 minutes, the Sage simply
walked with his hands behind his back, as he also searched the
Heart of the Eternal.

Breaking the long but far from uncomfortable silence, the Sage said "I have a prophecy for you from the Maker" in an even voice. "May I release it over you?" he respectfully asked.

Trizzen looked at him excitedly. He felt as if his body were suddenly light as a feather which was in danger of floating up on the winds. "Certainly!" he exclaimed. Trizzen felt as if all time stopped.

The Sage, who had been lighthearted in his conversation and mannerisms up until this point, stated to Trizzen in a certain but commanding tone "Everything will change in your life after this. With the knowledge I reveal to you comes joy and fruit, but sorrow and toil as well.".

Trizzen, taken a bit aback, nodded slowly. "I understand" was all he could muster to say in that moment.

The Sage, who was a good 4 or 5 inches taller than Trizzen even in his slightly bent posture from old age, placed his gentle hands upon Trizzen's lithe and lean shoulders. He kindly stared into Trizzen's inquisitive eyes. Then and only then did Trizzen recognize a shift in the Sage's eyes. It seemed as if those eyes turned into oceans of grace, peace and love. The presence of the Maker became palpable. The scents of aloe, cassia, and myrrh mixed magnificently in the air around them.

"My son. I have called you for a season and a time such as this. You are of My chosen ones. The people of this land have great need of your strength, as they have an even greater need of My Mercy. Think it not an accident that the entire land now knows of you and your heroics upon the battlefield, and they know that you have called upon My name."

"You have been empowered by My Glory, and your destiny in Me is just beginning. The War was only a foreshadowing of the troubles to come. I am raising up a remnant to fight for the souls of Aretz and other realms beyond."

"Will you lead My army in this conquest?"

Trizzen, tears streaming down this cheek, dropped to one knee. He could hardly mutter the word "Yes" as his heart felt as through it would leap out of his chest and fly into the Highest Shamayim (Heaven) to personally tell the Creator "YES!", face to face.

The Sage, reached into his belt pouch, and took out a vial of glowing oil. As he opened the stopper, the scent of cassia, myrrh, and aloe mixed with the scents of peppermint and lavender. Trizzen lowered his head instinctively, and the Sage poured out the contents upon Trizzen's head.

Trizzen stood and let the oil freely drip down his face. He stared deep into the eyes of the Sage, and realized that the Sage was operating purely as a vessel of the Holy Phantom. Knowing that his Creator was staring back at him from those merciful orbs, Trizzen looked even deeper. A fiery feeling radiated deep inside Trizzen, and he vowed internally at that moment that he would find this level of fellowship with his God. He set a command from his spirit to his soul and body to seek the highest attainable relationship with the Eternal Father. No stone would be left unturned in this quest to achieve as such.

The Sage intently listened within the silence of the cool

night air. After a few moments, he said "I am preparing others in this season. You have performed your previous task well, as a warrior and a ranger. Now, My beloved, you are assigned to a season of reflection, solitude, and seeking Me. Report to the library tomorrow morning. Your new journey has began. Know that I will never leave or forsake you. Even in the tough moments, when you feel that I am not with you, remember My promise to you."

He continued, "The powers of darkness plot incessantly against you. Stay grounded in My Word, and press for more sensitivity to My Spirit. In future seasons, you will experience great warfare, far more intense than anything you experienced in the war. I love you, Trizzen Stealthkin. You are and will always be My ranger, and I will show you great and mighty things which you know not. You have not only the heart of a ranger, but you've the heart of a king, my son."

And as sudden as the prophecy had began, it was over. The Sage's eyes returned to normal, and he smiled warmly at Trizzen.

"So, the great adventure of our time has begun, aye." quietly stated Caldolmork.

Trizzen, emotionally broken and simply wrecked under the power of the Eternal, simply leaned into the Sage's shoulder and began crying like a child. Tears of deliverance and joy streamed down his face similar to the rivers which flowed into the Heart Valley.

It was a long time before Trizzen and the Sage walked away from that place. No other words were exchanged between them that night.

***

Jaza headed for the door. This just wasn't her scene anymore.

All of her friends were laughing, drinking, smoking, partying and enjoying the festive night.

Jaza tried to relax and enjoy the good company of her longest standing friends, but her mind was elsewhere. She had hoped that she would get to finally get to the bottom of the mystery of this recurring Trizzen dream, and perhaps speak to the ranger today.

But after he had arrived to town, he hadn't been seen again that day. Unable to mentally put the matter to bed, which was quite rare for the cerebral beauty, Jaza slipped out unnoticed from the tavern.

She enjoyed the cool air, and she began walking near the river front, the opposite direction of her pad. She had so much to think about.

She had ran down every possible lead from the Sages and soothsayers, wizards and other practitioners of the curious arts. She admitted that the advice and wisdom from the Sages made the most logical sense. This stirred up many questions inside her. She generally had avoided the followers of the Eternal, and she had good reason for doing so.

Their teachings defied logic and reason. As a Quantum Researcher, there were many laws which she knew for a fact were true and verifiable. She had conducted over a thousand experiments in the past three years alone. The wizards and soothsayers and even some of the witchfold (although they were just as off in their worldview as the followers of the Eternal, in her own opinion) all understand these concepts which she based her livelihood and career on.

But the Eternal followers claimed that He had created everything. And in addition to that, everything tangible and visible was created not even six thousand years ago! Impossible!

She herself had used quantum entanglement diodes and capacitors to date hundreds of fossils and remains to at least tens of thousands of years, here in Heart Region alone. She was well versed in the writings from other continents of Aretz which referenced even older fossils and debris which could date back millions of years!

In addition to the general self righteous attitudes which most followers of the Eternal seemed to possess, the fact that the lot of them disregarded proven knowledge left her with no choice. She had regarded them long ago as essentially misinformed at best, delusional at worst, and had few dealings with them.

But something, or rather someone, had been troubling her today. Trizzen.

He was clearly a follower of the Eternal. And now none of the spiritual sources she had sought could tell her anything concrete of the dreams she was having beyond the wisdom of the Sages. To further add to the mysterious dilemma she was facing, several of her dreams had foreshadowed perfectly the afternoon she had as she waited for Trizzen to arrive.

Something that Jol said earlier that afternoon as he walked her from the wall back to her pad had resonated with her. Walking back from the wall, he mentioned that it seemed that she lived her life like a follower of the Eternal.

At first, she scoffed. Ridiculous!

But then, she begin to ponder as the day wore on. She had long ago taken a self imposed vow of celibacy. It was her personal choice, as she had great respect for marriage as an institution. Her own parent's marriage had outlasted many others, and the two were still lovebirds. Furthermore, she had a solid understanding of the quantumical phenomenon which transpired with the joining of two people in intimacy. When two souls drew near to one another in such a manner, every quantum mystery which she intimately understood would surely be magnified to a scale beyond her own considerable reckoning. Lab tests with several species had surely proven that to her. Therefore she had no intention of joining herself to another, unless it was permanent. And she had no plans of getting married any time soon. She was the only one in her University circle to demonstrate this life principle, besides the followers of the Eternal.

Also, she respected all living things to the best of her ability. She was always honest, sometimes brutally so, if her tongue got the best of her. She very rarely indulged in anything that harmed her body. Smoking the peace pipe or drinking the strong drink held little to no thrill to her. She did not like feeling that she was not in control of her own mind.

As she thought about the life of the disciples of the Eternal, she had come to realize today that generally they promoted a life well lived. Line upon line and precept upon precept, she naturally agreed with many of the principles which they adhered to. She had little use for the man in the sky part, as that simply defied all logic and reason.

How she had never noticed this before this day was beyond her.

Although Jaza was a creature of reason, logic, and depth, deep down something had stirred in her this day. In her youth she had studied the Book of the Eternal as it was required reading for all adolescents in Heart's education system. After that, she observed and watched many around her who claimed allegiance to the Eternal. Judging them logically by her own understanding of the words from the Book, she found the majority of them lacking in sense and prudence. Few professing disciples, if any, actually demonstrated anything remotely similar to what she had read. Due to that reasoning and some of the unresolved questions she still had with the subject matter and stories within the Book, long ago she had decided that it simply wasn't for her.

"The winds of change blow, and the seeds of change grow" the young beauty mused. Those where some of her favorite words from one of the poems of her favorite poet, Mazwell. Jaza then thought about how water which sits still too long in a flask begins to grow mold, whereas the waters from Heart's waterfalls stayed fresh eternally. Jaza knew that if she never challenged her own beliefs, her mind would eventually grow dull, which sadly enough, she had seen happen time and time again in her twenty four summers upon Aretz.

She determined that tomorrow she would head to the Great Library of Heart to start some research. She settled in her heart to get to the bottom of this. If the spiritual representatives she had consulted could not figure it out, she knew of one more resourceful than them all put together. Herself.

She grinned to herself. Yes, she would indeed get to the bottom of this mystery.

In the spiritual world, a certain saint and a certain Task Angel smiled. Their task was complete this day.

In the natural world, two blocks behind and carefully blending with the shadows, Jol kept watchful eyes upon the young woman.

***

Upon the highest mountain in the range surrounding Heart, Katheros stood overlooking the city. He prayed for the citizens. He was happy to hear that Trizzen had returned, as well as numerous other heroes over the past few years.

He had been praying everyday for their safety. He doubted at times that The One God was listening to him. However, in this specific moment, Katheros knew that on some level his prayers had been heard.

"Thank you Merciful Father! You are a merciful God. Help my unbelief. Help my doubt. I simply want to please You!" he spoke aloud.

He shivered, the frosty wind nipping at his skin. The monk was bare chested as he offered his prayers as well as his body to his God. Every muscle honed to perfection, the physical aspects of the discipline of the Order was certainly Kath's strong suit. He focused inwardly and forced his body temperature to adjust by warming up a few degrees. Instantly he felt the heat from within release throughout both his spiritual and natural bodies. As a monk, having control of one's temple was a key aspect to maintaining a virtuous life.

He thought back to the many months of prayer he and several other of his monk brethren had offered and smiled. The war had given him such purpose. Oh, how he enjoyed those moments of time when he could feel the Heart of the Creator. In the same instance, he also remembered the tearful nights wondering if his Savior had forsaken him, had forsaken them all. It all seemed so easy for the other monks. They never had any doubt. They never had any fear. They were full of the utmost faith at all times. Katheros waffled and doubted more than he liked. He couldn't understand it for the life of him. He had joined the Order of the Monks four years ago, and now his time of service was up. He had learned all their ways. He was fondly thought of as a promising young monk with a lot to offer the Brotherhood.

He had progressed rapidly through the monk training, and was considered a prodigy among many. He was offered a spot on a traveling caravan of monks, which would visit the lands, even those far beyond the borders of Salvatia. He had always dreamed of visiting the many other continents on Aretz. This was considered a high honor amongst the monks, and an opportunity he would have once relished and seized.

But how could he take such a noble position? He knew deep down in his heart of hearts that he was not qualified. Yes, he loved the Creator, through and through. Yes, he wanted to spread the good news to all who would listen. But how could he? What if he couldn't reach the One God with a critical prayer of healing at a crucial time? What if he didn't discern a force of darkness properly, and someone was tormented by said darkness for far longer than they should have been?

No, Katheros loved the Creator and all of His creation, but in his own mind he was not strong enough to represent the Creator to the people.

So instead, he would help the Creator in a different way. He would travel the lands by himself, and show love to the Creator's people. He would pray secretly in His heart and maybe share a message here or there. But beyond that, he would blend in with the people. He had some skill in woodworking and tent making, and was quite prolific as a gemologist. He would use these skills to support himself while secretly impacting the world around him.

This happened to be his first night out of the Order. The brothers were sad to see him go, as many believed that he had great potential. Even that saddened him a bit. They never knew of his doubts. He had never told them. He was always too ashamed to confess that although he greatly loved the Creator, his heart still doubted at times that he was called and chosen.

So instead of following the call, he would be like one of his personal heroes, Trizzen Stealthkin. He would be stealthy. He would befriend citizens of Salvatia, and show them the love of the Father. He would serve them like Yeshua served in the Scriptures. He knew the Holy Phantom was with him, at least at times he could be certain. When he could feel the presence of the Phantom, he would do the bulk of his spiritual work. When he couldn't he would just retreat in meditation and prayer, and focus on his natural skill sets along with keeping his temple primed for the pinnacle of strength.

That much he knew he could do, even though the doubts at times would strongly hinder his prayers. He was young, barely twenty two summers of age. He had time to figure it all out. He would go to the great Library in the Sanctuary tomorrow. He needed to research a few things before he left for his great journey. He smiled.

"Thank you Creator for understanding. I will serve you one way or the other, all of my days. You are worthy of more than I can provide, but I truly hope that this is a pleasing scent of worship to your nostrils." he said. He then began to softly sing a spiritual hymn.

At the precise moment he began to sing, a dark spirit flew from his presence, and landed on the mountaintop adjacent to Katheros. In the spiritual world, the demon took shape. It grinned, an ugly and menacing yet triumphant smile.

A bigger demon appeared before it.

"Well done! You have completed your assignment!"

"Thank you dark one. Where are my wings and what is my next assignment. There are rumors that time could be drawing short for us, and I plan to cause as much havoc as possible in that time" responded the smaller demon.

The bigger demon stretched forth her hands (as it preferred the female guise) and uttered dark magical words. The smaller spirit grew two feet taller, and more power was bestowed upon it. Choose your gender and name, my dark pet." she commanded.

"I will be known as DoubtFyre, to commemorate this great victory for our master. As far as gender, give me elements of both essences. I believe I can cause more confusion that way." he answered.

"So be it."

The evil spirit became a parody of both male and female, with great dark bat wings. It howled into the air! Finally! A prophecy of the Creator was diminished in some capacity. For years DoubtFyre had attacked Katheros relentlessly. It had penetrated deep into his heart. DoubtFyre had taken fiery darts of Katheros' passionate prayer and been singed time and time again. It had withstood the pure heart of Katheros, and even in the furnace of awful torments from standing within close proximity of heartfelt prayer to the Creator, as Angels came and went at the behest of Katheros' prayer, it had stayed hidden from the Light. If Katheros would have simply confessed the doubt, things would have been much tougher, maybe even impossible. Nevertheless, DoubtFyre had completed its mission. Now it was promoted. Four years was a long time. Other lesser demons frolicked around purposelessly causing mayhem. DoubtFyre looked down pridefully on those spirits. DoubtFyre had advanced. They had not.

DoubtFyre wanted more. DoubtFyre wanted to be a great name amongst demonkind and DragonBorne besides. DoubtFyre wanted legacy. So, it had attached itself to this Katheros, and helped prevent him from reenlisting in the Order of the Monks. Katheros had great power inside his heart, but due to DoubtFyre's dark arts and whispers, had never come to realize just how much the Creator loved him. DoubtFyre grinned wickedly as it reflected on its success.

Now, DoubtFyre had new dark powers to master and a name amongst the demonkind. In the portals of Gehenna and at the waypoints of the second heavens, its name would be written.

The senior demon, known as CastleBreak, smiled. "You have done well. You have been imbued with a twisted reflection of all the power you stole from Katheros. This young Monk has some special place in the Creator's heart. Your next mission is to subvert the sexuality of a young princess from the Isles. She is nowhere near as pure as Katheros, but she is willful. Her great will and drive concerns the master greatly. Ensure that she never turns that will towards seeking the Creator. Beware...." she paused as she ensured DoubtFyre was giving her its full attention. "There have been massive stirrings in the Third Heavens, of which we do not have full surveillance of yet, but our dark scouts are on it."

"Just like you did with Katheros, go out and spiritually assassinate this princess. Steal her power, and in your next promotion, you will receive tenfold what you currently have. It is written, that to those who are faithful with little, they will become rulers of much. Remember, the more you know of the Scriptures, the more effectively you can twist the truth to cause havoc.", she continued.

"When I next summon you, you will then return to Katheros. You have averted the prophecy of Katheros joining the Monks and subduing evil in Salvatia, but this one has a pure heart. He will need to be hindered again, and you will be stronger when that time comes. Next time, you will lead that pathetic fool to suicide, and we will claim his soul. Oh the tears of grief when the foolish Monks hear of his fate." she roared with laughter, and DoubtFyre joined.

"Any words of wisdom before I depart on my wanderlust, mistress?"

CastleBreak soberly thought for a moment, then stated

"Beware of Trizzen Stealthkin. There is something strange about that one. The higher ups are strategizing, but the oracle spirits and warlocks have seen bright futures in the realm of his possible futures, affecting all of Aretz and even beyond. Even Earth, some have claimed. We can't understand all of the Light, as you know, but all of the forces of hell are buzzing. We will obliterate this puny mortal and stave off the Lake of Fire, at least a little longer. Beware of him."

***

Trizzen awoke the next morning in his new quarters.

He had arranged a private lot of land, with a furnished stone cottage located deep in the northern intersection of Heart and its surrounding mountain range. The dwelling suited him perfectly.

The previous day had taken an emotional toll on the ranger. He had fought for so long. He had contended against dark beings in the netherworld for so long. He had scouted the forests and jungles of DarckNex for so long. He had strategized to stay alive and keep others alive for so long. Now that chapter of his life was over.

And beyond that, he was a bona fide hero. The peoples of Heart knew of him and his exploits. He had left so many years ago, an orphan and essentially a nobody. Now, he was known as a hero. The magnitude of that struck him very profoundly. He had joined Heart's Militia for several reasons. Yes, he did want to serve and help, that was certainly part of his decision to leave.

But truth be told, Trizzen's decision to join the Militia was centered on running away from his previous life, at its core. He wanted to flee a life of disappointment and abandonment. He had wanted to get as far away as possible from a life of grief and sadness. He wanted to leave the city where he had been abused, mistreated, and on some level scarred. It was too much to think about. He shifted his thinking. He was now a hero.

He had earned a considerable sum of golden coin for his part in the service of Salvatia. Before the Militia, he had survived in the undercity of Heart, which was likely and often more dangerous than his time serving at the front lines of the Militia's defense of Salvatia. He smiled as he thought of those days. It was in that dark place that he had first heard the voice of the Father.

Reflecting on it in this moment of time, he began thinking about that fact, which had been buried deep in his subconscious mind. There were clearly many benefits to joining the Militia to someone of his low status. However, it wasn't until after he had first distinctly heard the voice of the Father in his heart that he had actually considered inquiring about the Militia.

Things moved pretty rapidly after that. Interesting. It was very interesting to him, as he thought about all of the words shared with him from the Sage the previous night.

"Ouch!" exclaimed Trizzen. He was preparing a breakfast of fowl eggs and a strip of salted meat in a pan. The oil from the fat had sizzled and lightly burned his arm. He wiped the spot and brought his focus back to the present. Plenty of time to reflect and think now, he reminded himself. On the front lines of battle, such moments to ponder the past were rare.

He finished preparing his meal, and poured himself a

cup of delicious Heart Coffee, which happened to be one of Heart's chief exports. The rich aroma of the coffee took him back to the campfire breakfast meals in DarckNex. He smiled as he thought of all of the memories over the campfires and his comrades' antics and tales. Although he was glad the war was over, he felt like the stone walls were suffocating him. He honestly yearned for the open road. But, a season of rest and study would do him well, he knew.

He prayed and blessed his food. "Father, thank you for this nourishment. Thank you for seeing me through to this moment and allowing me to live through all of the things I've lived though. May your Blessed Name be made known in all places."

He ate his food while he looked around his new pad. It was comfortably high up and overlooking the vast majority of Heart. As he ate, he thought of ten years ago when he often slept in the gutters, sometimes even near the waters underneath Heart. He mused to himself, " I started from the bottom, now I'm here". He laughed and silently asked himself, "Where is here?".

***

Jaza arrived the the Great Library of Heart early that morning. She had ran ten miles at the crack of dawn. She had eaten a quick breakfast of vegetables, and meditated upon deep Quantum principles. When she meditated, she could see pieces and parts of the Quantum world operating and manifesting, due to the Law of Observation. Her meditative practice always steadied her mind.

She always followed that routine when she wanted to advance in knowledge quickly. That is to say, that was her daily routine which she never missed, without fail. She had primed her brain for understanding vast arrays of knowledge by developing and honing this routine, and she cherished her process dearly.

"Okay Jaza, today you find answers to this mystery" she told herself. She giggled aloud. It was strange to talk to herself.

But in a parapsychology tome she had recently finished, the author strongly urged the readers to do so. It would unlock new methods of thinking, allowing a person to ultimately think outside the box of all of one's internal references to the threshold of their individual memory.

And Jaza was determined to crack this mystery by any means necessary. Nothing will be denied to one who won't be denied. She smiled as she briskly walked up the stairs to the great Library, located within the central region of Heart, known as Sanctuary. "My knowledge will serve me well in this quest" she thought to herself.

"Perhaps something more than your own knowledge is needed to complete some quests, aye?" she clearly heard audibly.

She stopped and looked around. Seeing no one, she asked aloud "Who said that?".

Silence greeted her. The mysterious voice had unnerved her, then disappeared. She shook it off as her imagination, and hurried up the stairs.

In the spirit world, a certain Task Angel and saint smiled at each other. It had began.

***

Katheros Kardia walked through the streets of Heart, on this way to the Great Library. He smiled as he passed a family of four setting up a fruit stand. He walked over to them and made some conversation and purchased a cupful of fresh grapes. "May the Creator bless your business and all that you touch." he spoke over them as he finished his purchase. The father of the family smiled at the blessing. "Well received, man of God", thankfully responded the father of that family, who then went back to his preparations.

Katheros smiled, and walked away. Man of God. He liked the sound of that. On the morning of the onset of his greatest adventure, the Creator had used a humble manservant of His to title him as a man of God. Katheros believed that the Creator worked though all of his people, so every blessing and word spoken was subject to higher spiritual principles. Death and life were always in the power of the tongue. Although hesitation and doubt had plagued him ever since he had decided to leave the Order of the Monks, that one statement had settled it in his heart for good. He was following the Creator's will, and the Creator was with him, and would never leave or forsake him.

He hummed a spiritual song and prayed in his heart for the father of that family to receive wisdom and favor unlimited. His journey had began.

***

Trizzen walked to his back porch, and grabbed the rope hanging over the ledge. His grip as secure on the rope as his faith in his God, he wildly jumped off the ledge into the treetops below his home, and swung safely down to the mountains edge with a controlled landing. He followed a trail up about a half mile to a clearing in the forest. He removed his cloak, exposing the many weapons strapped to his leather armor. He grabbed his two ranger axes, and starting swirling and jabbing and slashing. He threw the axes perfectly in to the dead center of two different trees at eye level, using his momentum from the second throw to tuck into a roll and grip his bow. He shot one arrow which pierced the tree inches above the location of where the first axe had landed. He dropped his bow and pulled out his two swords, and danced around the clearing. Within minutes, he was sweating profusely and a little winded. He then performed a series of acrobatics, most defensively themed. Still, more sweaty and even more winded, he began a series of calisthenics, which would keep his body limber, loose and powerful. Once he had finished the entire routine, he sat cross legged in the middle of the clearing, and focused all of his attention on his Father. He searched with all of his being for a divine connection with the Holy Phantom.

Trizzen had developed the routine under the tutelage of his mentor, Parag. Parag had trained Trizzen and worked Trizzen hard as the Master Ranger. Before he had died at the cruel hands of the DragonBorne, Parag had imparted all that he knew to the young Trizzen within the first year of his Militia service. Parag was the closest that Trizzen had ever come to a real father in his life. The multitude of things which Parag had instilled within him had stayed in his heart. Parag had trained Trizzen to be thoughtful in training. Be thoughtful in training, for when battle is upon you, there is no time to think, only time to react.

The words echoed in his mind. Trizzen thanked the Father for his time with his mentor. He always thanked the

Father for Parag first, as a means of honoring the departed ranger trainer. Then, Trizzen went through every thing in his heart which he could think to be thankful about.

This was his walk with the Father. This was the relationship he had formed with his Maker on the front lines in deep enemy territory for so long. Everyday, as Trizzen made Targilim, (which was the name that Parag had taught him for this sort of practice), he always ended it with a meditation of gratitude to his Maker. Sometimes, with his eyes closed and his heart fully focused, he felt as if the Maker was standing right before him. Sometimes he would hear words and phrases and the Holy Phantom spoke back to him. Always, Trizzen left that meditative state feeling refreshed.

The feeling Trizzen experienced that day was beyond anything he had ever felt. With the flood of emotions still coursing through him, Trizzen meditated a long time. Tears freely streamed down his face, as he had entered into a sense of perfect peace. He knew his Maker and his Father knew, loved, and acknowledged him.

After awhile, the things that the Sage had told him began playing through his mind. Trizzen knew his Maker, more by Spirit as opposed to Word. He had been afforded little time for the scholarly pursuits as a ranger. He did have a few scrolls with scripture, which he had read every day, but he had understood there were entire volumes of teaching from the Maker. He knew of them and could quote some and had heard summaries of many of these teachings. And still there was the knowledge of the last set of scrolls which were penned by the hand of the disciple Yochanan. His heart leaped within himself as he thought of the prospect of getting his hands on such a copy. Derius had mentioned it was far unlike the rest of the Book, but somehow summarized all of the rest of the Book as it merged past, present, and future together. Amazing. However, DarckNex was not the most ideal place to find such volumes, to say the least.

But now, he was free from the call of war and had time to study and come to know more about this Maker whom he had formed such a strong bond with. He was ecstatic of the implications. The way the Sage had connected directly to His heart to relay the message to him. Woah! There was so much more to learn! Trizzen opened his eyes, looked up into the clear blue sky and let out a deafeningly loud ranger woop!

He finished his meditation, and sprinted back to the rope which led to his dwelling above the tree tops. He bathed and then dressed himself in simple traveling leathers. No leather armor was needed. No need to arm himself. He kept a throwing dagger in his boot, but other than that left his weapons hanging on the wall. As he stood at his front door and stared at his weapons which would not be going with him, the thought hit him quite profoundly. His life would be very different from now on.

"I have a weapon for you, the likes of which Aretz has never seen." the Holy Phantom whispered, at that moment directly beside him. Trizzen felt the love in every word.

He smiled, and fell to this knees in pure adoration of his Maker. He had no idea what Father was talking about. He always seemed to be speaking in riddles and mysteries and dark sayings to him. He had long ago just starting receiving the inspiration and stopped trying to figure it all out at once. He had realized he couldn't, and he acknowledged that was just part of the Maker's personality and steelo.

He was encouraged as he raced to the Library of Heart.

There was another friend and mentor there he would reunite with this day.

As Trizzen walked through the streets, he realized that being a known hero had perks and minor drawbacks. One perk was that everyone was very kind to him and hailed him and wanted to speak blessings over him. Many believers of the One God greeted him and let them know that they had been praying for him during the war. Many offered to pray for him right there on the spot.

This was great and was greatly appreciated. But, then he realized that he had only progressed about a mile within an hour. He loved the peoples of Heart, but he decided to try a different strategy. Dipping into an alley, he pulled his hood over his face and did what he could to hide his identity. Walking back out, he wasn't immediately recognized, and was thus able to move much quicker. Stealth suited him well.

Up until this point, he had been so immersed in his hero's welcome, he had hardly noticed the changes which had took place in Heart during his long absence. The war had taken its toll. He looked to the shadows and lower branches of the city as he walked, and his heart was immediately broken. He saw many who were desolate and begging alms and generosity for food for the day. Trizzen had grown up in the undercity and knew what it was to go for days on a hungry stomach. He gave generously to everyone he saw in such a predicament.

But, within himself, he knew that for the several that he helped with enough coin for a week or more of food, there were likely many more across the city in need. He pondered that if Heart's desolate population had grown, then the situation of the outlying cities, towns, and villages must be grim. He had earned considerable coin for his service in the Militia, but he was far from wealthy enough to provide a solution for all of them.

The stress began to dampen his spirit and his heart was sunk low, at least momentarily. "Oh, Father, how can I help them?" was his passionate plea to the One God.

Immediately, he felt the strong presence of the Holy Phantom manifested upon him. It was so powerful that it brought him to his knees, right in the middle of the roadway. What a sight he must have been to onlookers! For a moment, he could not move. He strongly felt and discerned that something had been deposited into him, although, he knew not what.

"Study My ways. To the measure of your study and diligence, will I provide for the least of these which you hold in your heart." he clearly heard spoken to him.

Immediately the heaviness was gone. He trusted the words he heard. He smiled as he continued his journey to the Library. In that moment of his purpose being restored, he felt a level of completeness.

Trizzen, equally pragmatic and adventurous, was a creature of purpose. In his youth, his purpose was to simply survive. In the Militia, his purpose was to stand against evil with his blades and bow. Now, he realized that his purpose was to help those who had not the means to help themselves.

"I will not fail you, Father." was his only response as he quickened his pace to the Library.

***

Expelled from the presence of the dangerous ranger, the chief Grief demon afflicting the region of Heart revolted at the encounter. Never had he felt pain than at that moment. The moment that Trizzen spoke out in his heart to the Creator, a powerful Archangel had appeared brandishing a spear of pure light. The spear was thrown as lightning, and had cracked through every defense of the grief demon.

This was a major setback. This armor of his had been forged through the suffering of many souls for many years. Those who lost loved ones in the War but did not trust in the Maker had minted that armor. Those who suffered financial lack in the region had strengthened that armor. Wherever there was sadness, this demon had feelers and tentacles (minions, beings from his very own essence) in place to receive.

However, with that one blow, a shift had taken place. Some of those whom Trizzen had blessed with coin that morning began to be strengthened against the spirit of grief. Their mindset had changed from a mindset of poverty to a mindset of blessing. Instead of rushing to find meat and bread for themselves with enough coin to do so for an entire week, many of those who were blessed sought others who were hungry to help them eat or obtain new shoes or clothes.

"NOOOOOOOOOO!" screamed the demon.

This was happening impossibly fast. A standard human mind should not be this quick to change after it had been in his grasp. He had waited for eons to garner this much power. In the blink of an eye, over a century of patient and grueling evil work was undone.

The demon looked across his vast empire which lived in the minds of men, women, and children in this region. He had been warned to be wary of this Trizzen Stealthkin. Now, he absolutely knew that he would need to be proactive. He sent one of his demonic underlings to fetch the chief Occult demon in this region. He would willingly barter with other evil forces by giving up some of his control over the minds of humans in order to stop this Trizzen. No, stopping would not be enough. He would assassinate this Trizzen. No human was a match for Grendor, the demon of Grieving Hearts.

****

Jaza arrived at the Library, and promptly filled a cart with books, twenty seven thick volumes. She was going to do the unthinkable. She was going to research this mysterious One God throughly, critically, and scientifically.

It wasn't so much that she doubted there could be a possibility that a central Creative Being of some sort existed. Even from her youth, she had doubts about the Mega Explosion theory, which stated that eons ago a huge blast had occurred from volatile gases which preexisted and planets and dimensions and realms and eventually life had formed of that. It just seemed so far fetched.

However, due to the antics and theatrics and operations of some of the people she had known who claimed to be supporters and followers of the One God, she had little reason to believe that they had the right God. To further compound matters, when she had studied the teachings of the One God in her adolescence, she had come across a rare scroll which contained scraps of parchment from a scroll which was rumored to belong to the Apokalypsi volume of the Book. She had translated the ancient language using a deciphering tool which she was familiar with. She happened to come across some writing that indicated that the world was flat and had four corners, and that beings known as angels stood at those four corners.

This greatly perplexed her. Even at that age, she knew that Aretz was round. In her Quantum meditative practice, she sometimes left her temple and was able to move about with her inner being. She saw many things as she had traversed the world in those times as she was connected to her physical body by a silver cord which tethered her. However by meditating on the principles of Quantum Reality, she was able to move about freely. She had found certain places she could not go, but for the most part she had free reign to explore. On several such journeys, she floated up into outer space! She saw how massive Aretz was, and it appeared to be a great brown and white ball! From there, she could see a great star which Aretz orbited via a magnetic pull, although she was very afraid, for it was massive beyond wonder and appeared guarded by forces which she did not understand. She could also see portals and doorways and many other things she did not understand. However, she was encouraged by this and knew what she saw was true.

She had strong suspicions that the other planets in the other dimensions and realms were all round as well, and not sqaure. Eventually, she heard tales of a wizard who was traveling in the Quantum realm, who had his silver cord cut by a DragonBorne mage. That wizard was physically alive, but his soul was lost to him. He laid in bed for many years as a vegetable. After this, Jaza had decided the risk of traveling in such a way was too dangerous. There were other ways to solve mysteries.

Ever pragmatic and curious, she was one of the few

upon Salvatia that understood much of the greater Quantum realities. Aretz was just one of the many untold number of dimensions. However, she also knew that the place called Earth was essentially what was known as the Prime Dimension. Somehow, although still mysterious to her, the other dimensions were all attached to the beautiful blue orb known as Earth. And from all of her extensive research, she knew for a fact that the Earth was round, blue, and orbited the same star she had seen.

So, the passage which referred to a planet as a flat place with four corners guarded by four angels would have reflected the belief of the peoples at the time that worlds were flat. If the disciple had truly seen the Earth and was taken up by visions of the One God, then he would have seen a large blue orb. She knew more about the Earth than most, for her studies were deep and her intelligent curiosity was vast. Her rejection of the faith of the One God was partially based on that one point, along with the ignorance of His believers. How could she, a being from another lesser dimension know more about the Earth than one who had been given some great revelation. She had asked some followers of the One God for advice, including her own parents. However, no one could give her any guidance. Therefore, she began to reject everything else from the camp of the One God as well.

She decided to place that obvious blunder into a small corner of her mind, and refocused all of her efforts and concentration on her study. A footnote had caught her eye, which referenced an interesting passage which in turn led her to another interesting passage. Some of the writings actually lined up with Quantum principles, she began to notice.

Unknowingly to her, her assigned Task Angel, and smiling saint to its side was holding a gift package labeled as

"Jaza - Word of Knowledge" right behind her. The Angel dropped the package at her feet. The package began to shake violently then exploded.

Jaza immediately straightened up her stance and attentively listened to the cacophony of thoughts that suddenly flooded her mind. She couldn't make sense of it at first, as it seemed like there was a voice of a multitude speaking (in a whispering still small voice) inside of her and then one thought was highlighted and magnified.

"And if Yochannon who knew more of the dimensions than even inquisitive Jaza, was simply relating to the people of his time? And if the language was purely symbolic of the Quantum Realm and even deeper Realms? What then, inquisitive Jaza?"

As soon as the thought completed, the cacophony of thoughts, images, and expressions stopped. She was stunned in the silence of her own mind.

The answer to her own question broke her. She knew she wasn't hearing things. She knew within herself that she had heard the Voice of the One God directly somehow. The control of knowledge and packaged wisdom was ecstatic, surreal, and ultimately unexplainable.

As tears began to pour down her face, she said aloud. "You're real. You're actually real."

The only reply she head was the same majestic Voice saying "I love you, Jaza."

The statement broke something else inside of her. She felt a warmth inside herself, as if deep inside her stomach a furnace had been piped and fanned several times. The warmth seem to then emanate through out her entire being. Although the sensation itself was brief, she knew within herself that what she had felt was not of a temporary nature. She closed her eyes then, and meditated on that feeling. Tears streamed down her face freely, and the realization dawned on her that she had been incomplete before, although she did not know it.

After that, her curiosity took on an entirely new focus. She had spent her life wrapped up in the theories and practices of the Quantum world, with no acknowledgment of anything deeper than that. Now she realized that even the mysteries of the Quantum world paled in comparison to something much deeper. She plunged headlong into the books, reading, understanding, and asking questions of the One God. Some answers came immediately in the form of fragmented thoughts from a still small Voice deep in her heart. Although the thoughts were barely whispers in her mind, she soon realized that every thought was packed with revelation beyond the surface of what she actually heard. Other answers she just heard distinct silence, but somehow she knew she already had knowledge of the answer. For other questions, she seemed to get nothing at all, but her curiosity urged her further inward, and the lack of any immediate answer didn't phase her.

After hours of furious studying, contemplating, journaling, charting, and marrying of old thoughts to new thoughts, Jaza had a brand new fascination in life emerge in the person of Yeshua. He was mysterious. He was powerful. He was humble. He was truly perfect, and she began to understand the great sacrifice He had made for her.

She became increasingly more and more sure that Yeshua, the Son of the One Living God, held the key to every mystery. She had heard some believers talk about Him, but the sudden passion she was feeling in her heart towards Him went far beyond words. He was truly magnificent!

Quickly and with great tenacity, she raced through the library shelves to put back the first set of books she had read through, and filled two carts with books which contained information relating to the one known as Yeshua. Some of the tomes were rumored to be translations of the very books which the advanced peoples of Earth had recorded of Yeshua. The ancient sages of Salvatia had many resources at their disposal. She began to wonder for the first time how the ancient sages could have accomplished such a task. She brought her attention back to the present. Plenty of time to ponder that later, she mused.

As she studied more and more about Yeshua, she wanted to know more. She couldn't get enough. How had she even lived her life without knowing about Him? No, she corrected herself. Knowing about Him, she realized in a moment of epiphany, was the quandary with most of the believers she had known. Knowing about Him wasn't good enough. She needed to know Him. Deeply and personally. She vowed to herself that she would not make the same mistake so many others clearly had.

Yeshua was polarizing, powerful, merciful, righteous, meek, and exceedingly super in every way.

"I simply must know everything about this Yeshua!" she said aloud.

She was smitten with Him.

***

Katheros arrived at the Library. He could feel the presence of the One God heavily, more than he had ever felt in his entire life. He knew something was astir.

As he walked up the stairs, he felt as if his feet were moving on their own. He realized that they were, and also that he was humming his favorite spiritual tune.

"Worthy is the Lamb who was slain" he quietly sung, following the humming in his heart.

His feet took him into the library, towards the top floor. He passed a beautiful young lady who was crying at a table full of books. He felt the mercy of the Creator strongly there, and although it was interesting to him, he pressed forward. He also saw a man in a deep hood conversing with the head librarian near the top floor, and they were laughing loudly, although they were trying to contain themselves. He felt pure joy emanating from that encounter, and wanted to join in for some odd reason. Still he kept walking. He arrived to the top floor.

His eyes were opened. At the end of an aisle of books, there was a blinding white light. An enormous angel stood at the front of the portal and smiled at him.

"I bid you, come." offered the angel, as she stretched forth her hands.

Katheros, as holy fear began to grip him from the wonder which his eyes were seeing, complied.

Katheros walked into the white light, and was seen no more that day.

Nor for a season and a time after that day.

Not that anyone was looking for him.

***

Trizzen moved with the renowned stealth and grace which he was known for. With his hood pulled low, he blended in with the early morning crowd walking up the stairs of the Library. Quicker than any assassin or ranger on a covert mission, he gracefully raced up the steps to the highest level of the library. That is where she used to start her mornings.

He spotted his target, and smiled to himself. He walked up behind his quarry with a mischievous grin on his face, and disguised his voice saying "Unacceptable. Who organizes this Library. Hmpph!".

Ninny Lynda braced herself and composed her face before turning around. She quickly internally recited the verse "Blessed are those who endure persecution for righteousness sake". She had been Head Librarian for a long time. Most patrons were extremely delightful and pleasant and thankful. There were always a few bad apples here or there. She was determined to not let this detractor spoil such a beautiful day.

She turned to see a man dressed in deep green and brown, with his hood pulled deeply over his face so that she could not see his face. But something was familiar about him, about his stance. The man pulled his hood back. She gasped.

"Why you ol' trickster, I ought to get me a switch from outside and take it to your backside!" she playfully exclaimed.

Trizzen just smiled all the more, and covered the distance between them in two long strides, and embraced Ninny in a great bear of a hug.

She squeezed him back harder, and they simply stood in the embrace for some time. She pulled back and said "Now now, let me get a good look at ya. My, you have grown up to become so handsome!" as she hugged him tightly again.

He kissed her cheek lovingly and said, "Oh, how I have missed you!"

Growing up as an orphan in the lower regions of Heart, Trizzen never really knew what it was like to have a normal childhood. However, Ninny Lynda had loved him from the first moment she laid eyes on him as a four year old young child, pilfering fruit from the fruit vendors. He had been caught red handed stealing some orange sweetfruit and was going to be exiled to a detention center and exported out of Heart. She saw him, and immediately vouched for and loved him.

From then on, she let him live with her own household, and come and go as he pleased. There was a special bond between the two which words could not describe. She poured love into him, and he radiated it right back. She was the first to evangelize to him of the ways of the One God. Without her love in his life, Trizzen didn't think he would have made it.

As the years went by and since Ninny had her own life to contend with, Trizzen visited with her less as he survived on his own. He didn't want to burden her and her noble minded husband and four children and eventually grandchildren of her own. But he would visit her at the Library often and she taught him many things.

Trizzen reflected on the many nights in the jungles of DarckNex when his life was in mortal danger from a multitude of foes. It had often been the love of his precious Ninny that kept him sane and focused. He would give his own life before he let the threat of darkness come anywhere near his beloved Godmother.

Now she stood before him. She had aged gracefully, and the spark of love and humility seemed even more magnified in her loving eyes. They sat at a table and began to catch up. He told her many stories and described far away lands which Ninny was curious about. She had read of these places, and wanted to confirm that the recorded information matched the truth. She took many notes, as she was writing a chronicle of the ranger's life, although he knew it not. He was always very special to her, and she wanted the Chronicles of Trizzen to be a grand surprise, whenever she was able to finish it.

She in turn told him of her family and how they had prospered over the years. She went to her desk and returned with all of the letters which Trizzen had wrote her. She read them often, and prayed for him even more.

Their hearts were so full of joy at the reunion. Eventually they began to reminisce and laugh at all of the old memories of the life they had shared together, and of the antics of young Trizzen.

Ninny's favorite story was the time an aleecat had darted into Ninny's house while Trizzen was staying there. An allecat was a small somewhat feral and somewhat docile feline animal which lived on its own in Heart. This particular aleecat had caught a whiff of the delicious roasted fowl which Ninny had in the stove. It had followed the urges of its nose and became an uninvited guest in Ninny's house!

The aleecat, once it realized it couldn't get to the fowl, had began to gallop through every room, trying to get to the back door which would lead it back to the street. Everyone in the house was in a disarray, some trying to get away from the thing and others trying to trap it. Trizzen, no more than 6 years old at the time, was getting a reading lesson from one of Ninny's sons, Glin.

Seeing the quick moving animal dart into the room that they were in, Trizzen was even quicker to bolt to the closet and promptly close the door behind him. Glin tried to follow, but the terrified Trizzen wouldn't let him in! Glin pulled on the door and hammered on it pleading mercy, but Trizzen left Glin in the room with the creature. Seeing Glin get more and more frantic only excited the aleecat even more, so it starting hissing loudly. Which only made Glin bang all the more on the closet door. And Trizzen refused to let him in, hanging on the the back of the door knob and pulling the door shut as if his very life depended on it. It was quite the scene which Ninny's noble husband, Wane, solved by whacking the creature a few times with a broom and leading it "gently" towards the door.

Glin would never let Trizzen forget it, and the family laughed at the scenario for years to come.

Trizzen really couldn't express his love to her in words. Without her influence in his life, he would have never known the joys of family, even for the short time he was able to spend with hers. Her family had become his family.

On the journey back, Trizzen had bought a gift from one of the many islands which separated Salvatia from the continent of DarckNex. As he was about to give it to her, he noted a young man, clearly dressed as a monk walking past them and smiling. He could sense a strong presence of love and could discern that the Holy Phantom was doing a mighty work in the young man's life. He wanted to motion for him to join them to hear this tale, since surely it must be worth hearing.

However at that precise moment Ninny pulled a parchment out of her lady bag which she had found hidden in a mysterious tome. It was clearly ancient with runes and symbols the type of which he had never seen before. Everything in Trizzen's heart welled up at the sight of it, although he knew not why.

Ninny Lynda said to him "I believe Father wants you to have this. I don't know what it is, but the Glory of God is strong on it. I believe it is a key of some sort, based on the the pattern of the runes."

He examined it gracefully. "It's beautiful, and I can feel the very fabric of destiny." He had seen similar markings in spiritual journeys and dreams, although he also didn't know what they meant.

He gently placed the parchment in the table, and wanting to seize the moment, he told her to close her eyes. She closed her eyes as she flashed him a deep grin, which he couldn't help but to return. He stood behind her, and placed an opulent blue sapphire necklace around her neck. She opened her eyes and marveled at it.

She could feel God's warming presence with the gift, as if Trizzen had somehow bottled all of His love for her in the gesture itself. Ever modest, Ninny fussed "Oh, you shouldn't have! How much did you spend on this!"

"That's for me to know, and this is for you to enjoy, mamma."

She paused at the word mamma. She looked into his eyes, and hugged him. She had been the only mother he had ever known, and he was so special to her. Not wanting to tear up and cause a scene, she promptly switched from Ninny Glynda to Head Librarian to help her son in something she was beginning to think would become a grand adventure.

"Now, let me show you a few volumes which may help you understand the meaning of some of the runes and symbols you see on the parchment."

Trizzen's heart was full of the greatest joy he had ever experienced. He spent the rest of that day with her, and followed her home to generously bless all of her family members with gifts he had selected for them as well. They enjoyed dinner as a reunited family that night and it was nice to be home.

***

"Yeshua" mused Jaza, as she walked home that night. Something fresh had awoken and risen inside her. She felt more alive than ever before. She carried only one volume home from the library, "Exposition of The Gospel of Yochannon, he whom Yeshua loved", penned by the ancient Sage Wither Wather. She walked dreamily down the street.

It was a beautiful night, as the mist from Heart's watery undercity dreamily ascended ever skyward. She hardly noticed Jol approaching, seemingly walking out of the shadows as if he were made out of shadow himself.

"Good evening, Beautiful." he addressed her.

Instead of the usual contempt she felt for the man, she was delighted to have someone to share the good news with. She hugged him warmly, and began talking a mile a minute as they walked, expounding on deep truths which she had learned from the writing of the Sages.

Jol, used to her cool nature and witty although slightly menacing banter, was taken aback. In the decade he had known her, never had she offered him a hug, or hardly even a smile. A change and a shift had occurred in the young woman. She had softened in her stance towards him, and the smitten man was caught off guard by this sudden change of behavior.

He had teased her yesterday about being a disciple of the One God, but he had no idea this would be the effect. Followers of the One God were purely a boring people, never willing nor able to have any real fun, he thought to himself. He'd have to allow Jaza to go though this little phase, but use her suddenly soft heart against her for his own advantage. Yes, that's exactly what he would do, he thought within himself.

He smiled and nodded as he walked her home, scantly listening to a word she said. She was babbling about dimensions and worlds and angels and demons and gods and truth and error and a thousand other seemingly unconnected points. His heart couldn't understand what had happened to her, nor did his heart care to try. This was the kindest she had been to him in years. This Trizzen had come back to the city of Heart, and all of a sudden change came to Jaza. Jol resolved deeply within himself to keep a close eye on this Trizzen.

***

Katheros stood clothed in a shining white robe at the Throne of God. His heart experienced the greatest bliss and joy known in all existence.

The Maker smiled at him. An innumerable company of angels and saints surrounding him all sung one tune in a glorious heavenly orchestra. The Maker started speaking.

"My beloved servant Katheros. I have created you for a time such as this. Write all that I tell you."

A feather pen and a tome appeared suddenly in Katheros' hands. He began to write. The Creator told him many things which must come to pass. It seemed both only an instant and an eternity.

Six months would pass before anyone would see the young monk on Aretz again.

***

For the next six months, Trizzen was daily in Targilim, in the Library, and at his home studying. There was much for him to learn. Many sought him out as an honored guest, but the man was nowhere to be found. He used his stealthy ways to go and come, and no one saw him, save Ninny Lynda. The parchment she gave him was leading him some where, to something or someone, to some grand purpose. He was sure of it. He pressed into the One God and His ways even further. His heart missed the adventure he had become accustomed to, but he felt as if somehow he was being prepared for an even grander adventure. Day by day, he became more sure and pressed all the harder into his ardent studies.

***

Jaza had quit her job and sold all her possessions. Most thought she had gone mad. Even the other followers of the One God could not understand the things she was adamant about. Something was coming. All needed to prepare. The weekly services in offering to the One God weren't enough. The pretentious schedules and programming did not delight the heart of the One God nor His son Yeshua. She became to be shunned by most other disciples, but she didn't care. If Yeshua was for her, who could be against her?

She used all of the proceeds from the sales of her possessions to rent a small room at the Inn of the Hearty Folk. Daily, her routine was to wake up, pray, run, eat a small breakfast, then study the life of Yeshua. She yearned for Him.

At the end of six months she had a powerful dream which shook her to her core. Everything changed after that.

***

Lord MoonBane rested comfortably right at the parting of the veils of the realms of spirit, quantum, and Aretz. Physically, if it were possible to see with a human eye, he would have been seen as floating at the line between the atmosphere of the world of Aretz and outer space. But that special location which formed a portal high into the night sky was invisible to the natural eye. He watched over all of the goings and comings of the continent of Salvatia. As he had since the Creator had allowed for its creation. This reality was teaming with life, and MoonBane was blessed to have received such an assignment.

The powers of darkness were coordinating and communicating far more than normal which couldn't be good. Since Lord MoonBane had many duties in service to the One God which stretched him thin, he prayed to the Creator for assistance. Seconds after praying, his quantum signaler device received a new download from the Maker.

"Well done as usual, my trusted servant. This realm will be key in Earth's final battle. Drop all of your other duties to your subordinates, and focus on training Trizzen and the band I will bring to him. They are my Chosen Champions, and I will be with them. Watch them from afar for a time of six months. Then show them how to access the Covenant Armor."

Lord MoonBane blessed the God of Heaven. MoonBane was a multi-tasker and deep thinker and a strategic genius when it came to intrigue of any sort. Now, the end of all worlds was to begin with a battle upon his domain. He knew this was no coincidence. The Creator had chosen him for just such a time as this. This was a high honor and a privilege which could have easily been offered to another Watcher, just as talented as he.

And this realm was nothing like some of the other realms MoonBane had also been watching. Furthermore, this world of Aretz was a high frequency planet, which just so happened to be thirteen hundred times bigger than the Earth.

This would provide for interesting combat in the spiritual

as well as quantum worlds. Adding to the intrigue, this world had somewhat advanced quantum principles stabilized, whereas Earth had only some success in stabilizing that realm.

This also meant that the second heavens would soon begin tingling with more activity. This violent activity would likely equal more than the combined activity which had taken place in the almost six thousand years of mankind's existence. Ah, this would be even more intriguing than the time before Adam had been placed in the Garden of Eden. He had scores to settle with those nefarious water beings who were the inhabitants of the Pre-Adamite Earth. Ah Atlantis…how well will your water defenses hold against the Lake of Fire? Not well. He chuckled to himself and forced himself to focus on the tasks at hand.

MoonBane started praying for assistance in assembling the right team of special Guardian Angels for the special operations. MoonBane had many training rooms to build, and he sincerely hoped that this Trizzen Stealthkin, Ranger of Legend and Lore was a quick learner.

{ And thus, the first of seven-parts of the Epic Parable, "Herald of Knetashkan" is completed. To be continued in Chapter 6 "Grinder's Paradise" }

Devotional - 30 Days Journey to Greatness

∞ 30 Days - Journey to Greatness ∞

You are in for a rare treat, my friend! When my wife and I first decided to start a Christian Publishing company (Summer 2017), we wanted to make sure everything was done in God's timing. We wanted to make sure that He would always go before us and make every crooked path straight.

In the following pages, I present to you the first material my wife and I wrote together, 30 Days Journey to Greatness. We had a standing covenant with God in place to free form write for 30 days, and to accomplish some goal each day. We started the covenant being somewhat in a state of despair. It seemed as if our bank account had hidden holes in it from which money just disappeared! We were very unsure about which direction to take our ministry in. We were both clearly in a state of mind from which God needed to deliver us from. At the end of the 30 days….our bank account still had hidden holes in it! However, we had received direction and vision from God and knew which path to walk fearlessly……

This book which you have either on your favorite device on in paperback is part of that vision. This was written at the start of this journey, several years ago by the time of this writing. The Lord has since blessed us tremendously in every capacity! We invite you to use the same principles to launch your own 30 day journey into GREATNESS!!! The notes pages are included for you to launch your own 30 day covenant with God and be prepared for greatness within your own life!

Without further ado, we present to you 30 Days Journey To Greatness!

Terrell Potts (co-author)

Emely Capo-Potts (co-author)

July 28th, 2017

Lord God of Hosts, we make Covenant with you.
For the next 30 days, both of us will write
at least 500 words talking about the journey, how we feel, what
you're showing us, and whatever you lead us to
write. We will set 1 goal every day, for
the next day, in our writing. We will not
write each day until our goal has completed. We
expect you to open up doors of relaxation and
opportunity to us throughout the process, and expect
our situation to be turned completely around.
We will be obedient to your voice with all
our heart, might, and strength.

Terrell M. Potts
Terrell Potts   Emely Cupu-Potts
starting 28th July, 2017

189

∞ Terrell - Day 1 ∞

30 days until greatness...what a concept. I rush into this journey, excited, ready and willing. I have been craving great adventure for a while now. I have so many problems, both me and my wife do. But Jesus has not failed us yet. I've failed Him. We've failed Him. Yet, His grace remains on our life. Time after time, He has shown us His great mercy.

Now, our finances are busted. I've had a pay cut at the job, and it hurts. Our ministry has not attracted more than a few faithful followers, so we're debating on shutting it down and going a different route. I have dreams since I've been 12 years old of being a software developer, and it still hasn't been accomplished. I want a stronger, more flexible body. I want the relationship between me, my wife and children to be better. I want to have abundant finances. I want to make full proof of the ministry which the LORD has placed inside me.

I want to be an awesome, inspiring leader. I want to be so dialed into Heaven, that I never miss a queue from the LORD. All these desires.

And the only thing which keeps me out of success, I feel, has been that I haven't made the effort. I haven't made and followed through on putting in 12 to 16 hours a day. I take full accountability and responsibility for where I am in life. If I want more out of Life, I need to put more in.

I'm fed up with excuses that I make for why I didn't do this or why I couldn't do that. Why I over spent money. Why I over ate. Why I failed to exercise.

Why I let thoughts enter into my mind...which I am clearly better than.

So... I put accountability up in the only place that seems to motivate me anymore. I put the full weight of the accountability in Heaven. I made a Covenant with the Lord of Hosts. I've always honored those before, whereas doing things just because they are the right thing to do....is flaky at best with me. Sure...I'll do great for a week or even a few weeks. Then, right back to bad habits intertwined with some good habits.

But I've come to the realization that I'll never become who I know that I am inside, if I don't do it this way. The hard way. The only way in which there is no turning back. I can let my wife down easily enough. I'm only human. I can even let myself down without blinking an eye. After all, everyone has to take it easy sometimes, right?

LOL.

With the Eyes of the Lord on me, there is only one way to move, and that's forward. I fear Him too much to conveniently forget. Tomorrow, my goal is to do 100 pushups. The journey has begun.

♥ Emely – Day 1 ♥

Today has just been one of "those" days for me. If I could sum up today in just one word it would be REJECTION. I was excited about going to the flea market to sell my sugar scrubs. I thought that tomorrow I would just go and select a slot and sell. Unfortunately, it didn't work out that way. I found out that I have to register two to three weeks in advance. I am also part of an entertainment company. In this troupe, there are times where things are said and done I personally don't agree with and can't compromise to. I reached out to someone to let them know and I never got a response back. I can't stand when people do that. In my mind, I'm thinking perhaps the person has an issue with the fact that I am a Christian. Honestly, all sorts of things went through my mind. When we are for Christ, we are in all the way or not. I choose to be all the way in.

I was also hoping that people would want to buy my scrubs at my husband's job. One was sold which is great, but not enough. I am also having a logo done for my business Hephzibah Beauty Treats. Yesterday I was so excited to view my logo and it was completely wrong. The designer had to redesign and I'm still waiting on it.

I've been missing my best friend a lot as well. It would be nice to have someone in town I can hang out with. Sometimes I don't want to be home and want to have a friend to spend time with. I feel very lonely here. Anyone I thought was my friend here, turned out not to be. I'm not one that needs to be surrounded by friends but I like to have my chosen few. These days it's like disloyalty is an epidemic. Nevertheless I am taking each life experience day by day trusting in God to see me through.

In ministry, I am fed up with the same routine of always. I was upset about something pertaining to the ministry earlier but I'll get over it. God told my husband and I that we are pioneers. Perhaps He wants us to do something completely unheard of. We are different. We are looked upon as weird. We are quirky and that's alright. I am ready to do something new. To tell the absolute truth, I enjoy traveling other places to minister and deliver what the Lord wants His people to know. Besides, a prophet is not honored in his hometown. Now, isn't that the truth! It was nice to have a church building while it lasted but right now my mind says sayonara to that. I'm ready to launch into this season.

Finances are very bad right now which is another factor to my mood. I am really trying not to be down by this but I can't help it. I just need to keep it 100. I know God will provide. Sometimes it even sounds cliché. However, I know that He truly will provide so that helps. I pray that tomorrow will be a better day. Besides, things could be a lot worse.

Day 1 Notes

What is the Lord speaking into your heart today?

∞ Terrell - Day 2∞

I just finished my push-ups, and I'm super excited about this Covenant. The Lord showed me last night how I need to be using more of what I have. He used my daughter, as I was chastising her in a dream to be fearless, because I had put too much in her to let it go to waste.

Then the Lord revealed that he was talking to me, using the situation as a lesson. Then, today I worked for several hours, to understand database building in SQL Server Management Studio. All week long I tried, but today I had my breakthrough. I'm beginning to finally put the pieces together to the puzzle. Tomorrow my goal is to resume running. Today I had an excellent time at GodFaithMedia, and recorded the first verse for Kingdom Grinding. I learned quite a bit.

More than anything, I felt like time spent today was the most effective use of time on a Saturday, the Sabbath. I received new direction for Guardian Brigade, as well. The goal of ministry must be to be effective, and sow the maximum amount of seeds. The field is ready and ripe for harvest. The entrepreneur spirit is heavy upon me, and I'm ready to break out of the day to day pay check to pay check, and really live a free Kingdom life.

The Grind is the key to maximum transformation. We're out here on stage for the entire Spirit world to see, and It's time for the maximum Glory to go to my King. After only one day of the Covenant, I feel refreshed and ready, as if living waters are flowing the way they need to be, to carry me into the next season of my destiny…. the next season of both me and Emely's life.

I believe that those who read this book, are going to

connect with those same living waters. I decree that those who sow into this project are going to receive the same blessings that we receive for honoring the covenant. That's the way the anointing works. Think about the prophet, the widow, and the jars of oil. If you receive a prophet in the name of a prophet, you too shall receive the reward of the prophet. And the Prophetic and the Grind can't be separated. Grind, my friends, and watch how it works out for you and yours.

I'm beginning to see that the commitment to the grind is extremely helpful in actually accessing the open heavens which Christ secured for us at the cross. Submitting to the grind is step one. Respecting the grind is step two. Appreciating the grind is step three. Loving the grind is step four. Craving more of the grind is step five. It's easy to resist the grind, but once you get momentum going, you'll realize that the Holy Spirit will seem closer and closer as the grind life becomes second nature.

♥ Emely – Day 2 ♥

Today was a much better day. I was well rested and ready to have a chill day. I heard back from the person from the entertainment company. I must say I was worried for no reason, lol. She said there are other ministers in the troupe who feel the same way I do. That took a big load off me.

I had a sense of urgency to visit a church I haven't been to in a while. Sometimes you can feel strange or nervous when you go to a place you haven't been to in so long. You wonder if people are going to act shady with you. I did notice a bit of that, but it doesn't faze me. In the end of the day, God loves me. My husband loves me and so do my children. Things went well there so I thank God I responded to the unction of the Holy Spirit. It was all for a purpose. I got there right on time.

Originally, I was just going to go the mall to get a free lipstick. It was national Free Lipstick Day and Mac was giving out free lipsticks. Instead I went to the church first. I ended up not being able to get my free lipstick because they said it was just the first 100 customers who would get the free lipstick. I didn't remember reading that. I was totally looking forward to getting that free lipstick, you know what I'm saying?

I found out some info about things that the Lord had already revealed to me. I can't say I'm mad though. It's interesting how people think they can hide stuff. God will always bring to the light what is hidden. While on earth, I don't want to be affected by what foolish people are doing. Of course, it's easier said than done. However, if I feed in to the mess, I am just as foolish.

Later this evening, we went to GodFaithMedia studios. We had a great time recording tracks. Terrell got part of his song done. It took over two hours to get through the first part of the song. Writing and perfecting tracks takes a lot of work but the finished product is worth it. I also recorded part of my song as well. I wasn't sure what kind of sound I was going with until I heard a track they had. Instantly I was in love. This song was exactly my style. I was able to get in and flow. I had lyrics written last night but I eventually got spontaneous. I love spontaneous and prophetic worship. This song will definitely bring people to tears and repentance. It will touch the hearts of many people. I am looking forward to our next studio time to get both of our songs completed.

I truly thank God; my day was so much better. But now I am waiting on a miracle. We have a financial obligation that needs to be met in two days. I really need you Lord. I know that You will provide. Next time, please help us be better stewards of our finances. I am looking forward to sharing how we ended up meeting the need we had. My goal tomorrow is to get through the laundry in the living room. I'm pretty much tired of looking at it. I'm so not a fan of laundry but somebody's got to do it.

Day 2 Notes

What Scripture is on your mind today?

∞ Terrell - Day 3 ∞

To be a Champion of this Earth. The thought rung through my mind as I completed my goal for the day, the 5.75 mile run which I swore to finish this day. Oh, how I long for that feeling! I know what it feels like to win. I know what it feels like to lose. I've had my low moments, and I've had my high moments. Ultimately, victory comes as a result of the grind. A new thought occurred to me today during my run.

The hunt for the grind. The grind can be elusive to us all, at times. During those moments, those days, those weeks, sometimes we may fall away from the grind in its purest form. In its purest form, the grind is consistent. The grind becomes second nature, and the benefits of the grind are continuously apparent, whatever that may mean.

However, in those times when it's hard to stay on the grind, we must go on the hunt for our elusive prey. We have to approach the grinder's mentality with the hunter's mentality. If I can push my way (hunt) through three runs this week, I'll be back on my running grind by next week. If I can hunt down programming tutorials and hack and claw my way through them, long enough, I'm going to be on my programmer's grind. If I can hunt for Scriptures that fire me up today, I can be on my Scripture grind by tomorrow.

The hunt can be daunting. Human nature wants to kick back, relax and take it easy. However, we must be willing and ready to sacrifice who we are right now, to embrace and ultimately become who we will become.

I feel like a caterpillar, who's been crawling around for far too long. I am ready to enter into that cocoon and emerge as a butterfly. The caterpillar is on the hunt, and the cocoon is the grind. Truth be told, it takes a very unique mindset to enjoy either the hunt or the grind. But the promise of achieving the goal.... which is to say, becoming the ever-elusive butterfly is out there. It's going to take work to get there. It's going to take sacrifice. It's going to take loss, pain, rejection, and a host of other unpleasant feelings, experiences, and emotions.

But when you realize that you don't get out of life what you want; you get out of life what you MUST HAVE. When you need success as bad as you need to breathe, you're on your way to achieving it. One day, we will all stand before the Awesome Creator of this universe. I want to smile before Him, and have Him smile upon me, knowing that all of my Kingdom assignments were completed.

Tomorrow, my goal is to fast, at least until 6:00 PM, from any food.

♥ Emely – Day 3 ♥

Today was another one of my bad days. I woke up okay but the day got worse. Perhaps I am worrying too much about things I shouldn't worry about. I should trust God 100% all day, every day. If I told you that I do this, I would definitely be lying. I have to keep it real and say it is so much easier said than done. When it seems like you don't have a solution to your problems, that's when you see what a person is truly made of. Part of me whispers "don't worry." The other half screams out "You need to worry about this!". Nevertheless, I have no choice but to trust God. He always comes through for my family and I.

I completed my goal of getting through the bins of laundry I had sitting around for a week. I still have more laundry to do but at least I got through the first few batches. Our grass hadn't been cut in like 3 weeks and finally got cut today so that was nice. I put out an ad on Ebay, Letgo and Nextdoor Neighbor for my sugar scrubs. I get very discouraged when I post information about my products on Facebook and get crickets. If I post a new profile pic of myself, me and my husband, or a family pic, it seems like I'll get lots of likes. I guess when it comes to money, people are funny.

I know that God gave me this idea for this business. Therefore, it is already blessed. I know He will send clientele but I will search as well. I see this business going big and being branded. I want to help my family with additional income. I also want to enjoy some profit of what I'm doing. I don't want to make beauty products just to cover bills. I have fun making the scrubs and just blending different scents. The possibilities are endless!

I just contracted the graphic designer again that I had for my beauty business. This time she is re-doing my Kingdom Rubies ministry logo. It's time to do things with this ministry. It's been lying dormant for far too long. My goal is to work out for 30 minutes tomorrow and do 60 squats throughout the day. I must do something to get healthier. I was told I have pre-diabetes. I refuse to become a full-blown diabetic. It's going to be tough because of all the food I love to eat, so I will have to either eat in moderation or cut. I will be seeing a nutritionist next month. It's good to be accountable to someone in the weight loss journey, not just yourself. I ask God to really help me with this one because the struggle is real.

Day 3 Notes

What is your biggest challenge today and how can God help?

∞ Terrell - Day 4 ∞

Obsession with greatness is a must. I can't say that I was obsessed with greatness today, however. But the thought was there. One of the core reasons is that I was fasting until 6:00 Pm, which was my goal. Without food as fuel, it was tough to really put forth the mental energy which is required to maintain the mental clarity which is needed to work habitually towards greatness, atleast for me.

However, the Lord came through during the fast. There was something very specific that I needed advice and clarity on, and by 11:00 AM, a trusted friend had called and gave the confirmation which I needed. Under most circumstances, I would have ended the fast at that point, since the breakthrough had already arrived. However, since I was in covenant with the LORD God of Hosts, the decision to continue my fast until 6:00 PM was a no brainer. If I make covenant with Him, I never take that lightly.

I love how close the LORD is during such covenant periods for me! There was a time a few months ago, where for around two months straight I was in some form of covenant or another. I had planned to continue that after a short break, which ultimately became much longer than the week long break I had originally planned.

However, I believe in all things in due time.

One major life goal I'm looking to achieve on this path to greatness is getting to bed early to get out of bed early. I notice my energy levels are drastically higher when I'm successful in that endeavor. Also, I have a big 10K race coming up in 19 days. I've been training for months. I'd had some rough patches during my training period, usually around travel. Whenever I travel for work, pleasure, or ministry, it's always been tough to get back into the day to day routine once I get back.

However, I'm looking to change that drastically. In this journey to greatness, I'm looking to pull upon every strand of good habit within me, and take it to the next level. The battle against the bad habits is a very real battle indeed. But the price to pay for greatness shall be paid. Champion of this Earth. We all have one shot at life. If one can live a life which glorifies God, wins souls to the Kingdom of God, and master every challenge of life along the way, I would be willing to wager that that is a life well lived.

So many dreams. 24 hours a day to make them a reality. My goal tomorrow is to make it through my Seeker armor in meditation, and on my Scripture Typer App. My Seeker armor is a set of 12 groupings of Scripture, each referring to the command to seek the face of the Lord (or a similar concept).

.

♥ Emely – Day 4 ♥

Today I am proud of myself because I completed day 1 of working out. I did my 60 squats. I also did my 30 minutes of exercise. Today I walked around the block while on the phone with my best friend Gina. Tomorrow I will do a different form of exercise. As I look at a lot of these actresses on television and movies, I see how fit they are. I also think about my future babies. I want to be fit and not overweight. Well in my case, not only am I overweight, but I am in the obese category. I am 5 ft. tall and weigh about 195 lbs. That is way too much weight for me. This will motivate me even more to lose all this weight. My goal is to be at 140 by December. If I can lose 10-15 each month I will reach that goal. I know I will have to truly discipline myself and be consistent. That is where my issue lies.

I find it very hard to be consistent in anything I do. If I could say there is one thing I hate about myself, it's the lack of consistency. I don't want to be that person who starts off passionate about something and then stops after a few days. I'm so tired of that. I know God has placed so much in me. He has given me so much creativity that I can be putting to good use. I want to play with my kids and not get tired right away. I want to show other housewives out there in my shoes that weight loss is achievable if we apply ourselves. Cooking yummy, healthy meals that don't break the bank is achievable. Creating a desire in our husbands to desire us even more because we transformed our bodies, is truly achievable.

I also went to Hobby Lobby today and got some accessories for my scrubs. I got in some more essential oils and I'm excited about new scents coming soon. I also got in my beeswax and mica pigment powders so I will be making lip balms soon.

I must say it gets a bit discouraging at times when I think about not having enough clientele. I am also not a sales person. I don't see myself going from place to place trying to get people to buy my products. I will be going to the flea market Saturday morning to register so that I could sell. I know that I know this is a God thing, so He will definitely provide. Some places I will offer a slight discount of the product. I have an add on one of these apps where you can sell things. I lowered the price to $5. Someone actually messages me and asks me if I will lower the price. I simply replied no, it's the lowest it will get. It cost money to run a business. There is time and energy invested into a business. I need to make some profit too.

My goal for tomorrow is to work on the living room area and reorganize a few things. I will do another 60 squats and another 30 minute work out.

Day 4 Notes

How good has God been to you today?

∞ Terrell - Day 5 ∞

Today was a long long day, but a blessed day none the less. I didn't get as much sleep as I needed last night, so I missed my opportunity to wake up early. I could have stayed up when I woke up at 3:30, but I didn't. It just wasn't in me.

I finally went back to sleep around 5:30, then woke up for work at 8. The Champion that I am becoming would have woken up at 3:30, done my morning routine, then either tried for a nap before work, or just worked right on through. Sometimes, you have to call those things as they be not.

Steady progress, day by day. I haven't coded since Sunday. Unacceptable. Why? I'd chalk it up to laziness and or busyness, and it's probably a mixture of both. I so greatly desire an obsession to drive me to this greatness! But, alas, if it shall not, then I'll just need to keep chipping away at it, day by day.

Make War, not excuses. That's something I need to tell myself more and more. I need to drive that statement through the very core of my being! Time is so precious. I have 24 hours every single day to make my life better. It's up to me and no one but me (and of course, God).

God loves hard work. God rewards hard work. He is fair in His judgments and dispensations of events. I know that over the past few years, I could have worked harder and been where I wanted to me, even now. But, He's also the God of second chances. I'm ready to bring the plans in my heart for Guardian Brigade Prophetic Company to pass. It's going to take courage, wisdom, financial abundance, and ultimately, an extremely intimate relationship with God.

I enjoyed the Seeker Armor goal today. I completed it, and it always stirs me up to seek His Face like never before. Therefore, I'm going to make my goal tomorrow to finally put together a meditation that goes along with the 12 scripture sets. A long-term goal that I have is to "put" the Seeker armor on early every morning, then put on the daily armor for my Covenant Armor Scriptures throughout the day. I also usually pray for myself, my family/church, then the entire Body of Christ along with each Covenant armor meditation.

I've been working in different contexts towards an elusive prayer life, where my mind just by default goes into prayer when I'm not using it for something specific. I'm not there yet, but I urgently desire that sort of a relationship with God, the Creator. That's what is put before me. Now, I just need to go out and get it. Go out and take it.

I'm enjoying the journey, and I hope this blesses many people.

♥ Emely – Day 5 ♥

Yesterday I lost track of time and didn't get to complete my goal until after 12 am. I did put up the picture of Jesus I wanted in the Livingroom. I re arranged a few things for now. I was also able to complete my 60 squats and 30-minute workout. My goal for today which I didn't write was to make sure I got to Samirah's ballet audition on time and to be prepared. It may seem like a small goal but I am working on getting to places on time.

To sum today up, I had a pretty good day. I went to my mother's house and helped her with her phone. She has a smart phone but rather have a standard phone. I tried to convince her that the smart phone is so much better lol. We ended up swapping phones and she has an older model smart phone that I think will be easier for her.

I was proud of myself for being able to press through and do my exercises. I can see that I will soon get in the habit of doing it with no issue. I really do want to see results. I feel tired all the time again so I know I need to go through some type of detox. In this covenant I do not want to and will not fail so I will do all I need to do, to exercise for 30 days.

My friend Barbara gave us a painting of Jesus walking on water last month. It's so beautiful. I remember seeing something similar to it when the Family Christian store was still in business. I remember thinking I sure wish I could buy this. In my opinion, I prefer pictures that don't have Jesus face on it since no one really knows what He looks like. It's interesting because the painting captures Him from behind and you can see just a bit of the side of His face. My husband was trying to keep it in our guest room but no one would really get to see it. I can just sit and stare at that picture and imagine myself walking on water with Jesus. I appreciate the fact she gave us that painting because I know she really liked it as well. Such actions like Barbara did, I don't take lightly. May God bless her abundantly for this. I'll even throw this in there, I truly hope and pray that you will grant her desire to move to Charlotte Lord, In Jesus Name. Amen

It's important in this life to have a true personal relationship with Jesus. Nothing on Earth tops this. It's sad that so many people go to church every Sunday but have no clue who Jesus really is. People are just going through the motions. They are caught up in religion and tradition. There is no transformation in their lives. It is the same routine all the time. However, when we come to know who Jesus really is and how He was waiting all along to be in a relationship with us, it will change our life forever.

Day 5 Notes

What is the Lord speaking into your heart today?

∞ Terrell - Day 6 ∞

I was led into a mind-blowing revelation. The Ox, in Hebrew, is the root word of Champion. I've been preaching and teaching on the Ox a lot lately, and I've been meditating on it was well. Ox mode work is the key.

And the desire to be a Champion of this Earth stirs strongly in my spirit. Christian, by definition means Christ like. Christ is the ultimate Victor. He defeated death, hell, and the grave in one fell swoop. It cost Him His life. He poured everything into His mission, and He was resurrected. Therefore, being Christlike should mean that we are Victors in every aspect of our life. We may need to give up everything, just LIKE He did. We may need to pour everything and labor unto weariness. But if we do so, we are assured that resurrection and glorification is the next leg of the journey. And ultimately, the last leg of the journey includes new glorified bodies in Heaven, in which we'll be perfect. I've seen and felt what's it like to have a glorified body in a night vision once. Powerful!

And this is the time to WORK. One thing I'm learning/remembering is that constantly inquiring of the Lord, and requiring His presence is the key to that intimate relationship with Him. So many Scriptures spell this out perfectly. Today, during the goal of putting together my Seeker armor meditation, I had the sudden blast of inspiration to structure the mediation to use certain parts of my testimony, starting from the onset of my Christ walk. It is very exciting. It will help me to remember daily all of the awesome things I saw the Lord do. And it will inspire me to crave Him with my whole heart, and require intimacy with Him to an entirely different level.

Tomorrow my goal is to actually go through the meditation for the Seeker armor, all in one fell swoop of time. I want that to be a morning habit for me.

Today, I had a chance to play basketball with some co-workers. It was a lot of fun. Since I've been doing pushups (usually around 50-100) a day, and have been running for a while, I really wanted to see how well I did. I was impressed and happy with myself. I constantly called upon the Lord, and time and time again He showed up. Especially during the last game. I had a lot of hustle in me. We were playing the last game to 15 points.

My team was down, 13 to 8. Everyone was tired, and everyone wanted to win. I remember praying down in the paint. I prayed that the Lord would give us the victory. Then, I went out and make two big defensive and hustling type of plays. A team mate who is good at 3 point shooting scored 5 straight points to tie the game up. We were playing win by 2.

The advantage shifted several times, and it was truly a battle. I never stopped praying. Down the stretch, I was able to score a few buckets and make some strong hustle plays, which helped my team ultimately win 19-17. It was legendary, and I'm glad that the Lord saw fit to allow me and my team to win. Glory to the Lord of Hosts, forever!

♥ Emely – Day 6 ♥

Today was a great productive day. I was able to get Samirah to her audition on time and all paperwork completed. I hope that she did well in the audition. I kept telling her the whole way there that following directions is most important. That is exactly what they instructed right before the audition began. Unfortunately, I didn't get to see them audition but we will see what happens.

I also got a good deal at Walmart with super fruit powders. I got acai, cacao and pomegranate powder and goji berries for $2. Those usually go for about $6-$7. There was no way I wasn't going to get it! I am thinking about putting some of those ingredients in my scrubs.

I went to my neighbor's house to tell her about my scrubs. I ended up being there for about an hour with her. We had a good time chatting. I am usually not one to just go and sit in people's houses. I am more on an ambivert. I do appreciate that she invited me in. We talked about various different topics. She spoke about her dad and some of the moral values he had taught her. My neighbor got emotional as she began to talk about him. It was sweet to see that after so many years, she holds the memories of her dad dear to her heart.

My father will be living in North Carolina in exactly five days. I can't say that I ever had a tender father daughter relationship with my dad. I got to the point where I didn't even miss the fact I didn't have it. While my father was in town a few weeks ago, I had never spent an entire day with him and had a great time. As a kid there were a few good times. However most days I would remember my dad being grumpy and unapproachable. This time around now as an adult, married and with two kids, I saw my dad in a different light. He was not this super strict, tough guy that was unapproachable. He was cool, easy going and easy to talk to. I am looking forward to building a new relationship with him.

I am proud of myself because once again I have completed my squats and 30 minutes of exercise. I started getting tired in the end of my dance game but I pushed through. Even if you move like a slug it's okay just keep pushing. Something is better than nothing. Instead of eating something heavy so late, I made myself a strawberry banana shake. Earlier this year, Terrell told me that if we both lose weight, we will plan for the wedding of our dreams. That is even more motivation for me to work out. My goal for tomorrow is to begin making a picture wall.

We are now in the month of August. The number 8 stands for new beginnings. I can definitely feel we are coming into the "new" in this season. I am excited about the remainder of this year. We will see what the Lord has in store for the Potts family.

Day 6 Notes

What Scripture is on your mind today?

∞ Terrell - Day 7 ∞

Today was the first day during this Covenant that I would have to say has been AMAZING! God simply showed up, showed up, and showed me what was really good. This was the first day during this Covenant that I woke up at 5:00 Am, and was instantly awake and ready to go. I got my breakfast in. I got my Word in. I got my prayer in. I got my reading in. I got my run in. I was on fire for the LORD all day.

The LORD even gave me the strategy for the next season of ministry, and wow. It is a big dream that would scare small minds. In fact, I'll need to stay on my own grind to make sure I'm able to hold on to the vision. It's that big, and that's not something I'd say lightly.

I finally have that feeling that if I choose to sleep in just one morning, then I could possibly set the plan back six months, easy. I have momentum going like I wouldn't believe, so I must continue.

This Bride of Christ stuff is so real. He is literally coming back for a bride without blemish, spot or wrinkle. Being in Him is the only way to make it, plain and simple. Deep in Him, at that. In scripture, an agent was sent to get Isaac's wife. The Bride of Christ has an Agent which brings us to Him. The Holy Spirit is that Agent. Having a close relationship with the Holy Spirit has many many benefits. Inquire of and for Him, constantly. He literally walks beside us and is always excited to relay the Father's Will to us.

I've also tapped into something powerful. Every morning during prayer, praying heartfelt prayers which results in tears, to humble ourselves before the Lord and all of Heaven should be a necessity. I did that this morning, and I felt God like never before. A few weeks ago, when I was traveling out in Seattle, I had a similar experience. Starting a day with that, as part of your routine, seems like one of the most powerful ways to walk in some true anointing, power, and demonstration of the Spirit. I will be researching this and following that path. Amazing, is all I can really say.

In other good news today, I received a great compliment from my mentor in software development. He said I was exceeding expectations at this point. That one comment sparked something fresh within me. I met my mentor, Parag, by "chance", that day that I began my day with praying to the Lord with tears.

Working through my goal of meditating my Seeker armor was also amazing and took me on an internal journey! My goal tomorrow is to practice my Kingdom Rap song. "Kingdom Grinding" for atleast 30 solid minutes. I really want to nail it in the studio on Saturday.

♥ Emely – Day 7 ♥

So far, it's been a good day. I was up early today and took the kids to a free day camp. The camp was sponsored by American Red Cross. Every week I get emails from a company named Charlotte on The Cheap. They basically post everything that is free for kids and adults throughout the week. They also post discounts for certain businesses. I love this website because I stay in the loop about what is going on in town. Every dollar I can save the better! After I dropped off the kids, I went home to relax and have some much needed me time.

Originally, I was going to sleep for another hour and then get up and go to Hobby Lobby. It totally did not end up that way. I kept hitting my snooze button until it was like 12:30 pm. I kept waking up just thinking about how I wanted to work on my picture wall in the living room. My body on the other hand was not having it. I felt bad because I could've started on the wall earlier and didn't. I was so fatigued and sore. Getting back in the flow of working out daily is going to be a process but well worth it in the end.

I had two sales today with my scrubs. My mom bought two. My nephew will also be purchasing some as well. I still need to get the labels to place on the product with my logo. After leaving my mom's place I went to Hobby Lobby. They offer so many beautiful things and ideas I can put together for my wall. I noticed after I left that the total was more than I expected. I believe that some of the things that were on sale did not come off at the register. Anyhow, I will go back tomorrow to return some of those things I didn't end up using.

When I got home I looked at the bare wall and thought to myself how in the world am I going to design it. Eventually I got into my flow and started putting things up. There is a bit of a pattern I'd like to keep, but I will still freestyle it. This is how I feel sometimes when I am going to minister through worship at another church. I often feel like okay God, what in the world should I sing? Sometimes it will take a while to get it. Sometimes I get the song list the very same day I'm supposed to minister. However when the Holy Spirit gives it to me I have a song list but then I will freestyle and go into prophetic or spontaneous worship as led by Him.

The wall is starting to look like a beautiful collage of our love for God and each other. This house will always glorify God as best as we can. I love how the kids incorporate God into their lives as well. There are times when my son Jeremiah is scared about something and his sister will tell him to pray to Jesus. My son will say "well where is He I don't see Him." Sami will say you don't have to see Him, Jesus is in our hearts. That is just too cute.

I didn't complete my 30 minutes or the rest of my squats, I had 20 left to do. My body was simply not having it today. Even working on the wall, was a mini workout for me. Tomorrow my goal is to do a 45 minute work out and do 80 squats.

Day 7 Notes

What is your biggest challenge today and how can God help?

∞ Terrell - Day 8 ∞

It's been another beautiful day. I finished my goal, and then really got into it and went above and beyond. I really want this is be an awesome rap song which expresses the Gospel and the Heart of God. I am going to make my goal tomorrow to do two sets of atleast 25 pushups, both until absolute muscle failure. I'm also going to have a secondary goal, of making it through my Seeker Armor mediation, since it's the Sabbath tomorrow. Of all the commandments, He commanded us to remember the Sabbath. I intend to.

This has been a great journey with my wife. She is growing so much, and I absolutely love that. Being accountable is important. And when you love God, and you know that you told Him you were going to do something specific on the next day, you have the highest motivation to make sure you accomplish it.

I'm very excited about coding (computer programming). I have so many ideas which circulate through my head, and I'm really looking forward to being able to bring the ideas to the forefront. God is extremely creative. We are made in His image, so I believe everyone has a creative nature somewhere inside them, because He made us. He wants us to create the things which are inside of us, as long as they do not involve wickedness. God likes new. God likes new wine. He likes new songs. He likes new.

I feel so much more encouraged over this past week in God. I feel like this covenant is really making a difference. Through this project I feel that what me and my wife are doing is going to bless many people. In fact, it wasn't until today that I had the inspiration to make this a workbook format for couples and for singles, as well. That's the thing about following God. Think about Abraham. When he left his father's house into a strange new land, he had no idea where God was taking him. But he believed God, and that was accounted to him for righteousness. Righteousness is right standing with God in every relation. Abram, as it were, traveled until he was renamed Abraham, which means father of many nations.

So, when we enter into covenant with God, we can always expect great adventure to await us. Now, if we don't want adventure, then, well, I don't know what to tell you. Literally, I'm an adrenaline adventure seeking misfit who just wants to go on quests with God. So, I probably couldn't give you much more advice than to trust God because He is awesome.

However, if you are seeking adventure, then I think you are in the right place. You are reading the right words and the right book right now. As God downloads fresh new revelation to my wife and I, you (and your spouse, if applicable) will benefit and grow in Him. Trust Him.

♥ Emely – Day 8 ♥

Today was another productive day. I went to my interview with the renaissance fair. I'm excited to announce that I got hired on the spot! My job will be to take tickets right at the front gate. I will be praying for every single person that comes through that gate. This will be a fun job but I will also look at it as an assignment. I like to think that I am undercover agent in the kingdom of God. There many different kinds of people coming to this event. There are witches, warlocks, wiccans, satanists and so much more that are drawn to the renaissance era. However, Jesus came so that all people would be saved. They are most certainly not exempt. I am looking forward to my experience there.

I took my time making my way back towards my side of town. I went to Publix and bought something to eat. Sometimes it's nice to just chill out in my car away from people and quietly enjoy a meal. I went back to Hobby Lobby to return my things and got a flower garland to add to my picture wall. Walmart was my next destination and I think I was in there for a bit too long. Anyhow I went to see my kids and then went home.

I did a 45-minute workout and did complete 80 squats today. I will tell you, my body is still feeling it. My feet are literally throbbing right now. Earlier in the night there was a beautiful lightning storm in the sky. It looked like a light show in the sky. Eventually it began to pour. Some people hate rain but I don't mind it, there are times when it is soothing, especially for sleep.

Tomorrow we will be having our meeting to discuss the new direction of Guardian Brigade. I'm interested to see how that goes. Terrell and I will then be going to GFM studios to continue working on our songs. During our last session we had a really good time making beats. I am really looking forward to completing our tracks.

I am really tired today but I am pushing myself to finish writing this entry. It's so easy to just give up and just stop where I am. Many times, in our relationship with God we want to do things half way. Imagine if God did half way things with us? Think about what kind of effect that would have on our everyday life. What if God said, I'll let my daughter live today but she will no longer be able to walk." Or what if God said, I'll let my son get to work today but I won't grant him favor with his boss today so he will be fired." These are just some of the many examples I can give. God is so good that He would never do anything half way for us. God is a God of Order. Let's keep that in mind on our "I don't feel like it" days. I am speaking to myself first because I have had many "I don't feel like it" days. I thank you Lord for another day of life where you kept me safe and sound. I am grateful.

Day 8 Notes

How good has God been to you today?

∞ Terrell - Day 9 ∞

Today was another wonderful day which the Lord has made. Today I spoke with the members of Guardian Brigade about the path forward. I think they are going to prosper mightily in this season. I will be baptizing one guardian this Thursday, after work, which is going to be fun. Also, this week the 1:1 (1 on 1) meetings start with them all. I am looking forward to seeing them all transform.

Effort is required in everything worthwhile under the sun. I put forth a strong effort in learning to code today, and had a breakthrough. I was struggling to achieve a certain operation, then I remembered the Lord. I prayed and called out to Him. Within minutes, I was attacking the problem from a completely different angle. Not much longer, and the problem was solved.

This was after hours of trying it on my own. Of course I was learning during this period of several hours, but I was strongly reminded of the need to always pray ceaselessly, even and especially for those things that we don't really think that God cares about. He cares about it all.

A lot of people are depending on me, whether they know it or not. The hard work in learning this new skillset is going to pay off, and ultimately pay well in many different regards. Then, I want to teach others. As a pioneer, this new skillset is going to radically change my life. I'm going to finally be able to do the things I want to do with my family and ministry.

I have a heart and a strong desire to see people become what they hope in their heart to be. I have two awesome little children, and I look forward to seeing them destroy every limitation which the world would put on them, and flying high for Jesus Christ.

I finished my goals for today. The progressive push-up strategy where I am working to muscle failure really seems to be a good fit for me. I managed two sets of 29 straight, and hit total muscle failure which is the goal. I also had a nice meditation session using the seeker armor. Tomorrow my goals are to get a 6 mile run in, and also to push from 112 active scriptures on ScriptureTyper to 135.

Last weekend, I gave up relaxation time to increase my knowledge of coding. This weekend I'm doing the same. With these 24 hours in every day, I'm learning to stretch more and more and abstain from some of the pleasures of relaxing to make strides towards where I want to be. The Kingdom Grind is real. As a Grinder understands this concept more and more, great things are on the horizon. We, as Kingdom Citizens, have so much power and authority. It is time to grind until that is seen by the people of this world. It is time for the grinders to arise and make OX mode moves. Are you ready?

♥ Emely – Day 9 ♥

Today I was really sick. In the middle of the night I developed a cough. I fell asleep around 3 am and woke up around 6 am shivering with body ache. I had terrible flu-like symptoms. I thought it was so strange how that happened. I had to cancel all the plans I had for today. I was really excited about getting into the studio today and finishing our tracks. I was so stuck in bed that I felt like I was glued to it. Eventually I got some rest and felt better.

I forgot to write a goal last night. However, my goal for today was to catch up on one of my bible plans on you version. I did complete this goal, and I will continue reading this plan tomorrow. I will attempt to work out for 30 minutes tomorrow and get my 60 squats done if I'm feeling better. I am excited about my new Zumba games coming in. I'm looking forward to seeing what new workouts it brings.

Terrell did the meeting today with the members of Guardian Brigade. I was unable to go but I was listening in on the phone and it seems like things went well. This is definitely going to be a new season for us all and I am looking forward to it.

Next week I also have goals to start putting videos out there for my ministry Kingdom Rubies. I would like to have maybe 1-2 videos a week on my Facebook page. It is definitely time to do something with this ministry. I'm even asking the Lord to give me ideas as to what content to bring. As I write this, sometimes I am hit with thoughts of no one will watch my videos even before I go live. The devil is a liar. He doesn't want any Godly content going forth that can totally transform someone's life. Time is short. Life is short. We can't live our lives wasting time.

It would be a sad thing to get to heaven one day and have God ask what did we do with all the talents he gave us. I want to be productive and be the best I can be. I want to inspire others. Kingdom Rubies is about edification, exhortation and encouragement. I know I also need to get back to writing and complete unfinished projects. Often, I get discouraged in that department as well. I feel as if people won't read my books so why keep writing? Discouragement is one of the arrows the enemy is always sending my way. If I always give in, I am just slowing down my own destiny. I know I am destined to be a mouth piece for God. I know He wants me to speak His word and not only speak it but demonstrate it. That is my mission and I will carry it out no matter who likes it or not.

Day 9 Notes

How good has God been to you today?

∞ Terrell - Day 10 ∞

One third of the way through! How exciting. Today was a productive day. I logged in a solid two hours in my quest to become a coder. I have so many ideas, both for ministry and work, which I'm just waiting to bring to pass. I completed my goal of running six miles, and I'm happy that it was a covenant goal for me today, because otherwise, I probably wouldn't have got it in.

I took my family to see the new Wonder Woman film today after it's been out a few months. I enjoyed it. I took some good lessons away from it. Now, of course there is the whole matter of the character being a "goddess". I'm sure that those who are extremely religious would have many negative things to say. But, outside of that hyper religious realm, the fact that Love was discovered to be the motive for the character's interactions with human beings was a powerful fact indeed. For anything that I give my time too, I expect to be strengthened some way by it.

However, at some point, I would love to be a part of making films which are purely Christ centered, and blow away everything that the world is doing. I could see myself going on a last fast away from any sort of entertainment whatsoever. Whether I ever actually do or not all depends on whether or not I feel the Lord is leading me into it. The LORD is only one I aim to please with any fasting efforts. If I know that the LORD is going to show me great and mighty things, I'm willing to charge into just such a fast.

In the meantime, I'll be practicing moderation. I don't watch any cable television, unless I'm traveling and vacationing a bit. I'll watch some things on Netflix, and once again all of those things I expect to uplift me and encourage me to get more out of life. I think downtime is important, so I try to be strategic about how I spend the time that I relax.

For tomorrow's goal, I am going to spend at least 33 minutes reading within a single book of the Bible. I'll be led to the one which I feel the Lord wants me to read, and then time it.

This week is the week before my big race. So, I plan on working out harder than normal, to peak, then next week taper up into the run. I'm pretty excited about this, and it is going to be a major effort. I've put many many miles in training for this. Even through the weeks when it was really hard to even log a few miles, I was able to keep pushing. Endurance training makes every other aspect of your life better, in my own opinion. I've logged almost 469 miles using the app on my phone that I'm using now. I look forward to see the tick for 500 miles.

♥ Emely – Day 10 ♥

Today was a great day I must say. I had a sale from my Mary Kay foundations that I had left from when I was a consultant. Instead of receiving $3 I got $10. Later on in the day the family and I went to see Wonder Woman at the movies. It was such an amazing movie! The whole time I am just looking at the actress and asking myself, what do I need to do to get my body like hers. She is beautiful, exotic, fit and best of all humble! I sat there in awe and the thoughts in my mind working like clockwork. I told myself I need to set a routine to get fit. When I grow up I want to be just like Wonder Woman! Ok, get a grip Em you are not five, lol just kidding. No but seriously, as women of God think about this, we can represent who our God is in the way we carry ourselves and by taking care of our temple. Diana Prince (a.k.a Wonder Woman), represented her people the Amazonians. She was a princess and a goddess. I am not exalting "gods and goddesses". I am just trying to make a point. It was important to carry herself in a way that would bring honor to her people. We should be able to do the same with God. God is the only one true God. He is also, a king. Not just any king but the King of Kings. We are to represent Him well in all we do to the best of our ability. We are heirs of His kingdom so why not act like it?

I am also noticing that lately while eating junk food, it is just not sitting well in my system. That is definitely a sign it's time to cut it. I am so ready to start eating healthy again and setting up an exercise routine. I am going to set one up that I actually look forward to. I won't make it super easy but something that is really working my body and I enjoy. When it comes to daily exercise, I feel it is highly important to choose a workout routine that best fits you. There are so many kinds of workout routines out there. When you are ready to start transforming your body, choose a routine where you wake up and say, "I can't wait to get my workout in!" I am about to start this journey myself and will let you know how it works for me. My goal for tomorrow is to continue my 30 minute workout, drink up to 32 oz. of water daily and find a infused water recipe that works for me.

I also wanted to try making my own homemade lotion today. I had shea butter, sweet almond, beeswax and essential oils for one batch. My other batch consisted of shea butter, sweet almond oil, coconut oil and essential oils. The second batch had a better consistency to it but I feel it could be better. I ended up just bottling up what I had and saved it for me while I master this process. I am really excited about my business and eternally grateful to God for giving me the idea. There are times when you will get ideas in your mind for a business, just go with it. It doesn't hurt to try it. Always pray and ask God if He is the one leading you to it. If He is, you will definitely be blessed! Until tomorrow friends!

Day 10 Notes

What is the Lord speaking into your heart today?

∞ Terrell - Day 11 ∞

So, I chose the book of Zechariah in the Old Testament to complete my goal of 33 minutes of reading in one book. I was reading it pretty intently a few weeks ago, and something within in really stirred by soul up. It was several mysterious analogies that the Lord uses to make His points. Tomorrow, I will choose the goal of doing atleast one page of analysis planning on the new GuardianBrigade.com website. If I can't write it on paper, I certainly can't code it.

Today, I reflected on the life long dream I've had of being a coder. Ever since I was 12 years old or so, I've desired to be a software developer in some capacity. I'm 38 at the time of writing this, and I still haven't bought it to pass. I've done minor coding things in my career in Information Technology, but never have I pursued it as I am now. I watched several videos with people giving their ideas on what it takes to become a coder. As I was watching them, something within me was bought to life. I've always had the interest. I've always been able to atleast figure things out with lots of trial and error.

Something that really stuck with me was "it's not you, it's hard". Computer programming is a very tedious interest. In order to be good, some people may just have certain advantages or possibly be good from the beginning. However, for many it's a journey that comes with a lot of sweat and tears. I reflected on how I had one teacher who failed me in Community College, while I was in the Air Force. I took on the idea that maybe I just wasn't good, since one teacher didn't like me.

It stuck with me for many many years. But now, I'm seeing that it is within me to succeed. With so many other dreams wrapped up in developing this one skillset, I have every motivation to simply do the work and make it happen. Just like everything else worth having. In life, I'll need to fight to bring this dream into being.

The future home of Guardian Brigade, Guardian Keep, will arise from the completion of this dream. The finances to be able to have more children will arise from the completion of this dream. The life I envision myself in, in which I'm able to minister to people out of love and only work on projects which I'm truly passionate about, will be before me as I complete this skill set. There are moments where I feel like maybe it's too much to make happen.

But then, in other moments I know that God will never leave me or forsake me. I know that if I ask for Wisdom, even specific types of wisdom, and if I am persistent and hardworking, I will be successful. For someone like me who looks at life like one big quest, this is a major quest in a series of other quests. Time will tell how I fare. What about you, my friend? What are you passionate about? Read on, and I hope that my own journey will be a blessing to you in your own quest.

♥ Emely – Day 11 ♥

Today was another productive day. I helped my dad get settled in his place. He got an awesome deal in furniture for his entire home. God is good He totally blessed my dad. I spent the entire day with him. This is definitely something I was never used to in the past. I was a rebellious teen growing up. The more time I could've spent away from my parents the better. I did a lot of things in my early teens that I was not proud of. However I do feel I had to go through some of these things for a reason. Some things were simply foolish choices I made. God was truly watching over me because with some of the things I experienced in my past, I surely wouldn't have been here today to share this with you.

When kids reach an age of 12 and up typically, they think they know it all. These days, I think that age is much younger. There is so much technology out there used to educate our kids. Some information is good and some is terrible. This world is also very corrupt and not getting any better. It's important that we steer and train our kids in the right path. The bible tells us in, Proverbs 22:6 "Train up a child in the way he should go: and when he is old, he will not depart from it." I can truly say I am a living example of this.

Once the seeds are sown, they are sown. Our children can't say they didn't know. When I was out doing my mess, in the back of mind I often thought about what would God think of my actions. I didn't want to but I couldn't help it. I could hear my mom scolding me for something that God wouldn't approve of. Then in my early 20's the same thing was going on. I knew that living with someone and not being married was wrong but I did it anyway. I knew that fornication, cursing, stealing, and so much more was a sin. Every now and then the Lord would send a stranger or use someone I knew to get a message across to me. Sometimes He would even give me dreams about the rapture and how I would always be left behind. Of course, there are many theories on this event. However, for me, I grew up thinking that one-day Jesus will come back and the saints who were ready would be caught up in the clouds with Him. I also believed that those who are left behind will have to suffer doing the tribulation period. I would often think about those who will refuse to get the mark of the beast and the torture they will endure for Christ's sake. These sorts of thoughts went through my mind since I was a small child.

Although I was in a backslidden state for 10 years and did all my dirt and had all the fun in this world I could have, something was missing. I was missing having a true encounter with Jesus. When I was 28 I rededicated my life to Him for good. He is now the lover of my soul. Jesus is my best friend, my Lord and Savior, my King. He is simply my everything.

I did not do my workouts today or my infused water. I am literally so exhausted it took everything in me to write this today. Tomorrow I will make sure I make my infused water before I start my day. I will also get my workout in no matter what.

Day 11 Notes

What Scripture is on your mind today?

∞ Terrell - Day 12 ∞

Today was a day which was great, but it brought its share of challenges. At work, I'm a big advocate of consultants being able to work from home. I've been sowing seeds here and there, and today, the one person who is vehemently against it, was confronted, and of course the trail led back to me. Not that I'm worried, since I've done all things in the light. It's very soap opera like, however, so I look forward with interest on how this may end up.

These sort of challenges teach me a good bit about leadership, and I'm learning first hand that when you believe in something, put it in God's hands and go for it, using wisdom. I was tempted at certain times to say certain things to certain people. But one benefit I'm seeing for consciously seeking the LORD as much as possible in day to day life, is that during crossroads type of situations, you feel his unction leading you to not say certain things at certain times, or speaking up in a certain way. We must be cunning as serpents and harmless as doves, after all.

In other news, I was able to search my heart to put together the general outline for the GuardianBrigade.com website makeover. I'm excited about it, and set my first goal up for about 3 weeks out, which will be a login functionality. I've never coded anything like that, but I look forward to the challenge, may the LORD guide and help me.

I also officially had my first 1:1 with a member in this new ministry model. It went very well, and I'm looking forward to seeing that member's life transform. Also, this morning I woke up extremely inspired to take some bold actions towards my career as a software developer. Throughout the day, I completed what was in my heart to do, and I feel strong about my possibilities.

Honestly, whenever I see resumes or accomplishments of people who have been doing it for a while, a strong sense of inadequacy comes upon me. But then, I remember the dream that's in my heart. Plenty of others have the technical skill to accomplish what is in my heart to do; but the dream is in my heart. So what's the resolution? To learn from every source that I can, and bust my hump until I accomplish that dream. We have control over how we respond to any and every situation which may occur within our mind.

I was also thinking about a situation at work where there is one person at my job who can't stand my presence, although I've never done anything to deserve it. The Lord gives us these situations to love our way through it, similar to a body builder who uses free weights to train his muscles. The bigger the weights, the more benefit is conferred to the body builder. The more we are strengthened in our spirit man when we choose love.

Tomorrow my daily goal is going to be to perform 3 sets of at least 25 push-ups apiece, with the requirement that I work until muscle failure. I did a full body workout today, so this one should be interesting. The goal, now that I have some momentum in the physical category, is to push myself.

♥ Emely – Day 12 ♥

Last night I had a terrible time sleeping. When I laid down, I felt as if my entire body was vibrating. It was so uncomfortable that I needed to find a solution for this and fast! I looked online for possibilities of why this was happening. I am always trying to find a diagnosis through google lol. I really like the Dr. Axe website because he gives really good, straight to the point information. I read that I should try some frankincense and vetiver oil and apply it behind my neck. I tried it and the vibrating stopped. Here is the catch, my body stopped vibrating but my brain was all the way live!

All I wanted to do was go back to sleep. I was now tossing and turning. Being transparent here, I then began to hear a voice in my head screaming. If you know anything about spiritual warfare or demons, they are notorious for this. I thought to myself, do I have any demons trying to hide inside of me? So, I simply asked God did I have any demons hiding. He didn't directly answer me but the next thought was to cast them out, just in case. Since hubby was asleep I placed my hand on my belly and I began to command any spirit not like Jesus Christ of Nazareth to come out in Jesus name. I heard the word anxiety so I cast that out. I also commanded anything hiding to leave as well.

Listen, after I did this self-deliverance, I began to yawn. I yawned once and felt so light. I yawned a second time and felt even lighter. I heard no more screaming and I was feeling much more relaxed. In deliverance, you can be demoniacally oppressed which means that demons will surround you and try to influence you to sin. If we leave an open door for sin to creep in, this is where the oppression begins.

Here is an example, if I am angry about something and I don't pray and try to take matters in my own hands, I have opened the door to the spirit of anger. I can hear a voice telling me to stay angry, to be mean to people because I'm angry, or even put my hands on someone. If I give in, once again I have opened the door to anger. If I begin to think thoughts in my mind of what I would like to do to someone because I am angry, once again I have opened that door. If I actually act on what I am thinking and feeling, yes you guessed it-another open door. My actions have allowed for the spirit to have a temporary victory on me.

The key to getting free of this oppression is quite simple. First off, I need to acknowledge I have a problem and do something about it. Second, I need to pray and repent wholeheartedly before God. Third, I need to give my issue to Jesus, trust Him and let Him work it out.

In the kingdom of God, we need to understand that we are not exempt from deliverance. We also don't need to go to the special conference with the prophet or apostle who came from out of town. We don't always need a well-known or "famous minister coming to lay hands on us. Go to your quiet place, have a sincere heart and ask God to purge you. Look at King David, he did it. If he did it, so can you. No one needs to know you need deliverance if you are doing it yourself. If you don't know what to say, google "self-deliverance". I'm sure you will find something.

I am proud of myself because I completed my 32 oz infused water goal and my 30-minute workout. I am going to change my goals up a bit. I will do 60 squats 4 times a week. I will drink my infused water for 7 days straight and see what happens. I will also complete another 30-minute workout tomorrow. Until next time!

Day 12 Notes

What is your biggest challenge today and how can God help?

∞ Terrell - Day 13 ∞

Today was a challenging day. I'm being loaded up pretty heavily at work, and dropped a ball, which was escalated. It's the second one this week! Not what I like to see from myself, but I'm not sure what else I can really do. I am a representative of the Lord, and everyone knows it. So, with that being the case, I want to be better than anyone worldly, since I'm representing the light of Christ, Himself. No use of dwelling in the failure(s), but use it as motivation. I've noticed before that when I hit my lowest in the workplace setting, I'm able to respond/bounce back and redeem myself pretty quickly. So, I'll keep all of my trust in the LORD and not in myself.

I heard from my member which I wrote about yesterday, who began his first day of stretching today. He said it was actually painful because he hasn't stretched in a long time, but after wards he felt great, so that was encouraging to hear. One day at a time.

As for my own physical fitness, I managed to complete the challenge of 3 sets of 25 pushups, plus more until muscle failure. I also ran 6 miles after work. So, needless to say, my body is feeling it right now. Tomorrow my goal is going to be to push from 131 active scriptures on ScriptureTyper, to 155.

In addition to it being a challenging day at work, I battled against a spirit of discouragement for the dreams that I have. When I say battle, I don't mean the offensive warfare, as in me recognizing that I was even under attack. I mean my mind was buffeted with the thoughts while my mind was racing and trying to focus on other things. Sometimes the warfare is like that. In retrospect, God was preparing me on the way to work this morning, by highlighting a work van for a company with the name "TruGuard". I am reminded of the battle of the Guardian when I see that van, periodically. In fact, on the way home, I saw another one of those vans.

I feel like God was encouraging me to guard the dream in my heart. One must guard his or her heart with all diligence, for out of it flow the very issues of life. The desire to continue at all costs; the passion to ultimately succeed; the will to use drive, commitment, and every ounce of energy devoted to the goals that one has purposed in his or her heart. There will be absolutely fantastic days when we're sure that our goals are just at the end of our reach. Then there will be other days, when we are tempted to ask ourselves why are we playing around and shooting for something far outside of our grasp? On a journey like this one that me and my wife, and ultimately those who will join us in ministry, we will be tested at many corners.

It is during these battles that one must STAND! Because the answer is near.

♥ Emely – Day 13 ♥

Today was a chill day for me. I didn't go anywhere. I just relaxed for today. Later on in the day, I began designing a new flyer for my business. I added some new scents that I will be making soon. I am looking forward to starting my lotion candles soon as well. I am excited about the new phase in my business.

School is right around the corner. This summer has definitely flown by fast. Samirah is going to second grade and Jeremiah is going to first grade. I am going to try and get them into a better school this year. I am so over the bullying they went through last year at their school and on the bus. There are a number of schools in the area that offer a better curriculum or have activities for kids who like the arts and such. Time truly flies so fast. One minute these kids were babies and then they were in school. I often look at my children and get lost in thought thinking about how they will look and sound when they are teens. I like how they are at this age. I love to see their little personalities develop. They both are very close which I also love. That is how it should be since they are all they got for the moment.

I did my workout today. Boy was it intense! I was playing Just Dance on the Wii. I will say that the workout today was the most intense of all. I sweated like a pig! I did my 30 minutes but I also pushed myself to put in an extra 5 minutes. I have still been sipping from my infused water but I will definitely drink it all. I am very proud of myself for pushing myself even when I could be doing something else. Oh wait, like nothing!

Tomorrow I have an appointment at a staffing agency. I

will see what kind of work they have to offer. Right now, I am looking for something simple that does not require too much of my energy. Being a homemaker is a lot of work on its own. Being a mom of two very active children who crave my attention is number one. I have two pets, a cat and dog. My dog likes to follow me everywhere I go. He also demands my attention. Of course, there is house work like cleaning, washing dishes, cooking, laundry, etc. I am also a wife, so making time to spend with my husband when he is free has often been a challenge. We don't get to spend much time with each other during the week. I would say after my husband gets home from work it's about 7 pm. When he comes home, he wants to sit, unwind, eat and a few minutes of something uplifting for him. He has other things he has to do and so do I.

It's important to get that time in with your spouse. If you are single get that time in with God. It is therapeutic and very helpful. Take time for you as well and unwind from a long day. Tomorrow I will continue drinking the infused water. I will continue my 30-minute workout and it will be a squats day for me. There won't be a set number, but just how many I can do in the day.

Day 13 Notes

What Scripture is on your mind today?

∞ Terrell - Day 14 ∞

I finished my Scripture push on ScriptureTyper. Tomorrow, my goal is to continue that momentum, and jump from 155 to 200. I'll need to make it a focus throughout the day. Today was a good day. My heart was filled with dreams on the things which will be bought to past.

So many times in our life, even on a given day, we come to crossroads of decisions. I would surmise that even the best of us don't always make the best decision. However, over time, if we honor that which is in us which is noble; if we honor that which is in us which is good; in short, if we honor the Holy Spirit and the Wisdom of God....we will make the right choice more often than not.

As we live life and watch for these specific moments in time, always preparing our subconscious mind to make the right decision at these crossroads, we will be able to move towards our destiny. However, if we allow our minds to become full of garbage, we will make bad decisions at moments which we will pay for later. If we allow indecision and hesitation to win due to doubt and fear, we will find ourselves as easy prey to the attacks of the enemy. If we allow sin and disobedience to take root in our hearts, we will go around and around those crossroads like the children of Israel.

All around us are fragments of both good and evil. Choosing good is certainly much better than choosing evil. Even as light excels darkness, and wisdom excels folly. However, God isn't just good. He's Holy. Holy means separate and consecrated. That is why it is so easy for a man to choose a road that he thinks is good and right, but the end of that way could be death. We must rely fully on the LORD.

As we commit our hearts to Him, He will guide us gently through those crossroads. Sometimes we want Him to reassure us at every moment in even the small things. Nothing is wrong with that, natively, but we must realize that the Lord always wants to partner with us. He wants His life to be reflected in our lives. As we allow the Light of Christ to shine though us, even in the daily tasks of our human experience, we can rest fully assured that at the major moments of our journey He will guide us and be there for us.

However, if in the little moments we do not honor Him, it makes it difficult for us to hear Him in the major moments. Therefore, the investments in ourselves to build Him up within us, day by day lead to security and confidence in the crossroad type of moments. This covenant lifestyle, this goal-setting, this constant seeking of His face, allows us to exercise our senses and seek His Face (His Presence), and really begin to require it as our vital need, as we are commanded in Scripture.

♥ Emely – Day 14 ♥

Today, I had a pretty good day. I went to a staffing agency. While I was there I felt out of place. I felt like I wasn't trusting in God. Two years ago, I had a full-time job. I quit because I heard the Lord tell me to quit my job and go into full time ministry. Since then it's been sort of rough. Often I would wonder if I missed God. During those times, God would send someone or use anything to confirm His word. Still, there would be issues within my husband and I. Its important to have a plan for finances during your marriage. I was used to always working since I was sixteen years old.

My first job was at a McDonald's. If there was something I wanted, I simply bought it. After I was single with two children, I had a job and made ends meet. God always provided and then He sent Terrell into my life. I say to have a plan for finances because it can really tear a relationship down. In my opinion, I would say finances are one of the top reasons for divorce. Talk about finances, create a budget, adhere to the budget as best as you can. Cut out unnecessary spending if you can. You will feel better about yourself when you don't buy that cute thing you saw at the store but you've got tons of cute things at home.

I went to see one of my friends today. I had a good time just hanging out. I needed that and so did she. While I was at her house, I thought about how I lived there for a few weeks as I was waiting to move into my very first place back in 2012. A bit of nostalgia always hits me every time I am in the neighborhood. I have come a long way since 2012. God is good He always took care of me and my kids no matter what.

I went to Walmart to pick up some supplies for my business. I was so ready to just get home relax. As I was putting the cart away, I hit my driver mirror and it broke again. It first broke last year when I was in a small car accident. Anyhow, I had to go right back into Walmart and get a roll of duct tape. That will give it a temporary hold. I did good for several months with the temporary fix I had on the mirror. As I am writing this I think about how many people use God as a temporary fix to their issues. Once they are done with God they move on. They forget they once had a problem. When and if the problem returns, or there is a new issue, God is called upon once again. I think about my car and how I shouldve got it fixed last year and didn't. I just kept putting tape for temporary hold. Several times driving around I noticed the tape getting loose. There was one time on the freeway, where the mirror actually got loose from the mirror and was hanging by a cord. I still didn't get my mirror repaired. Here I am again with the same issue. Since I no longer want to deal with this, I will just get it fixed asap. It is the same concept with God, we can keep putting tape on our sin, but one day enough will be enough and we will be ready to permanently fix the issue. That sin issue is repaired by building a solid relationship with Christ and living a holy and consecrated lifestyle.

It was very hard to work out today. I still pushed and did it even though it was a light workout. I also had my infused water. Tomorrow my goal is to get everyone's things packed for our beach trip Saturday and make more sugar scrubs. I will also do a 15-minute workout and continue with my infused water.

Day 14 Notes

How good has God been to you today?

∞ Terrell - Day 15 ∞

Wow, now at the halfway point for this journey to greatness project. Today was Friday. Everyone who works a classical Monday to Friday, 9-5 sort of job knows what I'm getting at, naturally. Awesomeness.

I just finished my Scriptures so I'm sitting at 202 in ScriptureTyper. Tomorrow, my goal is to get a PrayFit physical body workout in, and also to code for at least 1 hour. I received some very encouraging feedback from my mentor yesterday, and so now I'm ready to show the world that I can code. I want to build an application that my workplace can use to transform itself to the next level. I've been in Information Technology for over 15 years now. I've also had the hope and dream of owning my own business, but this is really the first point that I've felt that I must own my own business. I must be my own boss. Life is too short to spend it furthering other people's dreams, as opposed to my own dreams.

There's so many things to see. There's so many things to do. There's so many lives to impact for Christ. I'm at a point where there is almost a physical longing inside me to approach life from a different angle. I want to be able to spend more quality time with my extended family. I want my children to have the best opportunities as they grow up. I want my wife to know what it's like to move into a new house which she owns. I want, I want, I want.

And the thing is, I believe that God is my friend. I've been through the process of going from a slave to a sin, then to a slave to righteousness, to being a true friend of God. He shows me many things. There's been seasons where the ball has been in His Court. Now, I feel that the ball is in my court in this season. He is on my team. He is encouraging me to take the steps necessary to transcend from where I am, to where both He and I know that I am capable of reaching.

I was listening to something earlier, about education. Oprah Winfrey. Bill Gates. Steve Jobs. Mark, the Facebook creator. Many others. Never completed college. But yet they are multi-millionaires or billionaires. They had a dream and something inside them that wouldn't quit. They focused their mind, on something they saw internally long enough...and applied themselves, likely with everything they had inside them. And it worked well.

It's certainly not all about the money. But, knowing what's in my bank account right this moment.....if I had a few billion dollars to spare, surely I could help a lot more families and people then I could right now. Wisdom is a defense, even as money is a defense, but the excellency of knowledge is that wisdom shields and preserves the life of him who has it. As a guardian, defense is key. I would choose wisdom over money, any day of the week. And wisely, I would choose wisdom and money if given the choice. The beauty of it, my friend, is that we have the choice to have both.

♥ Emely – Day 15 ♥

Today was a pretty ordinary day. I was well rested. Later in the day I just began to clean my house and get rid of some clutter. I also got my trunk cleared out which desperately needed to be done. I took the kids with me to drop off some things at Goodwill. I got there about 8:45 and I know I wouldn't be there long. However, there was an obvious disgruntled employee sweeping in the back of the store where I was. The kids and I were looking at DVD's and this man decided to want to sweep where we were standing. He actually said, "Excuse me I need to sweep there." So, we moved from that spot and moved to another. He then came to that spot and repeated what he said. I was started to get annoyed because this man could've swept anywhere else in the store.

As I went to go stand in line, I was just thinking about how annoyed I was. I also thought about how it was almost closing time and I know how it is when you want to go home and people come in close to closing time. I thought about complaining to corporate about the man that was sweeping because I thought he was very rude. Even on my drive home I thought about his actions.

For my goal today, I was going to be spending 45 minutes with God. I began to listen to music and read my Bible. First, I read the entire chapter of Hebrews 11. This particular chapter is all about faith. Paul mentions people like Moses, Abraham, Sarah, Noah and many more. I love how he briefly points out how they put faith in action in their situation. Reading and meditating on this chapter was just a reminder to increase my faith. Currently we have a $855 water bill that we have no idea why it's so high. About half of it is due in two days. Yes, you read correctly in two days I need to come up with $400. The bill says the water may be disconnected if the payment is not received.

The Lord reminded me to trust Him. He has always made a way for us. Once again, I received some money today. A few days ago, I mentioned that every day I have received a financial blessing. I am believing and trusting God with all I have, that we will be okay. That our water will not be shut off. In fact, I speak it now, that it won't be shut off and someway somehow, we will not have to pay the full amount since we did not use that much water.

Also in my time alone with God He reminded me to have mercy on that disgruntled employee from Goodwill. He had me think of different scenarios and how I would've responded. God reminded me of my days when I worked in retail and how I would feel when people came in at the last minute. I chose to just bless the man and keep it moving. I like to be transparent when I tell my stories because I am not going to act like I got it all together. Truth is, God is still working on me. He is still stripping me of my old self and small things that would affect me for a long time.

Here is a tip, always remember that Jesus WILL return one day and we need to make sure that at that moment we better have a clear heart and mind to be able to go with Him. There is no horror movie in this world that can out do getting left behind when Christ returns.

Day 15 Notes

Halfway point! What have you learned so far?

∞ Terrell - Day 16 ∞

Today was a great epic day. On this journey to greatness, I'm examining how I spend my time very closely. Every day is 24 hours of opportunity. Harnessing your will into productive endeavors, day after day, hour after hour, is how a person taps into their potential. The LORD has put so much of Himself inside each of us, and one of the greatest features that the LORD has put into us all is the great gift of imagination.

Everything is created twice. First, the mind's eye sees something. The imagination can craft impressive things, whether they be good or evil. After the imagination has crafted something internally, the next phase is the grind to bring it to pass. The principle works whether it is something Godly, something demonic, something worldly, something noble, etc. In order to stay focused on the grind, in order to bring the dream to pass, it takes discipline and consistency. Otherwise, the dream will just be a dream, forever.

The dreams which are in my heart stir me to action. Some days, it's easy. Some days, it's hard. But in a sense, I've landed my ships in a foreign land and burned them. The only way to victory is forward. There is no going back to who I used to be. At times, it can be uncomfortable. At times, it can be disconcerting. The waiting to see the actualization of the dream coming to pass seems to be taking forever and a day. It's one hour at a time. The question to ask myself, at the beginning of each new hour is this; Did I make that last hour count? If the answer is no, the thing to remember is not to dwell on it. There is no time machine, and the goal is to press forward bravely and get back on track.

If the answer is yes, then the next question is this; Will I make this upcoming hour even better? Hour by hour, minute by minute...... the Lord JESUS Christ has given His own life so that we can access heavenly places. Heaven is a great place of strength. A great place of mercy. A great place which is inside of us. As we bring Heaven to Earth, with daily work towards bringing what is inside of us out, Heaven itself will manifest around us, and we will grow closer to Him. Abraham did great things with his life. As did King David. As did Samuel the prophet. And the list goes on and on.

Tomorrow, my goal is to read 33 more minutes in the book of Zechariah, and also to spend time in a 15-minute meditation/prayer session using my Seeker Armor.

With so many ideas circulating and swirling through my mind, I'm ready to see them actualized, so that the LORD can get glory. Because when I make it, whatever that may mean, it will be the LORD whom I give all the credit to. The journey to greatness is truly what He wants to be a part of with all of His children.

♥ Emely – Day 16 ♥

I had a pretty good today. I am excited that Terrell got rid of some junk we had in our backyard. I feel there will be a shift at night when I sleep. Usually 3-4 times a week I always feel that people are outside in the backyard. There are times when I actually wake up out of my sleep. I definitely feel it is something spiritual. I am a firm believer that where there is a mess it is likely for spirits to hide or dwell. There have been times when the Lord has told me to clean certain areas of my home. It has been a sense of urgency to get it done. I believe that when its clean I can hear the Lord clearly. The less clutter the better.

I am proud of my husband for working on a new skill set that he has always wanted to learn. Although I had to sacrifice spending time with him during these past weeks, it is worth it. He put a resume together and a portfolio for his work. That made me think about brushing up on graphic design. I have an associates degree for graphic design but I am doing nothing with it. When I was in college I didn't take it serious but still managed to graduate.

I went to rehearsal for the troupe I am a part of. I had a great time. I will definitely practice more so I can get used to the scripts.

During my time with God, He gave me the words to a new song. It is a remixed version of a song called "Dance Like David Danced". It will have a Latin tune to it. I am looking forward to hearing how it will sound when it is complete. I am looking forward to a new fresh week. I speak that my family will continue to receive blessings. I speak that my husband will hear from jobs he applied to and go to interviews, this very week. I ask Lord that you reward him for his hard work and consistency in learning a new skill set to help the family, in Jesus name. Tomorrow my goal is to work out for 30-minutes and spend 30 minutes with God. 15 minutes in worship/prayer and 15 minutes reading the word.

Day 16 Notes

What challenges have you overcome today, in Jesus' name?

∞ Terrell - Day 17 ∞

What a wonderfully productive day. I woke up this morning with divine direction. I woke up early while my wife and children slept, and worked toward my dream job. I woke up inspired, started moving forward and never looked back. Although it is my dream career and lifestyle that I'm working towards these days, I'm also looking forward to a higher quality of life for my family.

Sacrifices must be made in order to grow. I laid down my free time in pursuit of applied knowledge as a software developer. I created a portfolio with a few websites that I've done, demonstrating what I can accomplish at this point. I realized that there was nothing holding me back from doing so. I could have done the same thing years ago. However, my mental state was in an entirely different place. I was of the mindset that I needed to have something significant under my belt before I could even try. Now, I realize that I'll always be in a state of learning.

I find it intriguing how that also applies to my spiritual walk. I used to think as a young Christian that there would just be a certain point of recognition from man and from God, to show that I was called and sent. Now, I know it's simply a pioneer's walk which the LORD has called me to. I've seen Him answer prayers even as I was praying. I've seen dreams, visions, and have both received and given powerful prophetic utterances. And gradually, I become more and more seasoned in Him and His ways.

So in the natural world, the gradual approach to all things is the same. Daily, persistence, dedication, grit, perseverance, tough nosed Ox mode. That's what it all boils down to. If you can take the hits, and keep moving forward, eventually, you will be a Champion. It doesn't matter what it is specifically that you're aiming for. The process is always the process. The grind is always the grind. Having the mental state of being ready and willing to continue to press forward until your dream is actualized, is a MUST. This is a MUST have mindset.

It is said in some circles that self-discipline is the only skill required to master any other skill. Self-discipline doesn't come in a day or a week or a month. However, over the course of many months and years and seasons and times, self-discipline can be built and harnessed, and used to craft you into the diamond which God has called you to be.

I finished my goal of reading 33 more minutes in the book of Zechariah. Very interesting reading. All of the minor prophets have some gems in them. I also meditated using my Seeker Armor, and it was a real blessing.

Tomorrow, I will move from 202 ScriptureTyper scriptures to 230. I have a busy week coming up, as I prepare for my race this Saturday, minister at a prison on Tuesday, speak with several ministry members throughout the week, and possibly baptize a member on Wednesday, should they remain willing. I love being a servant of the Most High God.

♥ Emely – Day 17 ♥

Today was a blah type of day for me. I don't have much desire to do anything. I had started working in the kid's room. That is a very annoying and tedious task. I can't wait until we are able to move so the kids can have their own room. I feel like every time I get rid of things, more just appear. I feel very slothful today and I just hate it. There is so much I want to do and its difficult when I feel this way.

I wrote the above paragraph earlier this afternoon. Shortly after writing this paragraph, I began to spend time with God. I put on my soaking music and began to just listen and talk to God. I began to feel better as I was in His presence. The first scripture He gave me was Proverbs 23 the whole chapter. That chapter is just jam packed with so much wisdom. I encourage you to read this chapter when you get a chance.

I paused my time with God when Terrell got home. I was at the 15-minute mark. I left to go get my nails done to have some "me" time and unwind. At first the employees at the nail salon were looking at me sideways as if they weren't going to take me. It was 7 o clock when I got there and they close at 7:30. I was starting to get annoyed but I held my composure and was patient. Finally, after about 10 minutes, it was my turn. The guy was polite and very gentle. I had a great time getting my nails done and watching tv in there.

Terrell called me earlier in the day to tell me that he was getting calls from recruiters for some of the jobs he had applied to. It was just yesterday he put in applications and updated his resume. Remember I asked the Lord to bless him and declared new beginnings and triumphs in the work field over his life. I was excited to hear that God was honoring some of that.

When I got back home from the nail salon I began my workout. I will say I had to really push myself today. Feeling as sluggish as I was didn't really help. Nevertheless, I completed my workout and was actually sweating. Tomorrow I will not be doing a workout but will resume on Wednesday. My goal for tomorrow is to spend 1 hour with God.

During the second half of my time with God, I had a powerful experience. I resumed the same song I was listening to. There was a point in the song where the man speaking starts talking about Moses at the burning bush. I then ask the Lord where He wanted me to read next. I immediately heard Exodus 3. It just so happens that Moses 3 spoke about Moses at the burning bush! I was so blown away that God did that! That is a miracle on its own. We must learn to appreciate what seems to be the little stuff that God would do for us before we can graduate to the big stuff. That is not to say He won't bless us with huge miracles like $1000 in our mailbox, etc. What I am emphasizing is that we often miss the small miracles. Let's keep our eyes open for what God is doing in our lives. He always has our best interest at heart. Until next time!

Day 17 Notes

What is the destination of the journey you are on?

∞ Terrell - Day 18 ∞

What an amazing day! After putting in numerous applications to many online coding jobs, I had an interview directly with an awesome local company. I was sent a take home "test", which will show that I can code. Of course, it's referencing some technologies which I haven't seen yet, but none the less it looks very doable. Other than that, I heard from a few other companies. So, I'm excited. I still have so much to learn, but it's nice to see some immediate progress in that area.

Otherwise, I'm realizing more and more it is time for me to make a serious career change. Lots of stuff which I'm seeing at work is seemingly more and more pointless and vague, and I'm really not growing as much as I would like to. Now the excitement of a new career is causing me to really have a strong sense of wanderlust flow out of my soul. I'm ready for the next major adventure in my career.

This deep into this covenant, I'm happy to report that I can see some definite growth in my wife, and even growth within our marriage. God is showing her some things, and she is excited about this adventure in God, and has great faithful expectations of the LORD.

4 more wakeups before race day. The adrenaline courses through my veins, even now. As a runner, I train for months and months for most races. Since the last time I completed a 10k road race was back in the mid 2000's, and it is now 2017, this is a pretty big deal for me. A few years ago, I was out of shape and not really motivated to get back in any sort of shape. Then, God used several people in several different situations to plant the seed in me. I remember when I first started, running for 5 and then 10 minutes were considered

breakthroughs! Now, I can run for an hour and be only partially winded.

Such is the same in the spirit world with spiritual things. If you don't evangelize often, you may have trouble doing it effectively when it counts. If you're always doing it, you'll have evangelistic stamina. If you are only used to praying in short bursts, several hours of intense prayer at once will seem unreasonable. If you don't memorize Scripture often, being able to memorize long passages of Scripture to "nibble" on throughout the day would likely be out of the question. The goal is always steady, consistent progression. Using your 24 hours wisely.

I had a good time today, working through my ScriptureTyper scriptures. Tomorrow, my goal is to find time, at some point, to simply be quiet for 7 minutes, uninterrupted. During that 7 minutes, I want to just concentrate and listen for God's heartbeat.

As a new season (Autumn) approaches, a new season is on its way for my family, ministry, and myself. I can see the natural signs. The leaves have already began falling. The day's end sooner. The temperature drops. The Fall is going to be gorgeous. I prophetically decree and declare the same over all that which the LORD has put within my territory, and yours as well!

♥ Emely – Day 18 ♥

Last night was not a good night for me. I woke up on two occasions throwing up. It wasn't like the episodes I had in the past with heavy acid and not being able to breath. I felt like some kind of a demonic attack was going on. I dreamed that I was at a barbecue party in a park. I saw a couple that Terrell and I know who are also pastors. When I stepped outside as I was getting ready to leave, I saw a long green python snake hanging high in a tree. From where the snake was at, it had a good view of the park. No one else had seen the snake until I pointed it out. I said well it's time for me to go! I told everyone else to be careful.

In the morning I dreamed that I was at an event with some friends. We had to go to the bathroom. In the bathroom was Jay-Z and some of his friends. I would say there were about 5 of them all together hanging out in a corner in the bathroom. At one point I was looking in the mirror fixing my mascara. I could feel them all looking at me. I can feel Jay-Z trying to get into my mind and putting thoughts I clearly was not thinking. He had a piercing eye type of stare. I was asking God to help me as all this was going on. All of a sudden one of the guys attacked one of the girls I was with as if he was a vampire. I knew that it was time for battle so I needed to find Terrell. Jay-Z was sitting on the top of the stairs in the building we were at. Terrell appeared and when Jay-Z saw him he was like "oh its you" with a disgusted tone. Terrell was the only one who could defeat him. After that, Terrell walked away and told me to leave from there and he walked away with a determined look on his face. He reminded me of Duncan Mccloud from the highlander. I also saw he had an invisible sword on his back that only I could see.

I didn't leave but hid underneath the stairs to see what

Jay-Z was doing. He sat looking out into the horizon. With his mind he told the skies to become dark and to produce lightning and thunder. He didn't say a word. Then I woke up. I definitely know that dream meant something and I am seeking the Lord for interpretation. I try to write down my dreams often. I must admit I have been slacking lately. Always try to write down your dreams or keywords that may help you remember them. You never know if you may have to revisit it in the future.

I helped my dad go to the DMV and handle getting a North Carolina license. I saw the power of God move once again. He was worried that he wasn't going to pass the signs exam since it has been so long. He was going to wait and study the book. Meanwhile as we waited to be called, I asked God for favor on my dad's behalf. It was a quick smooth process once it was his turn. The person assisting him was nice and even gave him clues as he took the sign test. There were a few times he got stuck and I also asked God to please help him. I saw God honor that prayer immediately. My dad passed the exam. The person gave him hints. I feel that someone else who could care less wouldn't have done that.

I had a good time with my dad again. I am getting to know him more and more each time we are together. I am also seeing even more that we are very much alike. Overall it was a good day. My goal for tomorrow is to work out for 30 minutes. I am also going to work on laundry and my picture wall. Until tomorrow!

Day 18 Notes

Have you been as consistent as you would like? Why or
why not?

∞ Terrell - Day 19 ∞

A fantastically productive day in both the natural and the spirit. I had an idea to continue this writing trend between Emely and I. This time, in a fiction book which is aimed at teaching people about deep spiritual things, while being entertaining at the same time. I'll pitch it to her in a few minutes.

This morning, my alarm went off again at 5:00 AM, and it was a battle. My body was so tired, but my spirit took command. I have a song as my alarm sound, and the song talks about not wanting to go through the motions in our walk with Christ. It was as if I heard the words, and felt the power behind those words for the first time in a long time. It's funny how we can hear something every day, and it really just be noise in our busy everyday lives. Then, we hear the same thing and our understanding is quickened (brought to fresh life) in that moment.

Ultimately, in the Grind, even though it may seem as if things aren't changing rapidly enough to fit our desires, when we grind long enough a quickening happens in our spirits. When our spirits are quickened (meaning suddenly brought to life, or suddenly brought to a new higher level of abundant life), the change begins to manifest in our soul and body. Our soul (mind, will, emotions) will begin to express who we are on an entirely different level as the previous version of itself. The body will long for good things which it did not used to. Humility will become second nature, and we are able to avoid fleshly lusts which so easily bound us previously.

Let that word encourage you, friends. Although the grind may seem to be wearing you out, if you stick in it long enough, the quickening will be like a breath of fresh air, and well worth it. Try to imagine that every day you are working towards your next armor of God. Working towards greater endowments of the fruit of the Spirit. Working towards a greater impartation of the gifts of the Spirit.

If you can accept that the grind of loving your human enemy with everything you have in you even when it's hard, will ultimately result in you truly loving your fiercest human enemies with the totality of Agape (God's own) love with the same ease as tying your shoes or riding a bicycle.

The 7 minutes were a blessing as my goal for today. Early into it, the revelation come to me "the doors of your house are getting bigger/(wider)". I meditated on that promise, and both the natural and spiritual ramifications of it. I meditated on the future and present ramifications of it. It really poured more life into me during a day when I've been doing lots of pouring into others. My goals for tomorrow are to complete at least 100 pushups, with preferably 3 sets. If I have to go to 4, I want the 4th set to be a very small number. Also, I'll increase from 224 updated scriptures in ScriptureTyper to 242.

♥ Emely – Day 19 ♥

Man, today was an exhausting day for me. I don't understand why I felt so tired. More and more I am seeing the effect extra weight has on my body. I have not been making a big effort to eat healthier. Its like I get amped up to eat right but I go back to eating junk. I really need to do something about this because I am really not feeling well.

It was so hot today. I think it was close to 100 degrees! I finally got to take the kids to the sprinkler water park. Before I did that, I had to take some things to my husband's job. I decided to start early on some of my goals to have less work to do when I got back home. I worked on my picture wall, sorted through some laundry and cooked my husband's dinner before I left. I was proud of myself because although I started late in the day, I got half of my things done.

After I returned home, I made a quick dinner for me and the kids. I was also on a bible study conference call that was really good. The class was titled "From repentance to regeneration". This is how I spent my time with God for that portion of the day. After the call, I continued working on the other batch of laundry I had and put the clothes away. I had the kids working on their own clothing as well. I am trying to teach them early how to be responsible.

I really had to push to work out today. I almost didn't do it. I was telling God that I would do an hour tomorrow. I told Terrell how I was feeling and he just told me to knock it out. I did my Michael Jackson game. I was able to do five songs and score pretty high and break records on some. My body was sore but I pushed. My goal for tomorrow is to drink my 32oz of infused water.

I am really looking forward to this weekend. I can't wait to just get away with hubby. I want to connect with him even more. I am looking forward to seeing Terrell's parents and spending time with them as well.

I can't believe how fast time flies by. We are almost done with this covenant! I am looking forward to putting this book together. It will be interesting to see both myself and Terrell's day to day outlook, experiences, etc. This book is not just to strengthen us but for you the reader as well. When we make a covenant with God, we definitely don't want to let Him down. We know that He loves us and would forgive us, but still we don't want to push it. That is what I tell myself every time I want to slack on my goals. I have truly been seeing God move during these days and I am looking forward to see what He will do on the last day of this covenant.

Day 19 Notes

Who do you say Jesus is?

So, today I was able to baptize a member of our church, and it was a completely blessed experience. Another member texted today and said that he is now thinking about what he wants God to do in his life more than ever. Hearing that really blessed my soul, because if he is thinking of what he wants God to do in his life, it will lead eventually to the mindset of what can he do to draw more intimacy in his relationship with God.

And ultimately that's one of the keys of this journey. Getting to the point where we know beyond a fraction of a shadow of a doubt that when we lay our heads down to sleep each night, we've grown in God through our efforts of that day. If we draw near to God, His Word tells us that He will draw near to us. **Intimacy produces the substance of transformation.** God enjoys walking with us. We have to strive to keep pace with Him. Paul, the Apostle, said that he labored unto weariness, with the superhuman energy which God so mightily worked and enkindled within him.

Ox mode work is superhuman. Working through the day to day grind, and always keeping God first will ensure that your labor isn't in vain. Keeping God first will keep us from pride. Humility allows us to receive the maximum amount of the deposit of that superhuman energy deep down in our spirits. After all, if God worked superhuman feats with Apostles Paul and Peter and so many others in the Bible and throughout history and modern days, and since God is no respecter of persons, superhuman energy is available to us all.

How do we access it? Grind every day to make the Earth more like Heaven. Make disciples of all men. Love the Lord our God with all our hearts, souls, and minds. Love our neighbors as ourselves. Bless those that use us spitefully. Essentially, do the Word. Be the Word. Be a living extension of the principles we read in the Word of God. Give in to the process of being more like Christ, as we understand more and more of Christ. Since Christ is the Word, and faith comes by hearing, and hearing by the Word of God, we can say that Faith comes by acting out the Word. Then, we can truly go from Faith to Faith, and from Glory to Glory. We can go from a certain level of understanding of spiritual things to a higher level of understanding. And here's the beauty of it all.

Whatever you have a lot of, it's usually easy to get more. If you have some muscles and fitness level, you can gain more muscle and fitness a lot easier than someone who has very little (by working out harder and putting more emphasis on certain parts of your diet). If you have a lot of money, you can invest and make more money much easier than someone who has very little to begin with (often by either taking risks or investing slow and steady and waiting for the due time to collect). If you have a high level of education, it will usually be easier for you to learn something a lot quicker than someone who has a low education level (if you're willing to spend the time to focus and use the learning skills you already possess).

So the more Christlikeness you have from time and energy investments in previous seasons will allow you to become more and more like Christ. The more often you make this a part of your day to day schedule, the more likely you can experience explosive spiritual growth.

Today, I completed my push-up goal. I did a set of 34, a set of 33, which left me with 33 more to obtain my goal. I powered through 37 straight for the last set, and it felt really good. I also finished at 246 in ScriptureTyper, a handful over my goal. My goal tomorrow is to get a 4 mile slow and steady jog in to keep my legs fresh for the upcoming race. Another goal for tomorrow is to break atleast 260 in ScriptureTyper.

♥ Emely – Day 20 ♥

Today I woke up feeling soreness in my body once again. I laid in bed a little longer and just relaxed. When I got up, I realized that the clothes I washed were still not dry even after letting them sit out all night. With my dryer not working properly, it's pretty tedious. I suppose I can just go to the laundromat and dry my clothes and all, but I'm used to doing everything at home.

I got an order for one of my sugar scrubs from my sister in law. She ordered a scrub that is good for sore muscles. I had some left over after making hers. I used some on my back and neck and my soreness was gone! I was amazed to see my product work so fast. I thank God once again for giving me this idea. I had previously made a batch of this particular scrub but this time I felt to change the recipe. I am so glad I did.

I took the kids back to the water sprinkler park. They had a blast. However, I told my daughter not to run and she didn't listen to me. She fell somehow and scraped her knee, legs and arm. Boy did she panic! My daughter is starting to act like a hypochondriac. She always thinks something is wrong with her. When she gets hurt she makes a big show out of it. I am always telling her that she shouldn't be such a drama queen because it's not a good look for her. I feel that in school it is a trigger for other kids to bully her.

With school starting in less than two weeks, I am already thinking about the bullying and how I hope they don't go through it this year. My goal is at some point to get them out of the school they are in. Then again, I need to stand my ground and be in prayer even more for my kids and that school as a whole. Parents, guardians, and other family members and friends, we need to really come together and pray for our kids. It's so paramount this day and age. The darkness in this world intensifies by the minute. However, we serve a mighty powerful God who can turn things around at any given second. Will you take a stand against the darkness for your loved ones?

Tomorrow my goal is to go to the laundromat to get my clothes dried and work out for 15 minutes. I also need to leave this house clean and in good shape for the time I will be out on vacation. Lastly, I will spend 30 minutes with God. I didn't write this in yesterday's goal but I will spend 5 minutes with God tonight and see if He has anything to tell me. Okay my friends, until tomorrow!

Day 20 Notes

2/3 Milestone! How do you feel?

∞ Terrell - Day 21 ∞

Today was a good day even though it was a really long day. One of the highlights of the day was picking up my race bib for Saturday (day after tomorrow). I'm excited to run in such a big race. It really has opened my eyes to the training process of a runner. I feel like I grew quite a bit during this training season, mentally, physically, and spiritually. The wait will soon be over.

Also, this was the first day that I forgot what one of my goals were. A goal was to run 4 miles. I did run the four miles, but I had doubted that I would have made that a goal even while I was running. I knew about the ScriptureTyper, but couldn't remember all day what the other goal was, when I had already finished it. I felt good to see that I was ahead of the curb for once, lol.

Today was a rough day from the standpoint of me and my wife having some serious financial challenges right now. As I was talking to God about it this afternoon during driving, a truck drove past me that said Knight Transportation. Another car at the same time was in front of me, which happened to be a Kia Soul. Then God began downloading into me that when God is bringing us through the fire, in order to make us a knight worthy of battling on the front lines, we have to be stretched. It is uncomfortable at times.

However, knowing that God comforts us in our weaknesses and trials is a good mindset for all of us to keep. Then, God allows us to comfort others, the same way He comforts us. God just revealed this to Emely with the Word of God. It was a perfect confirmation. I feel encouraged, but still ready to be in a different financial situation.

I believe God is stirring us up to become less dependent on other people financially. Right now, I'm the bread earner, and I work for a company. Although I'm not extremely passionate about what I do, I currently don't have another option. I look forward to the day that I have a multitude of finances available, and God centered projects to keep me busy for 16 hours day, all of which I'm extremely passionate about. To get to that glorious point, I need to be willing to sacrifice who I am, for who I will become. Then, once that is achieved, I'll be qualified to help and direct others to do the same thing.

So, patience is certainly a virtue. I often preach on how the busiest person in a restaurant is a waiter or waitress. When we wait on God, we should be busy serving Him, moving from assignment to assignment, clearing stations, preparing for the next assignment. God loves work, and He'll bless everything that is truly done in Him. We just have to really put forth the effort. If I had known what I know now, I would have become a qualified programmer long ago. But, all things work together for good for those who love Him. I will let Him hone my patience in the process. And you should do the same, my friend.

The goal tomorrow is to spend 33 minutes in a book of the Bible. I'll let Holy Spirit guide me into the one He wants me to get into.

♥ Emely – Day 21 ♥

Today I woke up feeling more sluggish than usual. I was moving so slow and didn't leave my house until after 3 pm. I had many things to do today in preparation of the trip to Florida tomorrow. Terrell is also running a 10K tomorrow. The last time he attempted to run a 10K he ended up passing out and was hospitalized for 3 days. It was pretty serious, in my opinion. He was dehydrated since he took an electrolyte gel which he wasn't used to running with. We also didn't get much sleep

Tonight, we will all definitely get to bed early and be well rested. I am looking forward to seeing my husband win a prize in his age group. I know this race is a big deal to him so I will try to be as supportive as possible, although I was tired and frustrated due to the heat today.

Lately these days have been very hot and humid. I hope the weather is not like that early in the morning tomorrow. I completed going to the laundromat and drying my clothes. I didn't clean the house as best as I wanted to but it's decent. I did clean certain things that were on my list of things to do.

My goal for tomorrow is to read my bible for 15 minutes and spend 15 minutes with God during the drive. I will also drink an entire 50 oz. jug of water I bought today. One thing I must say, being transparent, is I wish we had more money to travel with. Of course, it helps that we won't be staying in a hotel, but it's nice to have extra spending money. Nevertheless, we will make the best out of this trip.

Another small issue has been my vision lately. It seems that while driving either day or night its blurry. It gets difficult when I forget my glasses especially. I've had an eye exam recently and the doctor said my eyes were okay. I would just really like to know what is going on with my eyes.

I am also intrigued as to what God is going to do on this trip. He is always talking to us on the road in many ways. I can't wait to write about how He spoke this time.

Right now, I am so exhausted but I am about to complete my 15-minute workout. I will keep pushing myself even when I don't want to. Trust me, I REALLY don't want to right now, lol. Usually I don't go to sleep till after 12 am but today I am really looking forward to going to sleep. When I was out and about today, I felt like I was literally dragging myself and looking like an oom-pah Loompa. I hate that feeling and I know I MUST do something about it.

Day 21 Notes

What challenges have you overcome today, in Jesus' name?

∞ Terrell - Day 22 ∞

Tomorrow is the big race that I've been training for over the last 4 or 5 months. All the anticipation, all the running, all the exercising, all the meditation, all the dieting, all comes down to this. In less that 10 hours it will have begun, and in less than 11 hours, it should be over for me, and I'll see how I fare against some of the best distance runners in the city.

I'm looking forward to seeing the kids race in the kids run, as well. I want them to come to grips with athleticism at a young age, as I really feel that it helps a person though out life. After that, me and my lovely wife are celebrating our anniversary early this year by heading down to Florida to visit my parents. I'll have 5 days off of work, which is pretty rare for me. I'm going to enjoy myself.

But, first I'm going to exert myself! My goal for tomorrow is to give this run EVERYTHING I have, and cross the finish line. Also, I'm going to tell anyone about Christ that I can. Which reminds me, I was featured in a workplace newsletter for my company. In the bio portion, I mentioned that I was an ordained minister of the Gospel of Jesus Christ. So, somewhere between 600 and 700 souls received at least a tiny seed of the Gospel. Sometimes, it's just about getting His Name out there, and letting people know that there are believers out here still.

Tonight's a big night and I pray I'm able to get some awesome sleep. I'll be getting up at 5 AM to get an ab workout in. Then a quick sprint. Then breakfast. Then meditation and likely reading some Word of God, and prayer. Then waking the family up and making sure we get to the race early. The race starts at 7:30 AM, so I want to be there 30 minutes prior, at least. These events fill me with adrenaline, and I absolutely love it. Did I mention that this is one of the bigger races in my city, Charlotte NC, for the year!

There are so many parallels between running/racing and Scripture. Not only does Paul use several athletic references in the New Testament, but life in and of itself is a journey. Every skill that you can pick up adds to the whole picture. Therefore, pick up every skill you can along the way, as you never know what is actually going to help you. My goal tonight was to read 33 minutes in one book. I chose 1st Timothy, since we're launching a new style of ministry, and Paul is giving the young leader Timothy many words of Wisdom on how to build the church and keep it on the right course. I read it, and one thing that was discussed was exercising the spirit onto godliness. Bodily exercise profits a little, but godliness prospers all things. So, exercising your spirit, soul, and body together is a great combination.

♥ Emely – Day 22 ♥

Last night I was unable to get to sleep. We all had to wake up at 6 am for Terrell's race. Do you remember how tired I was last night? It was so crazy how I ended up being wide awake just out of nowhere. I prayed for a few minutes and even tried to sing songs to God in my mind. Honestly, I don't know what time I even fell to sleep. When I woke up I was tired but I could handle it. It also wasn't extremely hot yet when we left which was good.

We got to the race and after about 20 minutes Terrell began his run. I went around to different booths to get free things. I ended up getting solar eclipse glasses for the eclipse coming up on Monday. That was the highlight of that part of my day. It would've been nice to get another pair for Terrell. The kids and I found a spot to go sit at and wait for Terrell. Eventually he came through and finished the race. Last years' experience was bad and I really prayed and asked God to protect my husband this time around. He had went to the bathroom so the kids and I picked up our things and moved closer to the bathroom. I turned around a few times waiting on him to come out and didn't see him. I began to get worried because it had been about 15 minutes since I last saw Terrell. All sorts of thoughts crossed through my mind. I thought what if the race was tough and he passed out in the bathroom from exhaustion and heat. I saw Terrell about 10 minutes after that and was so relieved.

There was also a fun run for the kids to do. However, we ended up missing it because we didn't hear the announcer when the race began. Terrell told the kids that when we got home, they would do a brief race and win medals. I thought that was cute.

Later on, in the day we began our vacation journey down to Jacksonville. We ended up getting a flat tire which was not fun. Thank God, I still had my spare in my trunk and it was good. My back tire was bad last month and I had my spare on for a while. While I was driving in Georgia it began to rain pretty heavy. At one point I almost lost control of my car. Now that was scary! Nevertheless, I kept on pushing. The sky was so beautiful in the different areas we drove through.

Finally, we got to my in-laws house and we had a great time just sitting around and chit chatting. I am looking forward to going to the beach tomorrow a having a great time. My goal for tomorrow is to spend 30 minutes with God. I did not complete my goal today and I do feel bad about it. I completely forgot about spending time with God with all that was going on today. I must do better tomorrow.

Day 22 Notes

What is the destination of the journey you are on?

∞ Terrell - Day 23 ∞

Today was such an amazing day. I ran and completed my 10k. Boy, was it tough. I know for sure that I finished 13th in my age group. I believe it was 13th out of 80th, but I'm really not sure since the online reporting isn't reporting that specific statistic.

How did I feel afterward? The feelings were mixed. I do feel that I completed my goal for the day because I gave that race my everything. Do I feel that I could have trained harder/better. Certainly. In fact, I'm now more encouraged to up my dietary approach more than ever.

There were many runners at that specific race who ran marathons and half-marathons and use this race only as a training run. I was floored by the physical achievements I saw. I was also encouraged by what I saw. I was inspired by what I saw. The whole time in training, the whole 5 months of it, I was envisioning myself placing at least 3rd, if not 1st. I'm not disappointed in myself, because I realize that failure is a part of the process to becoming a bona fide Champion.

Now, I was able to bond with my children to a higher level after the race. It's as if God was really talking to me on a new level afterward. It seems that there is something about our weakness which really causes God to speak to us clearly. In this case, after the race I was separated from my family for a while, since there were so many people. During that time, I had some of the most profound conversations with God that I've ever had.

Afterward, relating to my children in this new dimension of communication was easy. I heard them and just listened to their childhood interests, and gave them some Godly pointers.

Also, me and my wife connected on a serious level. We took an early anniversary vacation this week, to celebrate our anniversary next week. So far, as usual, it's been a complete blessing to visit with my parents today, who are a 7 hour drive away from us.

Tomorrow, my goal is to really listen to my parent's heart in all things, and have a high expectancy of God to speak to me though them. They have lots of wisdom, which now more than ever I would love to harness and use for God's glory. Otherwise, I really want to relax. Relaxation, recuperating, and recharging are so vital and important. Without that, you run the risk of being burned out. After you've enjoyed some time working super hard and going above and beyond, you deserve a little break, so that your mind will be able to function at its peak capacity.

One thing that I've learned is that every day is a dynamic opportunity for growth. I've found that in any setting that is different than whatever your day to day process is, you will bring the most spiritual value into your life by allowing the differences of those day to day realities to shape your future.

♥ Emely – Day 23 ♥

Today was a very chill day. I got to experience seeing part of the solar eclipse with my eclipse glasses. Here in Jacksonville, FL we didn't get 100% totality so it wasn't as dark as it could get. In other places it was darker. It was cool to witness this part of history. I got caught up on much needed rest as well.

Earlier during my time with God, I was speaking to Him about something that was concerning me. During that He began to talk to me about how He felt about favoritism in the church. I was led to post on Facebook what was on His heart. I love when I can hear God and speak His heart. That is what prophets do. I am a woman seeking after Gods heart, so I enjoy this.

In some of my posts, it was interesting to see non-believers like the posts. Sometimes we may not know why a person doesn't want to serve the Lord, especially if we don't know them well. It is so easy for us to think that they are just being rebels and want to do their own thing. You never know if they were raised going to church and what they saw there. Many kids just go to church as a habit every Sunday but as they get older will see things they don't like. Often these things will cause them to backslide and not want anything to do with God or church.

When I was a kid, I went to church Tuesday, Thursday and Sunday morning then back again at night. Sometimes there were events on Friday nights as well. Since I hated being dragged to church, I trained my mind to think of church as a social club. I was looking forward to seeing my friends and catching up on the newest gossip. Of course, there were people I was cool with and those I was not cool with.

Although I was in the youth ministry and participated in different things like being the youth minister secretary, worship, and dance, my heart was so far from God. I had no relationship with Christ or fear of God. I went to church all the time, wore the clothes I was forced to wear, which was skirts all the time but what a fake I was!

Now I can tell you that I am glad I went through that phase so that I could talk to others about it. Often, I tell this part of my testimony to reassure people that although we are not living right, when and if we repent, God still forgives. If we choose to have a genuine relationship with God, things will be so much better.

My goal for tomorrow is to spend 30 minutes with God and just really listen out for what is on his heart. I will then share with the world if He wants me to. I am looking forward to visiting St. Augustine FL tomorrow and having a good time. I'll have details for you tomorrow!

Day 23 Notes

Have you been as consistent as you would like? Why or why not?

∞ Terrell - Day 24 ∞

Today was a fantastic vacation day. God is awesome. When you work hard, being able to play hard is a necessity. Being able to recharge away from the grind will make you come back to the grind and put even more of yourself into it.

This morning at breakfast, my mom gave me a book about self-publishing. Although I've only made it a few pages into chapter two, my head is already spinning with new thoughts. She also gave me a book which talks about Zig Ziglar. I've heard and read of plenty of references to him and his notable book "See You At The Top", but now I'm beginning to understand more about who he is and how God impacted his life. In fact, I'm really beginning to understand a lot more about God and motivation, including motivational speakers. If a person is motivated, virtually anything is attainable. In the Old Testament, the tower of Babel was being built into the heavens. God said that if He didn't intervene, nothing would have been held back from them. (Genesis 11:6)

This is a very mysterious scripture, in it's own right. But I want to focus on the fact that the motivation to have a certain level of control over the spiritual world pushed Nimrod (the champion of the earth at the time) and the people of the earth to push into uncharted territories. If God would not have decided to confuse the languages, who knows what Nimrod would have unlocked.

Why should only the forces of evil push with the motivation to conquer innocents? Shouldn't the forces of good push deeper and deeper with the ultimate motivation being to hear the words "Well done, My good and faithful servant?". With so many Eternal Treasures up for the taking, as people of the Most High God, our goals should ever drive us. This temporary dwelling place of being inside of a flesh suit on the expiring version of the Earth should motivate us to trade in this temporary concept of time for something exquisite and eternal.

Essentially:

Time =< Eternal Treasure.

This means that time is less than or equal to heavenly treasure. Keeping this formula in mind, we should constantly be turning the time on this Earth into heavenly and eternal treasure. Unfortunately, many people and even some Christians often live like:

Time > Eternal Treasure.

This means that time is greater than heavenly treasure. In all honesty, I spend some of my own precious time not grinding out heavenly treasure! Oh, the humanity! Literally, the humanity within us needs to express its own outlet. However, part of the purpose of constantly having a covenant with the Lord is that as you are constantly drawing nearer and nearer to Him, you're also constantly building heavenly treasure for yourself. As my goal today was to listen to my parent's heart in all things, and receive as much wisdom as I could, I was successful. The self-publishing book was honestly a miracle. Tomorrow my goal is to push from 263 to 275 on ScriptureTyper. Another goal is to do atleast one set of 25 pushups, then another set finishing with muscle failure.

♥ Emely – Day 24 ♥

Today was an amazing day. I finally got to go to Ripley's Believe It Or Not. There were a lot of cool things in there. On the flip side, there was a lot of straight up demonic stuff. We all went to the town of St. Augustine which is the oldest town in America. It is over 300 years old. There is a lot of history to learn about in this town. It was interesting to see the fort that was built there centuries ago.

Meanwhile at Ripley's, there were certain areas in the museum where I could feel a strange presence. Terrell and I had gone to one exhibit that had "fantasy" coffins. These coffins were built and used in Africa. They were hand made with different shapes. The ones we saw was a snake and an elephant. It was really eerie being next to them. We also passed by an African fertility statue. It is said that many women who touched this statue ended up pregnant. After we left that exhibit, I began to feel very ill. I was feeling dizzy and had bad cramps. It could've been a coincidence, but I think not. This spiritual world is very real. You can see it, hear it and feel it.

There were a lot of items in there used in witchcraft, voodoo, shamanism and much more. These were the authentic items not fakes. I say all that to say that we need to keep ourselves covered when we are around demonic paraphernalia. I am NOT saying to fear but do protect yourself.

After Ripley's I ended up getting a custom-made ring with Terrell and I's initials. That was my favorite material thing from this trip. The price was right which was even better. They had lots of shops, restaurants and other attractions as well. I would recommend visiting St. Augustine, FL when you get a chance!

Earlier in the day after 12 am, I went ahead and spent extra time with God from my 30 minutes the previous day. It felt nice to just be laid out talking to God. I am looking forward to doing this more often. When we lay out before God on the floor, we are showing God that we are in complete reverence and submission to Him. We present ourselves to Him so that He could do and say whatever He needs to. This is called having an intimate moment with God. God has many sides to Him and it is important to get to know them.

Tomorrow Terrell and I end our vacation and will be headed back home. We're going to hit the beach one more time. Part of me is looking forward to getting home quick so I could see my babies and animals. I am excited about seeing the kids start school again and soar above and beyond. Last year, I feel like I failed a little in my duty helping the kids with school and attendance. I feel I could've been involved more and stricter on attendance. I will do what I can this school year to do better.

Day 24 Notes

Who do you say Jesus is?

"That's the difference between men and kings." Wow, what a sentence. We watched the new King Arthur movie tonight with my parents. I enjoyed the movie, and that quote was used to encourage Arthur to see everything he needed to see, even when it was tough to do so. Men stop looking as it gets tough. Kings continue to press though.

Knowing what I know about the ancient world's definition and lore and expectation of a king makes this even more interesting. You see, the fact is that a king always had spiritual backing. Of course, Israel had Yahweh, the Ancient of Days as spiritual backup. The only True and Living God. But even the kings of other nations had spirits backing them up. So, by definition, kings are more than men. And then Christ has made all of us as believers into being kings and priests. There is so much within Christianity which guides us into taking our rightful place as kings.

As this project begins to draw to a close, my excitement level rises day by day. This book is a tool to help God's people take the path of most resistance. To help the kings which report directly to the King of Kings take up their power and use it to craft this world more and more into submission to the coming Millennial Kingdom. As Eternal Kingdom Publishing is just a seed and an idea right now, every day that I'm able to learn and work towards it, it becomes more and more of a reality.

Every Kingdom citizen has a God given dream. This book is a tool to help you bring your own dream into being a reality. I want to encourage you. You can do it. God wants to empower you beyond more than anything you can imagine. You are His champion. He has placed something inside you that needs to be unleashed in the Earth realm, for other Kingdom citizens and even unbelievers to see and partake of. Day by day, if you're willing to sacrifice who you are now for who you will become, your dreams are going to take shape and ultimately take off. It starts with you and you can do it.

Take a hold of your passion and your dream, and push to bring 1% of it into reality today. Tomorrow, push to bring 2% into reality. Don't quit. Reaching 100% may take you longer than 100 days, with the pressing matters of life being hurled at you from every corner of the universe. Trust in your Spiritual Source, JESUS Christ. He is able, and He is powerful beyond any measure which we can understand. Today was the day of a solar eclipse, and it was an awesome display of God's power and precision of control over the world of man.

Today, my goal was achieved. I finished my scriptures with 1 Corinthians 13, the love chapter. So powerful. I also finished my pushups and it felt good to even push myself while on vacation. Tomorrow, my goal is to show my wife a surprising level of romance.

♥ Emely – Day 25 ♥

Well today is the end of my anniversary week. Terrell and I on our way back home as I type. We had a pretty good day. We went to the beach today and had a good time. Before we got to the beach, I was met with a tough challenge. I figured that the enemy would try to come at me after how much the Lord blessed us this week. I had an issue with a customer service rep from the water company. She made me so mad that I said two curse words. Although I said it in Spanish and no one understood me, it was still a curse word. To pay $400 for a water bill really hurt. Then to hear that the balance went up to over a thousand was outrageous! This person was impatient and had no compassion whatsoever. After I got off the phone with her, it took me a little while to get over that situation. I told myself I would go to the water company personally and complain. As I began talking to God at the beach, I told Him I would let Him handle it. I also decided to ask God to bless her and hope she doesn't have to go through what I experienced with her with someone else. I took many deep breaths and did my best to simply relax. After speaking to God, I felt much better.

For my covenant, I did a little bit of exercise. I counted my steps as I walked back and forth. When you walk at the beach of course you are working your legs as you walk on the sand. It was a push for me since I was exhausted already from not sleeping right. Nonetheless, I did my exercise. Tomorrow my goal is to plan my plant diet for the next 7 days. I will start out with 7 days and see if I am consistent. I pretty much have no choice since this will be my next covenant. I will eat no meat but only fruits, vegetables and grains. This week showed me that I am extremely overweight and unfit. I already know that but it's like that was highlighted more to me.

Tomorrow I will work on catching up on much needed rest. I have a busy weekend coming up. I am really looking forward to going to the GFM studios on Saturday. I will pour my heart out in song to my Lord and exalt Him in my song. God has been so good to us this week. He met EVERY single need and then some. There were personal things I asked Him for this trip specifically, and He made it happen. My father in law bought me brand new tires for my car. That was a major blessing. We didn't have to stay at a hotel and stayed in a beautiful comfortable room in my in law's house. We didn't have to spend a dime on food or drive anywhere. Everything was provided for us. I speak blessings over my in-laws because they were such a blessing to us. Thank you Lord!

Day 25 Notes

Home Stretch! Will you finish strong?

∞ Terrell - Day 26 ∞

Today was a fun filled day with my wife and family. It is such a blessing to have both a loving wife and supportive parents. Sometimes we easily take these things for granted. Many things can be healed with laughter and good times with family. Ministry is really beginning to pick up, in a one on one setting. I talked to a brother who me and Emely occasionally help out, and I believe I'm going to be able to help him. One by one the desire within me to lead people into being the best version of themselves comes to fruition.

In order to do that, I'll constantly need to be on the top of my own self-improvement game, and constantly checking in with the Holy Spirit. I feel like there was a definite spiritual shift in the spiritual world last night, and new events have been set in place. Last night via dreams, I battled against several dark spirits. Nothing too threatening, but still eye opening. During the dream, praying in tongues was a major weapon against them. I now have a renewed desire to build up the gift of praying in tongues.

My wife, being a seer, is also going to see some strange and unusual things this season, I truly believe. It is very exciting to be on this sort of a journey with someone like her. She felt the romance effort today. Tomorrow, my goal is to speak at least 3 scriptures prophetically over our life.

The adventure of ministry is returning. Even as autumn comes quickly, so does my passion for fresh ministry to come forth. The thing about being called to a pioneer ministry is that you must actually be willing to pioneer into something that has never been done before. Moving into the supernatural, gearing up the soldiers, and preparing for a new spiritual foe. All reliance is on God. Holy Spirit measures success in terms of obedience. That's exciting to me.

New opportunities and new doorways open up daily. The plan of pushing and driving and knocking down every barrier with raw grind is empowering to the mental state. Taking responsibility for every aspect of your life, and focusing on becoming better every day, empowers by taking control of everything that you can control. That which you can't control is that which you can't control. Every day, anything out of the ordinary can be tossed your way. Being strong internally will manifest externally, and the world is going to realize that there is something different about you.

Physical toughness. Mental fortitude. Spiritual strength. God wants us to have all of these three traits as His children. And each one takes work. As we push forward into the murky gray of tomorrow, be brave. Let nothing deter you from the path of self growth. Not even self doubt. As Holy Spirit is allowed to grow inside of you, you'll become more like Christ, who is the epitome of physical toughness, mental fortitude and spiritual strength. As you read the Scriptures, think of how Christ exudes these traits.

♥ Emely – Day 26 ♥

Today I rested a bit longer before I started my day. I went to Walmart to get school supplies. They had some good deals too. I went to my kids open house and met their teachers this year. I really liked my son's teacher so far. Samirah's teacher I am on the fence about. I will keep a close watch and always ask how she is treated throughout the year. Both teachers are new to the school.

Although I slept in, I still felt so exhausted today. Everywhere I went, I felt like I was dragging myself. I went to the grocery store and bought my things to eat for the next 7 days. I am looking forward to seeing how different my body will feel. I will really be praying and calling on the Lord for strength. I know myself and I know I would want to justify why I am eating something I shouldn't. I don't want to do that. It would benefit nothing. It is not worth a few minutes of yummy bliss to break this experimental diet. My goal for tomorrow is to get the house partially clean.

This weekend I will try to push myself to wake up early and go to the flea market to register. I want to sell all the sugar scrubs I have now. I want to have income to make new products to sell. I believe in this vision that the Lord gave me. But as I mentioned before on another day I believe, it gets frustrating to share posts about my scrubs on Facebook, but no one interacts. If I post a picture I may get 50 plus likes. I just don't understand it. This shows me that I need to investigate where my target audience would be because obviously Facebook is not cutting it.

I am very intrigued as to how this will end since there are only a few days left of this covenant. This month has gone by so fast. Before we know it, it will be December already! I want to finish this year strong. It has been a tough year in my opinion. There has been lots of warfare, betrayal and struggles. We have laughed and cried. However, through it all, God has been my rock. My husband and I are still going strong and getting stronger. In the midst of our darkness, we remind ourselves that our main source of joy is the Lord. We remind ourselves in the midst of trials to rejoice. Our finances are still not where we would like them to be but we will continue to trust God. It could be worse, like being homeless and alone with no family. Fortunately, we are blessed to have a roof over our head, food to eat, a support system and decent health. Most of all, we have a relationship with Christ. He can be our Friend, Comforter, Advisor and much more. My trials always remind me to cherish the small things. Even though I am almost in tears as I write this because I am so tired of being broke, I believe that by the end of this covenant there will be a solution.

Day 26 Notes

What separates champions from non-champions?

∞ Terrell - Day 27 ∞

Today was the last day of me and Emely's anniversary vacation. It was my mother's birthday as well, and it was a lot of fun to be able to celebrate and enjoy that with her. When you don't live in the same town, sometimes you can't see important people in your life as often as you'd like. So, during the special times when you get to be together, it makes the memories that much more special.

My mother gave me a teaching series on the wisdom of God in the workplace. Listening to some of the teachings for several hours on the ride back home really imparted into me a fresh fire for the workplace, both current and future. I thought about missed opportunities in the past. These were opportunities that I squandered in the past. But, I know that God is a God of second chances, and I look forward to racing ahead to make up time and stand in the appointed place.

I accomplished my goal for the day of prophesying three scriptures over my life. I did this in the Atlantic ocean, and waves crashed all around me. It was a very memorable experience that I thank the Lord for. I come back from this blessed down time ready to take charge of every aspect of my life in the precious name of Jesus Christ. So many dreams, so many obstacles to make an example of, and so many souls to reach for the Kingdom of God.

The Lord has laid before me the choice of being a world changer for His kingdom. He has also laid that very same choice before you. Using the principles and exercises in this book, you will begin to see the world itself change around you and more specifically, you're going to get to know the God you serve better. Every day that you strengthen the bond between yourself and Him, you will see that everything you touch is blessed. This will happen the more you include the Lord in everything and in every aspect of your life.

Your work or school life is something you spend 70% of your waking life involved in. God is very much interested in His Glory being displayed and being evident on you. Are you happy with your current job? What is it that you desire to do? What small steps can you begin taking today to prepare you for the days which will surely come after tomorrow (Lord willing, of course). Every action adds to the previous action, and that is how momentum builds. As Kingdom citizens, we should be light years ahead of everyone around us in the workplace. LIGHT years. We have access to the perfect knowledge of God, and putting His knowledge and His Word into practice is wisdom. Begin to inquire of Him for every process and task which you are responsible for, believe what you hear, and be obedient. You'll begin to move into a new realm of effectiveness.

My goal tomorrow is to inquire of the Lord for every work process which I am involved in and follow the same advice I just gave you. I will also refresh at least 15 scriptures on ScriptureTyper.

♥ Emely – Day 27 ♥

Right now, I am wishing I was right back at the beach. It's been one of those blah days for me. My neck has still been causing me discomfort. It has caused me to be cranky and snappy. I don't like acting that way. Meanwhile on the road my vision is blurry and I feel so tired all the time.

Today was day one of starting my no meat diet. I must say that I was proud of myself for not eating meat. For the most part I did my best in eating healthy today. Tomorrow I will do better. It's amazing how many of us depend on meat to have a complete meal. For me, if I don't have meat it's not enough. I am now seeing that it will truly be a sacrifice to stay away from sweets, meat, sugars and junk. However, I must do it. I am proud of myself for completing day one. My goal tomorrow will be to make sure I have two servings of fruit. Today I just had half of a banana which is not enough.

I did clean up a little as well. I got rid of all the recycling trash which was accumulated in the kitchen and straightened up a bit in the living room. I will continue working in this house and organizing everything little by little and room by room. I want to have this house ready for when it's time to move. I have a major mission to de-clutter this house.

I would also like to see the outside yard looking better too. The shrubs outside look hideous. My mailbox is surrounded by branches and shrubs. It's embarrassing to be the only one in the neighborhood with tall shrubs and branches. I must get this handled asap.

I can't believe there are just three days left in this covenant. It has surely been a journey and a half. There have been days when I didn't want to write a word. Then there were days when I was excited to write.

This morning I had a very strange dream that I can't seem to stop thinking about. I dreamed I was back in NJ in the town where I went to high school. I saw two girls that I was friends with. I was at a dance of some sort. I then saw both girls were pregnant. I don't remember what they were having. I will definitely seek the Lord on this and hopefully I will figure it out.

Tomorrow I am hoping to have a better day. I really looking forward to completing my new song with GFM Studios. In the future I would love to have a bilingual album which both English and Spanish speakers can enjoy. That is one of my long-term goals. I would say within the next five years I would love to have accomplished this. I will also love to have completed my series of training manuals for my ministry "Kingdom Rubies". With God all things are possible even if you can't see it.

Day 27 Notes

What's the best thing you've seen Jesus do in the past 27 days?

∞ Terrell - Day 28 ∞

This was the first and presumably only day of failing to keep my covenant. After returning from vacation at 3 AM, sleeping until 8 AM, going into work, ministering to one of the members of Guardian Brigade, then finishing the day off with a job interview and coming home, I had no energy left. I literally laid down in bed and had not the strength to even concentrate on typing successfully through even one scripture. I gave it the ol' college try, but had not the strength to succeed.

I prayed to the Lord to forgive me, as I felt bad. In a vision of the night, the Lord visited me. The voice I heard was my wife's, but I knew that it was Him talking to me. He gently told me that He forgave me, and that I would learn not to fail in the future. It was endearing and powerful. So today I woke up and made it through my scripture goal. The previous day I had given my work everything I had as well, especially in the last hour of the day to play catch up. So, all in all, it's been a good and productive two-day period.

I've been coding for hours, working diligently on a take home test for a major employer here in Charlotte. I have two potential good opportunities on the horizon. However, I'm still working hard to improve my skillset, as I have many dreams to bring to pass.

I've began to have 1 on 1 sessions with each of my children. I recently purchased a book called "How to Dad", which includes a myriad of cool things that a father can teach his child. So far, they both really enjoy it, and it always puts a smile on their face. I want them to grow up and be interested in life, and be interesting themselves on top of that.

In other news, I've taken a strong stance on cleaning my home office area. Since I desire the work that I do to take me to the next level, I'm becoming a real stickler to a perfectly clean work environment. Also, I've collected my first castle. It's a sand castle, and it is fun to stare at. Many more shall join it, over the years, Lord willing. Also, I've recently purchased a book called "The Story", which puts the Bible in Chronological order. I'm looking forward to reading it and drawing closer to the Father.

Friends, this Christian life is an endurance race. At times, we may get tired, but we should never weary of well doing. There is an enormous calling on your life, and at times you are going to need to rest. If you rest when God says rest, and receive mercy for any failures, but pick yourself up and keep pressing forward, you'll get closer and closer. God is primarily interested in the state of your heart.

My goal for tomorrow is to perform two sets of pushups to failure, and also refresh 15 additional ScriptureTyper scriptures into being current.

♥ Emely – Day 28 ♥

This day started to be pretty relaxing. I got a decent amount of rest and was ready to start my day. I went on the hunt to find some nice affordable shoes for my kids. At the first store I went to, I ended up finding a nice outfit and shoes for my son. The next store I went to, I must say I was truly blessed. They had a clearance sale going on and I was able to get four pairs of shoes for my daughter. These shoes were all under $3! What a blessing!

The blessing continued when I took the kids to get their hair cut. I found an event on charlotteonthecheap.com where they were giving free haircuts at a salon if you donated school supplies. My son was able to get a haircut and my daughter got her ends trimmed. I was so happy I had found this event. Overall with all the deals I received, I am pretty happy.

Terrell and I went to GFM studios to work on our music. I was able to complete my song. I am really excited about this. It's going to be a great worship/soaking/prayer song. I can't wait to hear how it will sound when it's all put together. We have known the founders of GFM for two years now and I will say it has been a blessing to know them. I am looking forward to when we are making music videos and showing the world what the true kingdom of God is all about. Besides, all the content we are putting out is all about Him all for His glory. I know many lives will be touched. Unbelievers will become believers after they see the content that the entire team puts out. Keep your eyes peeled for GFM Studios it is coming soon!

I know that a few days ago I mentioned that I would not eat meat for 7 days. I actually decided that I would have one meat day, go figure. Today was my meat day. I believe that I need to be weaned off slowly not just all of a sudden. I will see how the rest of the days pans out for me. Ultimately, the end goal will be not to eat meat for an entire month. However, for now I will set a realistic goal.

Tomorrow my goal is to have everything ready for my kids first day of school on Monday. The kids are actually excited about going back to school. I will also continue with my meatless diet tomorrow. I will drink 3 bottles of water.

I am looking forward to seeing what this last week of the month will bring. I feel as if we will receive some kind of breakthrough at the end of this month. Usually when I get this feeling, something happens. Let's see what God is going to do. I am also looking forward to September and what it has in store for the Potts family. God is always faithful.

Day 28 Notes

What's the sweetest thing the Holy Spirit has told you today?

∞ Terrell - Day 29 ∞

Today was a tough day. The coding assignment that I'm working on has been tough and laborious. The media team that I'm working with went great for Emely's song, but my song didn't pan out, and I'll have to go back to the drawing board. I'm mentally drained, but I'm vowing to continue in my press. After all, is that not the difference between men and kings?

That's one good thing about always finding new ways to keep yourself and those around you encouraged. Those sorts of things have a funny way of creeping back into your head, and encouraging you down the road. Spending some time today to let something positively influence your spirit will pay huge dividends for you down the road, when you least expect it. Use time wisely. As this project draws near an end, I reflect on the ups and downs, the victories and defeats within the past 30 days.

I don't count it as a coincidence that just as this project is ending, I have a major test for my new career path which is due on the same day. Things which are prophetic are often that way, but many people miss it. It is a great journey which the Lord lays before us all. Being willing to submit to Him, and let Him guide us while we continually ensure that our hearts are always prepared for what is to come. That is equivalent to training wisely so that we will be able to fight the good fight of faith. Putting forth an effort which is considered good in that fight is key, day in and day out. We can't simply rely on yesterday's level of faith to get us through whatever may come our way tomorrow. Today is always the day to ensure that we're giving our everything to this faith walk.

Today is the day to love unconditionally. Today is the day to forgive, in person and in our hearts. Great things occur in our lives when we trust in our Heavenly Father to be working out all situations for our good. A fantastic way of constantly seeing the faith to faith and glory to glory promise manifest in your life, is by setting a goal ahead of time, making a covenant with the Lord, and then consistently fulfilling your end of the bargain, all the while stretching yourself.

We never want our spiritual life to get stagnant. We want it to always have a fresh edge to it. Relationship with JESUS is the sweetest thing on this entire Earth. Heaven is unending, constantly being stretched out by the Father. As we stretch ourselves spiritually, we'll be inclined towards never lessening our expectation of our Big Huge God. He is enormous in wisdom, enormous in strength, and enormous in His love and dedication to us. We should be dedicated to Him. This Journey to Greatness process will help you primarily in your dedication to Him, which will ultimately bless every aspect of your life.

My goal for tomorrow is to go from 303 active Scriptures in ScriptureTyper to 320.

♥ Emely – Day 29 ♥

Yesterday I went to the Puerto Rican festival they were having here in Charlotte. That place was packed! I never thought there were so many Puerto Ricans in Charlotte. My parents and I along with the kids went. I will definitely say that I see more of a disinterest in me for places that are packed with people. I have never been a fan of crowds. Especially when there is alcohol involved, some people don't know how to act.

My dad wanted to see one of his favorite bands that were going to be playing. We arrived at the festival after 2pm and didn't leave until about 7:30. Of course the bands my dad wanted to see was the last act. I guess they figure people would leave if they come out earlier. Nonetheless, the kids had a good time once they found something to do. At first, there were many complaints about being hot, but I can't blame them it was really hot!

Terrell didn't go he stayed at home. I was missing my best friend. I must admit I was bored and was ready to go home after about an hour. However, I tried to make the best of the day. I was able to win some things at a spinning wheel that offered prizes. I ended up winning the prize I wanted as well, so that was pretty cool.

I also decided that I was going to stop my fruit and vegetable diet and resume at a later date. I was honest with myself and saw I was not ready to fully commit to not eating meat at this time. If I am going to do a challenging covenant and I see that I may not be able to do it at that moment, I rather wait and do it right. Eventually I will work towards the goal I have and be successful. My goal for tomorrow is to spend time in the word for 20 minutes.

I amso proud of my husband and I for coming this far. I am proud for all of you in advance who will be doing the same thing. It's been quite the journey over these past almost thirty days. I have enjoyed sharing my life experiences with you. Moving forward, I strive to better myself in many ways and teach others as well. Life really is like a box of chocolates. You really don't know what you are going to get. One day could be awesome and the next day not so much. One day you could get blessed and the next day you have a super high-water bill like we do, lol. The most important thing is to keep trusting that God will provide. Allow God to stretch you to see what you are made of. No one said this Christ walk would be easy, but it is worth it.

Day 29 Notes

You are a warrior. You are royalty. Do you believe these statements?

∞ Terrell - Day 30 ∞

The finale is finally upon us. What a journey it has been up until this point. When we first began this self-entitled 30 day journey to greatness, I came in with an expectation of what the Lord will do in our lives. I was expecting a great break through and a change in many or atleast several situations.

What we got instead has been great vision, and a path highlighted for us to take to achieve those dreams. The warfare has been heavy, especially over the past few days. It is very clear to us that this covenant is the first of many. This covenant is the foundational covenant, the proverbial stake in the ground. The vision of where to lead the family and ministry has been given. I've seen the end, even from the beginning, and I look forward to the opportunity to weather the storm. At some level most of us don't really want to weather the storm. We want the reward and the results.

But as I've mentioned numerous times through this book, the grind is the key to it all. I have bigger dreams now than I've ever had in my entire life. I feel like my dreams are literally so big that they would scare small minds. I know that my dreams are far bigger than me. I know that it is going to take a lot of work to actualize everything and bring it into reality. If I truly had my way, everything would already be in existence and I would be enjoying the fruits of my (future) hard work now. However, not my will, but His be done. The Lord loves for us to be fruitful. I was actually withheld once again, and missed a covenant day, so this is officially day 32. The coding project I was working on actually took me so deep that I completely forgot about my covenant. I felt pretty bad lying in bed at 1:30 in the morning when I realized that, but I asked for forgiveness and kept pressing.

We have to make war, not excuses. We have to make war against the status quo. We have to make war against the desire to hold back. We have to battle fiercely against the tendency within all of us to take the easy road. We have to not make excuses for our weaknesses, but instead realize that all of us have work to do within ourselves. If we are willing to admit that tiny fact, and earnestly ask God for His help, I believe He always hears and puts a plan of action in place as long as we are willing to follow. It is us who is likely to turn back when the going gets tough. It is never Him who turns back once the dream has been given.

The download has been received. Now the application must be installed. During this next season, Emely and I are going to literally be putting our hands to the plow, revising this book, working our skillsets, and publishing this book for other Kingdom Citizens to enjoy and be edified. Oh, that the LORD would supernaturally strengthen us on our endeavors! Oh, that the LORD would supernaturally strengthen you on yours as well! Remember that you don't have a junior sized Holy Spirit inside you. You have all of HIM! And I finished my last covenant goal of reaching 320 Scriptures on ScriptureTyper, which just so happened to complete all of my Covenant Armor Scriptures, almost exactly. The journey to greatness is just beginning. Please stay tuned for Journey to Greatness part two.

♥ Emely – Day 30 ♥

Well, this is the final day of this covenant. It has been a journey these past 30 days. Today has been a very challenging day for me. I have spent most of the day stressed out. I dare to say it almost makes sense for it to have been that way since it is the last day of the covenant. Although I am going through a tough trial, I know that I need to keep my head up and trust God 100%. Of course, it is easier said than done but it is achievable.

It looks like it's time for me to go back into the work field. I have been a stay at home mom and wife for the past 2 years and a half. I will certainly have to get used to going to work again. I was used to being free with my time and always being available. Depending on what job I get, my time will become limited once again. My biggest priority is that although I am working, I still need to be around to spend time with my children. I don't want to get home when they are already asleep. I want to be able to see them after school and help with homework. At my last job, I worked long hours and was barely there for them. My mom lived with us at the time and I got a lot of help from her. Now she has her own place so it will not be as easy without her around.

Tomorrow I have an interview as a receptionist at a staffing agency. We will see how things go. I also applied to many other places and may possibly have a few good leads. Back in 2014 I quit my job because I heard the Lord tell me I would be going into full-time ministry. Since then finances where like a roller coaster ride. I will admit there are times where I wonder if I totally missed God on this. I would have people confirm what the Lord had said, but I would still wonder why are we struggling. I have struggled with this decision I made 2 years ago still to this day. I guess time will tell if I had made the right decision back then. My last goal will be to do the best I can to help my family in every way possible.

I have always worked hard for what I needed and wanted. When I got married it was a bit different because there was extra income. However, I always liked having money around that I earned from a job. Although when you get married you become one and what's mine is his and what's his is mine, there could be issues when it comes to finances. When there isn't enough money coming into the home, that can quickly escalate to a problem along with the blame game. I personally don't have time for that, and I do want to help my family so all of that will be avoided. This will be a new chapter for me and although you won't get to read what happens, perhaps there will be a second book in the future.

I pray that each of you that worked on this book are blessed abundantly. I also pray that the Lord will grant you your heart's desire according to His will. May you continue to shine in Him and display who Christ truly is in all you do. Remember everything and anything is possible in Christ Jesus! Keep calm and covenant on!

No one can ever take this away from you. How worthy is
God of all the Glory?

Epilogue:

So, within a year and a half of writing this, I (Terrell) was able to land a Software Engineering position with an awesome Health Care startup. Interestingly enough, the same company which hosted that 10K that I ran in is now my employer! Look at God's sense of humor! Between the skills I learned on the job there and in self training, I was able to build the first version of GTKPortal. As far as Eternal Kingdom Publishing goes....this Pre-Release of Shamar Meditation is our first book, and we're just getting started!

Emely is doing great and her website, https://www.etsy.com/shop/hephzibahbeautytreat, is constantly being updated with new awesome products. Please check it out! She still enjoys acting with her troupe, and I even join her sometimes now!

Our daughter Samirah is our budding artist. Our son Jeremiah is our little encourager. We have the feeling of Tribe within our family...and that's what we have been working towards. Peace and blessings to you all, and we really appreciate your support!

Section 2 - Occupy Until I Return

Chapter 4 - Occupy Until I Return (Mindset)

*** Construction taking place ***

In
The
Meantime….

" I'm planning on releasing a ton of private content as I build. Short stories and conceptual information. Check me out at https://www.patreon.com/GuardianBrigade if you enjoyed Salvatia and want to enjoy more before the full Shamar Meditation drops! I promise that if you support by joining the $1 a month tier, you have my Ranger's Honor that I'll make sure you get more bang on that buck than any other dollar you'll spend this month!"

Chapter 5 - Internal World Building (Application)

*** Construction taking place ***

In
The
Meantime....

" If you enjoyed the book, please leave a 5 star review. I really want to reach as many souls as possible with the message of the Kingdom, an empower souls to attain great destinies in the name of the Lord Jesus Christ!

Your 5 star review will be a TREMENDOUS BLESSING! "

Chapter 6 - Grinder's Paradise (Epic Parable)

*** Construction taking place ***

In
The
Meantime....

"My tribe members were all troopers that Christmas.
Knowing I had to finish this if we all wanted to head up
north for the New Years.... I got your six! "

Section 3 - Greater Works Shall You Do

Chapter 7 - Greater Works Shall You Do (Mindset)

*** Construction taking place ***

In
The
Meantime….

"As Human Beings, we were made to be naturally Supernatural. I love you and your show, Sid Roth! "

Chapter 8 - Seeking to Release The Gifts (Application)

*** Construction taking place ***

In
The
Meantime....

"So, I really want to get some solid teaching out there about what Jesus said in John 10:34, along with what is written in Psalm 82:6 "

Chapter 9 - Agents of The Savior (Epic Parable)

*** Construction taking place ***

In
The
Meantime....

"Be as bold as a lion. Be as cunning as a serpent. Be as harmless as a dove. Soar like an eagle. Grind like an ox."

Section 4 - Be Not Of This World

Chapter 10 - Be Not Of This World (Mindset)

*** Construction taking place ***

In
The
Meantime….

" When the Father whispered to me that He would be sending help, I honestly almost laughed like Sarai. It was a total grind, day out, day in. Then Joyce came along to breath fresh life into the project. And on the last day, Emz found the perfect font for the cover!

I felt like God chuckled as He reminded me of that. Now my heart is actually filled with wonder as I await Him performing all the other things He whispered. You can have the last laugh, God. You are indeed my Jehovah-Nissi"

Chapter 11 - The Best Offense Is a Strong Defense (Application)

*** Construction taking place ***

In
The
Meantime....

" In my experience, the greatest blessings of wisdom and revelation, bliss and joy, fortitude and quiet resolve in the face of grave danger....seem to typically come with a level of resistance. Navigating that resistance effectively is the key. That's when the warrior within us all is stretched. Keep your spiritual blades sharp, friend..... "

Chapter 12 - Realmwalkers (Epic Parable)

*** Construction taking place ***

In
The
Meantime….

" Eternal Kingdom Publishing is all about pioneering new content for the Kingdom of God. In the 2020's and the 2030's, we want to help the disciples of Jesus Christ attain full maturity. "

Section 5 - You Are A New Creation

Chapter 13 - You Are A New Creation (Mindset)

*** Construction taking place ***

In
The
Meantime….

" Yeshua is constantly beside us. Be willing to take risks."

Chapter 14 - Interfacing with Heaven On Earth (Application)

*** Construction taking place ***

In
The
Meantime....

"

Proudly Introducing the SuperNatural Humanity Series

All books will feature 4 sections. Mindset, Application, Epic Parable, and Devotion.

3 Phases, 7 Books Each Phase

Phase 1: Shamar Meditation { 2019-2025 }

Phase one focuses on the members of Christ's Body being strong in Christ at an individual level. Tips,strategies, research, testimonies, exercises, story, and other resources which everyone from seasoned spiritual warfare veteran to newbie can glean from. Look out for the second book:

Grinder's Paradise: Shamar Mediation Part 2

Coming - Summer 2020

Phase 2: Ro'eh Shepherding { 2026-2032 }

Phase two focuses on team building, in a Christ centered family unit in which every member is willing to bring individual excellence to the team mission of impacting the world for Christ. Aimed at developing the leader that is in all of us, even children. As we build strong unity across the Body of Christ, we will draw near to the moment of cultural transformation which is necessary to maximize End Time Harvest.

Phase 3: Shamayim Advancing of the Kingdom { 2033-2039 }

Phase three focuses on heralding the Kingdom of God effectively in the futuristic society which the world is quickly becoming. If Christ were to come back tomorrow, we need to have already literally introduced the presence of Jesus Christ (Yeshua) to all 8 billion worldwide peeps! However, if Christ comes back hundreds of years from now, we need to ensure that our lives today are still reaping a harvest in those future generations. This book introduces pioneering new ways to effectively accomplish that using technology to obtain higher level of unity at crossroads moments including the entire Body of Christ.

Chapter 15 - Heavenly Host United (Epic Parable)

*** Construction taking place ***

In
The
Meantime....

"Names were altered slightly to provide a meager level of protection for the somewhat innocent ;) "

Section 6 - Worship In Spirit And Truth

Chapter 16 - Worship in Spirit and Truth (Mindset)

*** Construction taking place ***

In
The
Meantime….

" If you're looking to get up to speed on the coming
advancements to SuperNatural Humanity, this book has a
fantastic teaching on The Quantum aspects of the Glory of
God. I 5 star recommend this book to you!

Quantum Glory: The Science of Heaven Invading Earth
(Mason, 2010)"

Chapter 17 - Returning Home to Heaven (Application)

*** Construction taking place ***

In
The
Meantime….

"Knetashkan is Hebrew for the English word: Victory"

Chapter 18 - Here to There and Back Again (Epic Parable)

*** Construction taking place ***

In
The
Meantime....

".... So this is what the situation all boiled down to, he thought about it one last time. MoonBane, and his charges were in grave danger, and it was his own false humility which had allowed the DragonBorne to get through the barriers. He was still spiritually injured, and in the very heart of the continent of DarckNex, with an untold number of fairly dangerous vermin hunting him. Their Head Quarters loomed before him in the jungle below.

Then Trizzen said aloud to himself "This will be the season I become known for. It's not about hubris, but necessity."

With a look of stoic determination upon his face and with out any further thought, he jumped off the cliff into the darkness of the dense jungle below. His grip upon Knetashkan was as firm as the faith in his God.

Even he didn't know the impact of his words upon his own world. In time, the peoples of all the worlds would feel them."

Section 7 - Transform From Glory To Glory

Chapter 19 - Transform From Glory to Glory (Mindset)

*** Construction taking place ***

In
The
Meantime….

2 Corinthians 3:18. We have a big God!

Chapter 20 - Completing Assignments and Levels (Application)

*** Construction taking place ***

In
The
Meantime....

Well, I wanted to make sure the reader had a good experience throughout. Reading should be fun. In other news, Greek word Thura is English for Door or Portal

In Aretz, we say Nexus to indicate the same.

Chapter 21 - A Hero Always Comes Home (Epic Parable)

*** Construction taking place ***

In
The
Meantime....

"Follow your heart in all things. If Jesus be for ye', my friend.....there is an unlimited adventure right before your very eyes!"

Jesus Christ (Yeshua) wants you to help restore Order to the Earth. As His disciple, He has anointed **you to be His noble warrior**. He has gifted you with **unique powerful weapons** to wage war upon darkness. He has given you access into a **Kingdom** with **riches** beyond wonder, and this book is a **portal** to that Kingdom. The practice of Shamar Meditation will help you to stretch your faith to new heights and help transform you into the ultimate version of yourself. As your spirit, body, and soul each reflect God's glory more and more day by day, you will transform into **something more than you've ever dreamed**.

18 And all of us, as with unveiled face, [because we] continued to behold [in the Word of God] as in a mirror the glory of the Lord, are constantly being transfigured into His very own image in ever increasing splendor and from one degree of glory to another; [for this comes] from the Lord [Who is] the Spirit. {emphasis mine}
2 Corinthians 3:18 Amplified Bible, Classic Edition (AMPC)

Travel to the **legendary land of Salvatia** and meet both **brave heroes** and dastardly villains as a new world is unlocked for you to pioneer. **Who will you transform into, mighty one?**

References

Jorgensen, T. (2011). Spirit Life Training: If You Knew What God Has Put Within You, You Would Train It To Become Your Greatest Asset (1st Edition). Shippensburg, PA: Destiny Image Publishing

Leaf, C. (2015). Switch On Your Brain (1st Edition). Grand Rapids, MI: Baker Books

Leaf C. (2016). Think & Eat Yourself Smart (1st Edition). Grand Rapids, MI: Baker Books

Mason, P. (2010). Quantum Glory: The Science of Heaven Invading Earth (1st Edition). Maricopa, AZ: XP Publishing

Kendrick, S., & Kendrick, A. (2015). The Battle Plan for Prayer: From Basic Training to Targeted Strategies (1st Edition). Nashville, Tennessee: B&H Publishing Group

Baxter, M., & Bloomer, G. (2009). A Divine Revelation of Healing: You Too, Can Receive Your Healing! (1st Edition). New Kensington, PA: Whitaker House

Oates, G., & Lamb, R.(2004). Open My Eyes, Lord: A Practical Guide to Angelic Visitations and Heavenly Experiences (4th Printing). Dallas, GA: Open Heaven Publications

Galloway, J. (2017). Secrets of the Seer: 10 Keys to Activating Seer Encounters (1st Edition). Shippensburg, PA: Destiny Image Publishing

About Eternal Kingdom Publishing

We are committed to creating content which glorifies God and expands His Kingdom. We are servants sent to the Body of Christ to uplift, inspire, encourage, activate, and ultimately edify. We hope our books, movies, and other media will assist disciples of Jesus (Yeshua) Christ become transformed more and more into His likeness!

We are authors, actors, publishers, ministers of the Gospel, graphic designers, veterans, athletes, readers, parents, entrepreneurs, software engineers, among other titles. However, more than the many hats we wear, we are disciples of the One True God, the Father of our Lord Jesus Christ! We are vessels of the Holy Spirit sent to let this world know that the promises of God are yes and amen!

Terrell Potts (CEO)
Emely Capo-Potts (Vice President)

www.ingramcontent.com/pod-product-compliance
Lightning Source LLC
Chambersburg PA
CBHW020820180626
46814CB00001B/43